CW01498484

The Dancing Boy

Roy E. Stolworthy

Acknowledgments

Janice, Always

Emma, for her computer skills

Justina Hurley, cover design.

Tommy, my cocker spaniel for taking me for a walk to clear my mind.

Edited by Sarah Cheeseman BA with Hons

During the writing of this novel, professional medical advice concerning the symptoms of Post Traumatic Stress Disorder was keenly sought; the source has asked to remain anonymous.

Other books by Roy E. Stolworthy

Coming Home

All In

Hidden In Plain View

The Dancing Boy

'It is only the dead who see the end of war.'

Plato

Caw Blimey Approved

For Alison

Best Wishes

Contents

CHAPTER ONE

Tom Gillet didn't need to be told that his regiment had no call for one-footed combatants, and he had no real desire to be anything else. It had taken the army six months to turn him into a soldier, and no time at all to reverse the process and turn him back into a man. He was a mister now, without parade, drums or bugle. After fourteen years' loyal service, the title of company sergeant major disappeared into thin air faster than his right foot did when he kicked in a booby-trapped door in Afghanistan. Then again, the title of mister didn't apply to the less than adult population of the small town on the north Norfolk coast. The younger generation, in their crass wisdom, took to calling him a series of intimate provoking names like Galloping Gillet, Tommy Five Toes or Toddling Tom. He knew he shouldn't have taken the bait, in itself a form of mental illness. But he did, and prayed for the opportunity to ram his aluminium walking stick down their throats until it appeared out of their arses ready for roasting over a fire like a pig on a spit.

"I'll sort them out, Dad," his son Luke said, looking up from his homework. "They'll soon get fed up and find someone else to wind up."

"Nah, let it go, you're twelve years of age and I don't want you getting into trouble. Anyway, the sooner I get used to the artificial foot, the sooner I can be rid of the walking stick."

"Homework, Luke, now," Amy Gillet interrupted, and turning to face her husband, "This came for you."

Showered, she pulled the silk gown tight against her nakedness. Gillet caught the scent of rosewater from her neck drift into his nostrils and looked up into her face. She wore her golden hair pinned up in a ponytail, the way he liked it back in the old days. He waited for the warm smile accompanied by the crinkled nose. It never came, not like it used to. Since his return from duty minus a foot she had become tactful and indifferent, not that he wasn't so stupid to know they only remained together for Luke's sake. Luke had been diagnosed with moderate learning difficulties. It was hard going at first, but there were days when he seemed better than others and made progress. To push him resulted in resentfulness, drifting into violent moods lasting for hours. Like father like son, Amy snapped at him in the heat of a blazing row. Nevertheless, Gillet displayed the patience of an African drought, settling him whenever he became angry or frustrated. Gillet tore open the letter and smiled.

"It's from Mickey Pink. You remember Pinkie? His mother's died and he's coming home for the funeral."

"How could I forget when he puked ten pints of Guinness down the toilet while I was having a bath?"

Gillet's smile thinned at the look of disdain sliding across her face.

"He says he'd like to stay for a couple of days after the funeral."

"Yes, well remind me when he's coming and I'll take a bath the night before."

Startled by the sharpness of her tone, he tightened his lips. Why the hell couldn't she just for once answer a simple question without throwing in a heap of sarcastic rhetoric? He looked up, observing her face as if it belonged to a stranger. It wasn't going to work between them. The in-fighting would begin like it had so many times before. Christ, he wasn't even in the army anymore and she still wasn't satisfied.

Five long, boring weeks he'd procrastinated in hospital, tolerating the indifference of bureaucracy and absence of compassion waiting for a removable prosthetic foot to be fitted.

Nurses and doctors, most who struggled to speak English, did little to help him come to terms with his loss. Further down the corridor in another ward lay a young lance corporal from a Scottish regiment with his kneecap shot off after a gunfight in Helmand. Nobody came to visit him for the duration of his time spent in the hospital. The day of his discharge they gave him a pair of crutches, and he left dressed in the same dusty bloodstained combat fatigues he'd wore on arrival.

Like others that had served in Iraq and Afghanistan, Gillet knew the British government didn't give a damn for the British soldier. What kind of country, he stated to anyone prepared to listen, squeezes the benefits of wounded soldiers, then slashes the pensions of the widows of dead heroes, while bankrolling entire ethnic communities to sponge off the welfare state? The same time, allow groups of Muslim extremists to stand unchallenged on the street corners of Britain, hurling abuse at marching soldiers returning home, and setting fire to the Union flag as if their unrelenting misplaced fervour might help to develop some miraculous powers of their own.

For two months he hobbled round on a crutch without complaint, never receiving any form of sympathy from Amy. The night he returned home from hospital they had slept as man and wife. Later, when she saw the stump for the first time, the sight had repulsed her so much she told him to sleep in the spare room. What had once been so strong between them had deteriorated. Deep down he knew she'd never accept him as he was. For her, everything had to be perfect or not at all. Instead, he lay in the next bedroom, listening to her gentle snores and murmurs. It took little imagination to realise that his marriage was beyond recall, and the inevitable separation drew closer. There had been times he'd considered telling her of his reoccurring nightmares hopeful it might revive her feelings for him. Of the times he'd woke in the night plastered in sweat and trying to push away the image of the Afghan woman holding a baby in one hand and a grenade in the other. Instinct made him to pull the trigger and watch the bullets rip into woman and child, tearing them to pieces. He wanted to tell her he'd sunk to his knees and cried like a baby, but there seemed little point now. Instead, he watched as day by day they drifted further apart. Time passed and hardened him.

Reaching for his stick he stepped out into the fresh evening air. An orange sun dipped in the west; dusk spilled dark blue and streaky pink across the sky, like a painting on an artist's easel. The season of spring was upon them. The season of renewal and rebirth, a time when the axis of the earth increases its tilt towards the sun and the length of daylight stretches until the hemisphere begins to warm, causing new plant growth to spring from the bowels of Mother Earth. Yet try as he may, it did little to disturb the shadows lurking in the corridors of his mind. He and Amy had reached the point of no return and there could be no going back. Her emotional and physical appetites were no longer his to satisfy, and he purged his body of all longing for her. All that remained of their once happy union was misery and despair.

"Maybe I'll skip dinner and go down to the pier and watch the lads fishing. Send Luke down when he's finished his homework and we'll get some chips on the way back."

"Maybe I won't be here when you get back," she said.

Gillet's mind tumbled with a plethora of memories.

"Maybe this, maybe that. That's all I seem to hear these days," he said. "So maybe it's the best thing you've said for the last few months, Amy. Lock the door after you."

She stared at him, replaying his words over and over in her mind, trying to isolate her decision from his reaction. When he turned away, something precious wrenched from her heart. Years ago, when she had dreamed of her perfect man, she knew she only needed to walk in the right direction and sooner or later he would be there waiting. Then the day came when God took her hand and guided her and her friend into the Neptune's Basket public bar. The moment he set eyes on her he asked her for her hand in marriage without even asking her name. She giggled like a foolish schoolgirl. Twelve months later, they married. Everything perfect, idyllic. Then things started to go downhill the day she learned of Luke's disability. Her world collapsed. He wasn't perfect like she wanted him to be and because of this she struggled to accept him as the son she had always wanted. At times she blamed her husband's line of work, in her mind no more than legalised murder. Gillet didn't find Luke a problem, dealing with him as best he could. Time passed until the onset of the war in Iraq and then later Afghanistan changed the dream into a nightmare. Week after week she waited for the knock at the door, worrying if he might ever return alive, until she could bear it no longer.

She studied her fingernails, waiting for the hollowness in her chest to fill. He was different, and it wasn't the loss of his foot that had changed him. She knew he possessed the strength of mind to take that in his stride; part and parcel of soldiering. Something deep and cancerous ate away at his being. His mood swings, the sullenness, an anger she had never seen in him. War had changed him. He seemed somehow disconnected.

*

"Mum's gone, she thinks I'm daft. It's just me and Dad now." Luke grinned at Pinkie.

"Go to your room, Luke," Gillet snapped.

"Sorry to hear that, mate," Pinkie said, listening to Luke stomp up the stairs.

"Been on the books for a time now, you know the way it goes. The army's no place for a woman these days, living like squatters in filthy married quarters, trying to raise a handicapped kid. Plus the uncertainty of whether their husband will turn up carried from a Hercules in a flag-draped coffin."

"It's still a bloody shame. Amy used to think the sun shone out of your arse, and Luke's a good kid. Pity he thinks whenever things go wrong it's always his fault."

Gillet allowed the remark to pass; no good churning the obvious.

"I'll get a couple of beers."

Pinkie, a lanky, raw young man of twenty-four, ten years Gillet's junior, nodded. Unlike the majority of soldiers serving in Afghanistan, who preferred their hair shaved to the skull, he sported a thatch of wiry straw-coloured hair. His large eyes were owl-like, with a tendency at first glance to make a person feel sorry for him, until they became better acquainted with his hard-nosed attitude.

Armed with an ice-cold six pack, Gillet slid the patio doors shut to keep out the mid-evening chill. Slumped in the brown velour couch, he ripped off the tab, pulled a long swig and stared into Pinkie's face.

"Hey, remember the kid who tried to warn you of the booby-trapped door? You know, for a few scraps of food he'd give us snippets of information concerning the Taliban movements?"

"Shafiq?"

"That's him. The Taliban discovered his game, beheaded his father and raped and killed his mother and sisters. The people in his village were too afraid to give him shelter for fear of Taliban reprisals and threw him out. News is he wound up in Sangin, north-east of Camp Bastion, begging for food, until he met a guy called Ahmed. The story goes Ahmed gave him food and a roof over his head... And now we come to the downside of things," Pinkie said, fidgeting with his can of beer. "I don't suppose the words *Bacha Bazi* mean anything to you?"

"No, should they?"

"No, they didn't to me until I made a few enquiries. Translated, the words stand for boys' play. It's an age-old cultural tradition banned by the Taliban that has reared his head again. Wealthy men offer money to poor families of good-looking boys between the ages of nine and fourteen, on the pretext they intend to train them to be dancers. Dressed with bangles and bells around their wrists and ankles, men pay to watch them dance, after which the boys are used for sex. No need to tell you access to women in Muslim countries is restricted, so these boys act as substitutes. It's pretty much a form of sexual slavery, with little chance of escape. Anyway, this guy Ahmed is a local pimp always on the lookout for a few American dollars to pay his way to the States, and he's found a buyer for Shafiq in Kabul – an ex-Mujahidin commander, a relic from the time of the Afghan–Soviet war with friends in high places, right up to the higher echelons of the Afghan government, so no one dare touch him."

"How do you know all this, and why doesn't he run away?"

"Word gets around, you know that. Anyway, where would he go? If the Taliban find him they'll torture him to death for helping us, and if he leaves the Mujahidin commander after he paid a small fortune for him, he can expect the same treatment. Rumour is most don't survive past the age of eighteen; from then on they are classed as adults. They're killed or they spend the remainder of their lives begging in the streets to survive."

"And this shit is legal? This is the kind of crap we are fighting and dying for out there?"

"Legal, what's legal? This is Afghanistan we are talking of. You know as well as I do they don't give a shit for anything unless it reeks of money. And from what I've heard the competition's pretty fierce between the owners of the best-looking boys; they are treated as status symbols."

Gillet sucked in his cheeks as a vivid image of Shafiq zoomed into his mind. The ever-smiling face framed by curly jet-black hair, the soft doe-like brown eyes, just another kid like millions of others all over the world. They didn't ask to be born in a godforsaken dusty shithole, existing in much the same way as before the Bible had been written.

"Why doesn't he go to the police or the Afghan National Army?"

"As if they give a shit."

"Okay. What about our lot? They rant and rave about hearts and minds, kiss the arse of every Muslim that walks on two legs. Tell them this kid and others like him are responsible for saving the lives of hundreds of coalition troops."

Pinkie grimaced. Whenever Gillet presented himself in this manner, common sense was never going to prevail. He glanced at the photograph of Gillet and Amy standing outside the chapel on their wedding day, a split second of joy and happiness frozen in time.

"You know the answer to that as well as I do. Come on, let's go down the pub and get rat-arsed."

"Yeah, that's not a bad idea. I'll see if Debbie will sit with Luke for a couple of hours."

*

As hard as Gillet tried, sleep wouldn't come that night. A skin full of strong lager along with half a dozen single malt whiskies did nothing to prevent the image of Shafiq visiting his troubled mind. Maybe there was something he could do- Children in Need, UNICEF, perhaps the Red Cross. He waited until his mood cooled. For some time he had sensed his pattern of life becoming distorted, leaving him wondering who he was and where he was going. He had put it down to fatigue, at the same time aware that he would never change. In the crevices of his troubled mind an ever-increasing urgency urged him to step away from the past. Accept the time had come to flow with the tide, make a go of his marriage and act like a responsible adult to his family, but Amy sensed the significance of the change of circumstances in his life. She'd watched him brood, realising sooner or later he would have nothing left to hold onto, no grasp of life as it should be. When dawn pushed away the darkness in readiness for another day, he closed his eyes ready for sleep.

Thirty minutes later, Luke leapt on him and ripped the quilt away.

"Come on, Company Sergeant Major Gillet, you are late on parade," he squealed.

Gillet forced a grin.

"Come here and give me a hug, you big wassock."

By the time Luke had left for school, Pinkie managed to struggle from his bed in the spare room. With bloodshot eyes, he made his way downstairs and spent the morning sobering up with endless mugs of coffee and, unable to kick the habit, chain-smoking Marlboro Lights. He'd never yet matched Gillet pint for pint, and more than likely never would, but last night Gillet went for the booze big time. He knew the reason why, time heals. At one o'clock that afternoon, the taxi pulled up and the two men did the man thing – a brief hug followed by a firm clasp of hands.

"Forget the kid Shafiq, Tommo, get on with your life and look after Luke. He needs you more than ever now," Pinkie said, jabbing his forefinger into Gillet's chest.

Gillet shrugged.

"Yeah, maybe I'll do that. If you hear any more of him, let me know ASAP. Take care of yourself, Pinkie, and keep your back covered."

For a brief moment Pinkie's temper rose at Gillet's nonchalant attitude towards his son Luke. He felt like blurting out that he should see a doctor, get medication to settle his nerves, relieve the stress. But knowing Gillet's stubborn nature; his advice would fall on stony ground.

"Yeah, you too, mate," he muttered.

Alone in the kitchen, Gillet felt hot and thick-headed from the night's drinking, and toyed with a fresh cup of coffee while flipping through Luke's video game magazine. In is present state it seemed pointless to try to read, instead he glanced at the pictures.

The harsh ring of the phone startled him and, thumbing the green button, he checked the number. It was his mother. Amy had called to tell her they had split and that she was sorry she couldn't be a better mother to Luke. Mrs Gillet told her to grow up and cut her off.

"If you need time on your own, Luke can stay with me and your dad; we are five minutes away. Apart from that, I won't say anything more on the matter," she said.

For the best part of the day he tried, without success, to slot Amy into a niche of his mind, somewhere he could summon or dismiss her at will. At night he slumbered in fitful spasms, waiting for time to stall and collapse. All the time, embedded in his heart the cold haunt of melancholy hung heavy like a wet blanket, and a sense of great sadness seemed to leap within him, leaving him feeling empty and drained. Out of nowhere the image of Shafiq loomed into his mind, pushing all away as if nothing else mattered. For hour after hour he tossed and turned, unable to sleep, and throwing the quilt to one side he made his way downstairs. Dressed in his pants, at the kitchen table he stared out the window as dawn brought forth the light of a new day. A vision of Shafiq persisted as if etched in his memory and he leaned and rested his chin on his steepled fingers. No matter how hard he tried to change, he saw most things as a form of provocation; the slightest disruption to his routine had become a pending confrontation. Separated from the only life he'd ever known, he needed something to fill his mind, something to grasp and channel his energies into. Then, at that precise moment, everything became clear. The answer had been there all the time, staring him full in the face. He had to find Shafiq, get him out of Afghanistan and help find him a new life away from those that treated life as if it were a piss in a bucket. His resentment rose, getting the better of him, then dipped. The brown waters that swilled though his mind were no longer murky.

*

The following evening he made the short drive into town and entered the Maharajah Indian restaurant. A couple of leaves ago he'd thrown out a bunch of drunken troublemakers, and Aziz, the proprietor, glad to show his appreciation, had been more than happy to give him the occasional meal on the house. Tonight, raucous laughter drowned out the lilting Eastern music. Half a dozen men on a fishing trip necked alcohol direct from the bottle. By a window a couple sat studying the menu. Others reached out for a glass of water to quell the fiery spices balancing on incandescent tongues.

"It is always good to see you, Mr Gillet." Aziz smiled, holding out his hand.

"And you, my friend. Is Ari around?"

"Of course, is something wrong?"

"No. I'd like a word, if that's okay with you?"

"No problem. Please wait and I will fetch him." Aziz shrugged.

Ari was an Afghan, or so he said. No one seemed certain where he came from, but he was an expert at Indian cuisine and that was all Aziz needed to know.

Ari scratched at his two-day-old beard as Gillet explained how Shafiq had saved his life. The moment Gillet mentioned the words *Bacha Bazi* his demeanour changed. His eyes dimmed and he raised his arms in a gesture of futility.

"Forget it, Mr Gillet, you'll never be permitted to get this boy out of Afghanistan. Not only is it dangerous, it is impossible."

"There must be something I can do. How about adoption?"

"Shaaria law does not recognise adoption. Cases regarding guardianship may be considered, but to a Christian family, it would be most unlikely. After thirty years of conflict thousands of orphans roam the streets in every town and city of Afghanistan and Iraq. People the world over are prepared to adopt these unfortunate doe-eyed orphans, but as I have already said, it is against Islamic law," Ari said, taking a long drag on his cigarette.

Aziz looked up at the no smoking sign.

"Maybe if I smuggled him over the border into Pakistan, at least he'd have a chance of a better life."

"Mr Gillet, please try to understand what I say," Ari said, staring into Gillet's eyes. "It would be as difficult as kidnapping one of your royal princes. Sure, these dancing boys exist, but they are the property of very influential people who exist beyond the realms of common morality. Should you be caught attempting to kidnap one of these boys, in all probability you will both end up dead, or at least suffer horrible mutilation. You would be wise to forget both *Bacha Bazi* and the boy."

Gillet pushed the cup away, watching Ari flick ash on the floor. Aziz ran out of patience, snatched the cigarette from Ari's hand and threw it from an open window.

"Yeah, I hear you; now tell me how I can get into Afghanistan," Gillet said.

In a moment of lucidity Ari rose without a word and, followed by Aziz, disappeared through the door leading into the kitchen area. Gillet shrugged. Maybe they had lost their appetite for the conversation, but he wasn't about to give up just yet. Outside, dark wispy clouds drifted past the half-moon in the darkening sky; maybe tomorrow would be another fine day. It was that word again, *maybe*; it sounded like a curse, sent to separate reason from hope. He knew hope was a good thing. In its own time it comes and goes, and never dies. Gazing out over the dark grey sea, he listened to the tide lap over the sand. The pain in his leg had eased and he decided to walk the last half-mile to his home. Level with an alley separating a burger bar from a health food shop, he dropped the aluminium walking stick into a wheelie bin. Then, pushing back his shoulders, walked away from the dimming town lights along the narrow unlit coastal road to the solitary row of houses overlooking the Wash. Darkness held no fear for him; if anything, they accepted each other silently in a mutual embrace. The flicker of determination in his eyes grew stronger. The impossible is always possible; you just have to sneak up and take it by surprise.

*

It rained the following day, a miserable drizzling pattern like a dull February morning. The elderly woman in the local post office peered over the top of her glasses, and with a superior smile informed him with a pronounced lisp he would need a visa to enter Afghanistan. A tourist visa valid for one month, she suggested. The length of time it took she couldn't confirm, maybe up to three months. His patience faded. The last thing he wanted was to hang around for three months while bureaucracy dragged its arse. Then, remembering the past he pulled himself erect. A professional soldier never acts out of fervour. He must remain sanguine at all times to avoid mistakes that might lead to his death. His immediate brief was to consider each risk down to the last contingency. He'd devise a plan that would not just get him into Afghanistan, but would get him out unharmed. This was a one-time operation, and the chances of remaining uncaught and undiscovered were minimal. Blind to the drizzling rain he considered his options. For the moment he had nothing concrete to work on, just a mix of loose fancies tumbling in his mind. He needed a straw to clutch at, anything that could give him a kick-start. From his festering mind came the makings of an answer. It was a long shot, but at least it was the embryo of an idea.

*

The next morning his begrudging eyes set dark with distaste. Gone the inclement weather of the day before, replaced by a bone-melting heat. Hands pushed deep into the rear pockets of his chinos, he gazed across the road at the converted cinema. Once upon a time, when Britain was great, people queued to watch extravaganzas as *Singing in the Rain* and *The Adventures of Robin Hood* starring Errol Flynn, playing to a full house. Now it was a mosque. In his mind a place that harboured a dark threat to a good and decent civilisation. The banner fluttering in the wind he presumed extolled the virtues of Islam. Time had passed since he'd given thought to the wanton butchery by the Taliban before the army pensioned him off, unlike time, his memory would never pass. But no matter of his other thoughts. In the main his mind concentrated on the problem in hand with little room for anything else. Yet the limp fluttering banner failed to repulse a flame of motivation searing into his brain. A rush of imagery filled his mind and stoked his temper. He was a patriot. A man convinced he would be doing his country a favour by slaughtering everyone inside the mosque.

Two young men dressed in jeans and sweatshirts, with a white skullcap-(*takiyah*)-pulled tight on their heads, left the mosque. The tallest hesitated, trawled out a packet of cigarettes and struck a match. Gillet pushed away his contempt, and made his way across the deserted road.

"Excuse me," he said. "Do Afghans use this mosque?"

The shorter of the two surveyed him, eyes slitted and sullen. His companion busied himself crushing the cigarette beneath the toe of his dirty trainer. Gillet watched, taking in the dark bird-like eyes, the hooked nose above cruel twisted lips. His temper simmered, ready to boil.

"What's your problem, mate?"

"No problem, I need advice," Gillet said, pushing back the urge to tell him he wasn't his mate.

"Tubeh, the Imam, he's Afghan."

"Where can I find him?"

"He's in the mosque. Wait here and I'll fetch him."

Tubeh was a slight man, approximately forty years of age with jet-black hair, and enquiring eyes bordering on insolence. He gave the impression of a man who knew all the answers before the questions had been asked. Dressed in a *jubbah*, a long white gown that reached from the neck down to the ankles unlike others of his ilk, he was clean-shaven. The thin straggly beard from which Allah would grab and pull him up to heaven when his time came, absent. His voice was soft.

"Good morning, how can I help you?"

"Is there somewhere we can talk, alone?"

"May I enquire the subject of our conversation?"

Gillet fidgeted. The first hurdle had been safely negotiated, now wasn't the time to show recklessness.

"I prefer if we spoke in privacy."

The Imam hesitated, and his eyes, intent on Gillet's face, seemed to strip away the flesh and peer into his mind, missing nothing. Gillet held his gaze; here was a master of chaos and turbulence. One with the ability to incite others to do things that shouldn't be done. He wasn't going to horse-trade his feelings with this man.

"Do the words *Bacha Bazi* mean anything to you?"

Tubeh's facial muscles jerked.

"These are not the words I would expect to hear from a man such as yourself, I assume you know their meaning, or you would not be here. But how could I be of help?"

"I'm aware of their meaning. *Bacha Bazi* is a form of sexual slavery using young boys, recently revived in Afghanistan," Gillet said, trying to sound casual.

If Gillet thought his effrontery so bold as to catch Tubeh off-guard, he was wasting his time. Tubeh face remained expressionless.

"Why would I have an interest in these matters? We are not in Afghanistan."

"I need a few minutes of your time, but not here."

"I can spare you a few minutes; follow me."

Elated at the rapid response Gillet was aware that once he'd entered into this world of the unknown there was a good chance he'd never leave untainted.

The Imam's room was small. A wooden table with a chair at either end stood in the centre. On one side of the table a worn copy of the Koran lay open next to a box of thick white candles. Without waiting for an invitation, he sat at one end of the table and told Tubeh the full story. How Shafiq had saved his life from the blast, the loss of his family, and his intentions to smuggle the boy out of Afghanistan in the hope of providing him with a better life elsewhere. Tubeh stared down at his slender hands waiting for Gillet to finish.

"A sad story, and I understand your reasons for wanting to help this poor, unfortunate boy, but what is it you want of me?" Tubeh said.

Gillet gritted his teeth; now was the time to push his luck.

"I need to get into Afghanistan, and cross the border into Pakistan without a visa."

"Without a current visa it is impossible."

Gillet had half-expected the answer.

"I need to get the boy out as soon as possible for his own safety, and I was hoping if you might be able to help speed up my visa application. As an Imam, the Afghan Embassy might make a special dispensation."

"It's possible, but even with a valid visa, how do expect to smuggle this boy you call Shafiq past the border checks?"

"Kids dodge border patrols daily just to stay alive, and as for getting him out of Pakistan, I'll deal with that when the time arises."

The atmosphere changed and Gillet thought he'd overplayed his hand. The Imam pulled a packet of cigarettes from his pocket, flared up a disposable plastic lighter and inhaled. Gillet watched in disgust. His time in the Middle East had taught him that all things rendered as harmful to a Muslim are forbidden under Islamic law. He also knew Islamic law induced by the Koran to be flawed, with confutations.

"You are a stubborn man, Mr Gillet," the Imam said. "Maybe I can help. Of course I make no promises. Across the road is a small newsagents shop. Be in your car at seven o'clock tomorrow night. A friend will bring you to the mosque where can discuss the matter further."

Hope flamed Gillet's heart. Best press home your advantage than to trample over it, Captain Frome once told him before a battle.

"I'll be there," he said.

*

Like most kids his age, Luke wanted things done his way, and the prick of disappointment hurt when his father said he must stay with his grandparents for a time. Not that he disliked them; he loved them to bits. After the loss of his mother he yearned for a strong relationship with his father. Feel the strong sense of security he needed. Most of all he needed his father to help divert his mind from his unwanted failings. At night-times, beneath his West Ham quilt, he struggled to work out simple equations using his fingers. Not once did he dare think he'd arrived at the correct answers. Even if he did, under the circumstances it's doubtful he would have known. Yet he strived in the hope that one day he could achieve something to please his mother, some small thing to make her love him as much as he loved her. That night, instead of counting his fingers, he listened to the wind rattle the windows. With clenched fists, he substituted his normal bedtime procedure to ponder the times he'd heard his parents argue over his progress at school. He accepted the blame for being the cause of their break-up and would have it no other way, regardless of what anyone told him. Other children got on well with their parents. He'd seen them at the school on parents' nights. His mother never attended, more important things to do, she had told him. As for his father, he was away fighting for Queen and country. Gradually he became less than a moderate scholar, with no leaning towards any particular subject. Aware of his mother's deep embarrassment at his failings, he learned not to feel uneasy at the way she avoided contact with other parents. But life has its compensations, as an athlete he was in a class of his own. Superb in track and field events, he towered head and shoulders above the other students, winning everything at county junior level. His biggest love was to keep goal for his school football team. All in all he led two lives as day after day he battened down his frustrations while struggling to live his life like the other children. During the nights he released those frustrations and sobbed himself to sleep.

"He needs you more than ever now Amy has left again. Get yourself sorted. This isn't the army, it's your son we are talking about," Gillet's father remonstrated. "Go and see a doctor, you're a bag of bloody nerves, you are. Damned if I know what's going on in your head these days."

Gillet let remark pass.

"Yeah I know, Dad, I've just a few loose ends to tie up. After that, we'll be just fine," Gillet said, his heart beating against his ribcage having to lie to his father. "I'll bring him straight from school tomorrow night."

"He doesn't seem the same to me since he left the army," his mother said to her husband after Gillet had left. "He seems troubled, intense and edgy. Still, I suppose he's always been a bit that way."

"I'll tell you what his trouble is, shall I? He's got that stress thing, or whatever they call it."

"Post Traumatic Stress Disorder, dear, that's what they call it, PTSD for short."

"Well, he should see a doctor then."

"See a doctor? Too stubborn for things like that, he is."

*

Barbs of guilt raked Gillet's heart as he made his way home. The thoughts souring his mind he tried to push away with an indifferent shrug, but as usual they lingered, chaotic and scattered. How could he tell them that he needed escape from the humdrum of civilian life before it drove him insane? Tell them that he needed to go on a wild goose chase in the hope it might dispel the demons dancing among his tangled nerves. Fuck the Taliban; they had taken his foot and now it was payback time. If he could piss off an immoral illiterate by taking a young boy from his filthy clutches, so much the better. He slowed and looked to the sea, knowing he was kidding himself. It wasn't Shafiq that gave him his motivation. It was a deep-rooted selfishness that prevented him from recognising his soldiering days were finished. He'd thought long and hard of

28

what else in life could replace the years of excitement, the adrenaline rush before the killing carnival began. Even better, the victory of survival after battle, when the enemy lay dead, covered in blood. This would be his war, his own private conflict, and no one would take it from him.

*

The next day he high fived Luke outside the school gates and made his way along the seafront. The comforting sounds of the breaking waves his only company. Legs outstretched on a rusting bench, he stared out over the grey North Sea. White horses charged from folding waves and crashed onto the foaming tide, washing the sandy shingled beach silky smooth. First one and then another, they charged again and again, defeat never an option. It was different here; the air, the sky more clear, brilliant, farther away, unlike the hovering grey canopies that hung low over major cities stifling the populations. The unmistakable smell of salt tangled with seaweed gripped the air and penetrated his nostrils, like it did when he and Amy had left their footprints in the wet sand. In better times they had walked the shoreline hand in hand the way lovers do. But that was history now. He cradled his head in his hands. His thoughts were not of himself, nor of the advancing tide or the shrieking seagulls diving and wheeling overhead. His mind was full of his son, Luke. What if he failed to return from Afghanistan to be the father Luke needed? If he did return, would it be enough to make him settle, or would he crave other speculative undertakings?

Morning gave way to afternoon. His mind blanked and he traced the horizon with his eyes, stopping to dwell on a passing ship. Passing ships have destinations, an exotic port far away from which to begin another chapter, plough another furrow in the field of life. Maybe the time had come for him to drop anchor, to ride out the rest of his life in peace and tranquillity, to ebb and flow with the rest of the world. Not just yet, later maybe. He smiled and wiped away the tears trickling down his face. That word, *maybe*, it never went away.

*

At seven o'clock, dead on time, a man dressed in a smart black suit strode across the road and paused in front of Gillet's car. His set of perfect teeth flashed a million dollar smile as he tapped on the window. Gillet stepped from the car with his eyes fixed on the hovering gang of Asian youths cocooned in oversized hooded jackets and fleeces. The man in the black suit caught his look, turned to the youths and spoke in a language Gillet didn't understand, then turned back with an extended hand.

"My name is Karim and your car will be safe, I can assure you," he said, shaking Gillet's hand.

"Lucky for them."

Karim was a handsome man in a film star manner. Light skinned, with warm brown smiling eyes, a well-proportioned nose and a full mouth, which in some cases might give concern as to his sexual genre. His voice was soft and precise, Asian-accented. By all accounts Karim was a man who gave orders and expected them to be carried out to the letter.

Raising his eyebrows he mulled over the meaning of Gillet's words. A cautious man by nature, he hadn't the slightest desire to be involved in clandestine enquiries from the local police over a minor fracas.

"Please follow me," he said, crossing the road towards the mosque.

It was a different room than the last time. The inside was larger. Books, maps, magazines and newspapers written in Arabic lay scattered across an inlaid table in abject chaos. In one corner a forty-two-inch plasma TV flickered a foreign news channel which Gillet guessed to be Al Jazeera. In another corner sat Tubeh, a satellite phone pressed tight to his ear as if having difficulty in hearing. Karim caught Gillet's disapproving glance, and as if suffering embarrassment began tidying the room, stacking magazines and books into neat piles. Finished, he sat and gestured for Gillet to do likewise. Gillet settled in a worn brown leather chair with split seams. Tubeh replaced the telephone in the battery-charging cradle.

"My apologies, Mr Gillet, we have been very busy. Might I offer you a drink, coffee or perhaps tea? Unfortunately, the Koran forbids alcohol."

Gillet pursed his lips to conceal the smile. Bullshit. He was aware Muslims possessed an inveterate habit of interpreting the Koran any way it suited them at any particular moment in time. If he took the time to search the room, he would in all probability unearth a half full bottle of whisky or brandy. He nodded his head and declined the offer.

"You said you might be able to help me."

Tubeh switched off the TV and pulled his hand across his mouth like a man unsure of what to say next. Karim sighed and spoke first.

"I shall be brief, Mr Gillet. Although we sympathise with your motives, our reasons are selfish. This man before you, Tubeh, is my brother by birthright. In his wisdom he chose to follow the path of Allah the merciful. I myself own a string of stores. I believe you call them *pound shops*," Karim said, frowning at Tubeh lighting a cigarette. "A long time ago Allah blessed us with a younger brother; his name, Aarash. Twelve years ago, at the age of seven, Aarash was abducted whilst playing with his friends outside my father's house in Kabul. The police were informed and, after extensive enquiries, we discovered he had been taken to northern Afghanistan and sold to a rich politician for *Bacha Bazi*. The police were afraid to help us for fear of repercussions. And despite further investigations, we have never seen or heard from Aarash since."

"If you expect me to search for your long-lost brother, you are wasting your time," Gillet said, raking his fingers through his hair. "I'm only interested in Shafiq."

"No, that is not what I am implying, Mr Gillet," Karim said.

Gillet shrugged.

"If we agree to help you find Shafiq, and get him out of Afghanistan, he must be brought to this country and be instrumental in the exposure of the practice of *Bacha Bazi* to the rest of the world."

Gillet turned and gazed out through the window. He hadn't envisaged bringing Shafiq back to the UK. Neither had he planned to use him as a political pawn in the hunt for revenge by two Afghan brothers with an axe to grind. Then there was the aftermath; what would happen to the boy when all the fuss had died down and the do-gooders had no further use for him? More than likely he would be sent back to Afghanistan as an illegal immigrant and end up having his throat slit in a filthy back alley.

"Then what? What happens when you have no further use for him?"

Gillet saw the tension lines in Tubeh's face. Karim remained cool and ran his tongue over his lips. Gillet shivered. Fourteen years in the army had taught him a certain amount of pride in his ability to weigh up other men's thoughts. And at this particular moment, he didn't relish the signals coming from either of the two men.

"We have considered all the aspects, with the boy's well-being our main concern, and we feel it would be to the boy's benefit to integrate him into our society. Papers, passports and visas in his name are a minor detail easily overcome," Karim said. "Naturally, it goes without saying he will be raised as a Muslim."

Gillet stared at each of the men in turn.

"You seem to have thought of everything, except for one thing. How do I get him out of Afghanistan?"

This time Tubeh spoke.

"Mr Gillet, you and I are from different backgrounds. You were a soldier, a man of action who lived under the banner of violence; your areas of employment are limited, I am a man of peace, free to move without suspicion or surveillance. Perhaps if we combine our recourses we can arrive at a suitable conclusion. I suggest you go away, digest what we have talked of and in three days' time we will meet again."

If Gillet was surprised by the words it never showed, yet wondered if somehow he had missed their meaning. No matter how hard he tried, he didn't understand Tubeh's words. Of course he was aware he was no longer a soldier and didn't need to be reminded by the likes of the Imam, or his brother. As for violence, the Afghans could teach him a trick or two in that department. At first-hand he'd witnessed a couple of examples of their handiwork on the remains of two captured American marines buried up to their necks in the desert with their eyelids slit.

An overpowering impulse to leave shifted into his body, and he looked at Tubeh silhouetted in the window overlooking the deserted street. He steadied himself, and pressed his outstretched fingers against the sides of his trousers and tapped his leg. Failure considered, but not contemplated. He needed to make a stand, something to let them know he wasn't going to be pushed around.

"Okay," he said. "I'll give you twenty-four hours to contact me with a plan to extract Shafiq from Afghanistan or I'll find an alternative way. This is my number."

They were attempting to manipulate him to suit their own needs, and he should have seen it coming. *He* would decide what was and wasn't best for Shafiq.

Outside, the Asian hoodies, lounged against the shop window like mindless morons. Maybe a little baiting might incite them enough to give him the opportunity to wipe the floor with them. Then again, his immune system didn't run to weasel-faced arseholes.

Back home he left the car on the drive and made his way to his local pub. Perhaps a nightcap might help him sleep and prevent the nightmares invading his mind. Olivia, the young barwoman aware of his tipple, started to pull his pint the moment he stepped through the door. After one sip he glanced across at the locals arguing over a game of darts.

"Hey, Tommo," one called. "Fancy a game of darts?"

"Yeah, come on, and put your best foot forward. Oh sorry, I forgot you only have one."

"Bastards." He grinned, picking up his pint and joining them.

*

When darkness had succumbed to light and sunlight streamed through the windows he opened his eyes. There had been times in his life when the thought of lying in bed until noon had been the stuff of luxury, fit for the rich and privileged. Awake, his head became filled with a myriad of questions followed by a mist of answers pushing all else away. Certainties were cancelled out by looming uncertainties, leaving him trapped in a limbo of distracted bewilderment. Gritting his teeth, he swung his legs from the bed and made his way downstairs, a heated can of peeled tomatoes on top of two toasted slices of bread served as breakfast. Finished, pushing away the plate he contemplated the best way to battle the relentless grinding teeth of time. Boredom had become his biggest enemy. No more patrols to cordon off and search a compound a Taliban commander had been seen frequenting. Apprehend him and bring him in for questioning were his orders, in the hope of gaining vital intelligence, they said. If he'd had his way, he'd have rammed a live grenade down the flea-ridden bastard's throat and given him five seconds to shit it out the other end before it exploded. He sighed, washed the plate beneath the running tap, and stuck it in the plastic sink rack to dry. Tomorrow morning instead of peeled tomatoes he'd have baked beans.

That night he watched Luke struggle with his homework, with corn-coloured hair and big blue eyes he was the image of his mother.

It had been on his mind all day how to tell Luke of Shafiq, how he'd saved his life and lost his family in the process. When he did and added he was considering returning to Afghanistan to help Shafiq seek a new life, Luke looked at him through bewildered eyes. He remained pensive, allowing his son the time he needed to gather his thoughts. Outside, the soft glow of street lights intruded upon the gloomy interior of the room and Gillet stretched out his legs. Luke folded and unfolded his arms, tapped his feet up and down, then contorted his face into a series of grimaces.

"He must be very brave," he said.

Gillet's mouth quirked; a wry smile changed the shape of his face.

"He can be my brother if he wants to, I won't mind."

The words caught Gillet below the belt and he knew the conversation was getting out of hand.

"Okay, that's enough for tonight. Sleep on it and we'll discuss it further tomorrow after school."

"Tomorrow's Saturday, Dad, we can discuss it in the morning."

*

Gillet leaned back as far as the high-backed chair would allow and pondered the situation. He knew nothing of Tubeh, or his brother Karim. Once he'd entered Afghanistan, he'd have to make enquiries about Shafiq in the knowledge it would attract attention from dubious sources. He had no intention of ending up with his cock cut off, sewn into his mouth, and left out on the desert waiting for a bunch of marauding dogs to finish him. Last but not least, he wasn't going to risk life and limb to leave the boy in the hands of a couple of strangers he'd just met. The essence of the operation was secrecy, and the fewer that knew, the better.

Halfway through the televised football results the following evening, Gillet punched the green button and waited for the message to crackle down the line.

"Mr Gillet, we have devised a plan to get Shafiq out of harm's way. Come to the mosque tomorrow and we can discuss the details of each planned stage until the boy is safely under our protection."

On the spur of the moment, either through petulance or sheer bloody-mindedness, Gillet called the deal off.

"May I ask why?" Karim said after a few seconds.

"This isn't just about the boy, is it? It's about him being used to uncover this *Bacha Bazi* affair. Surely you realise by publicising his existence you place us all in danger?"

"Mr Gillet, you are mistaken."

"I don't think so," he said. "It's likely there are more Taliban and ex-Mujahidin in this country than in Kabul, and I don't want them hammering on my door looking for revenge after you have sold your story to the newspapers. The deal's off."

Gillet pressed the red button. West Ham had lost to Bolton 2–0, Luke shuffled his way up the stairs ready to take out his frustration on whichever unfortunate victim wandered in front of the cross hairs on his Xbox.

The next day, Amy made a brief call to check if all was okay with Luke. Gillet didn't bother to respond, and instead tossed the phone across to Luke. Luke leaned across to pick the phone up, then shrugged and left it where it lay.

*

The weeks passed, each day much the same, monotonous and tedious. The only noticeable difference was that one day it rained, and the next the sun shone. And as if waiting for a reminder to begin its relentless search for destruction and annihilation of all that dared to stand in its way, time stood still. Gillet divided his time between waking and sleeping, with the occasional stroll down to the beach to break the boredom. As usual it was the thought of Shafiq that had occupied his mind with alarming regularity, until he admitted he'd failed. That was no great problem; men like him were never afraid to fail. Great accomplishments demanded the greatest risks, and history had been shaped by those that failed, and then rose again when moments of crisis were thrust upon them. Yet, irritated, he felt the wind shift to the south, causing a feral grey light to descend from overhead. He paid small attention to the conclave of screeching gulls' acrobatic manoeuvres during their incessant search for food, and realised perhaps he should have showed more patience towards Tubeh and Karim. It was alright for them, they hadn't been trained as soldiers whose lives depended on rapid decisions. Theirs was a country where life had stood still for centuries, stagnating with time. Then again, maybe it still wasn't too late, he mulled, attempting to raise his spirits. But he was kidding himself; where once he was vibrant, alert, now he felt spent, fading. For all he knew, between him and the dark grey rolling sea Shafiq might already be dead, rotting in a dried-out wadi minus his arms or legs, or even his head. Even if he were still alive it might prove impossible to find him. *Maybe*, the word haunted his mind and twisted his entrails. *Ready for Anything* was the motto of his regiment, and that's the way he had lived his life.

Kneeling, he tore off his false foot and hurled it into the sea. He wanted to be a man again, healthy, whole.

"Mr Gillet."

Still angry, he turned and fixed his gaze on Tubeh a few metres away. His face was calm with that ever-present smile of superiority. Gone was the *jubbah*; in its place a grey lightweight suit and black polo shirt, a black *takiyah* tight on his head.

"I sense anger, Mr Gillet. There are those who would say that is a sign of weakness," he said.

Gillet checked his temper and kept the bite from his voice.

"Yeah, well I'd call it controlled aggression," he grunted. "What do you want?"

"I have come to ask you to reconsider our offer of help, under different circumstances of course. Karim is emotional about the disappearance of our brother, Aarash. Unfortunately, in his mind he holds the world responsible."

"Yeah, well it's a pity he can't bring himself to blame the people who were responsible, instead of blaming his brother's disappearance on the rest of the world."

Tubeh's face twisted.

"For a man seeking assistance, your attitude surprises me. Plus, you are misinformed. Sometimes the world isn't always as we would wish it to be and we live under perplexing circumstances."

"That sounds convenient."

Tubeh's throat burned and he stared at Gillet with ill-concealed distaste.

"Mr Gillet, be assured, I am as appalled as you are by *Bacha Bazi*. However, I am here without Karim's knowledge. I admit his reasons for assisting may be wrong. What you do with Shafiq is none of my business. I would be more than happy to see the boy escape the clutches of these evil men," Tubeh said. "And do not speak to me in this manner. In the West you have a different term for *Bacha Bazi* – the word paedophile comes to mind. Your lax laws allow these men to walk the streets of every town in Britain searching for victims, male or female. It is *your* justice system that needs closer scrutiny."

Gillet remained quiet, and then gave his standard response when faced with a loss for words.

"Bollocks."

Tubeh crushed the cigarette into the sand.

Gillet looked down at the incoming tide, bent and picked up his false foot.

"Mr Gillet, do you accept my offer or not?"

"I call the shots," he said.

Tubeh's response was succinct and to the point. "It would be unsafe for Shafiq to remain in Pakistan. They are nobody's fool and would recognise him as *Bacha Beresh*, a boy without a beard that dances and dresses like a woman, and it would be just a matter of time before his Mujahidin owner learned of his whereabouts. For the sake of his safety, he must be brought to the UK."

"And then?" he grunted.

"That is your decision."

"I want to see the boy settled, nothing more."

"Then we are in agreement?"

Gillet nodded.

"Good. When you reach Kabul, you are go to the Mustafa Hotel – a room is reserved for you – and wait until you are contacted. When you discover the boy's whereabouts, you will be given an address. Take him there. A passport containing all the necessary visas will be waiting, and disguised as an Afghan woman he will make his way to Peshawar International Airport in Pakistan. On arrival, he will be taken to a place of safety and given another false passport along with the necessary documents allowing him entry into the UK. Do not worry, they will pass the customs' scrutiny. I must stress that it's imperative for your own security that you travel apart. Do not make contact until you are both safely in England."

"You make it sound easy."

"Mr Gillet, I assure you it will come as no surprise if I never set eyes on you again. Remain vigilant and stay close to him. As an English tourist in Afghanistan you will rouse suspicion enough for him to go unnoticed."

"When do I leave for Afghanistan?"

"Trust me with your passport, and your visas will be entered within the next three or four days and returned by post. In the meantime, I would suggest you see your doctor and get the necessary inoculation documentation to be on the safe side when passing through customs. Officials will demand money before you are allowed to pass without the correct documentation. And one other thing, from now on it will be wise to keep away from the mosque."

CHAPTER TWO

Leaning back in his seat, Gillet snapped on his safety belt and fidgeted as Flight 173 from Heathrow, with its nose pointed north-east, began the descent into Kabul International Airport. Below, white drifting clouds gave the appearance of sheep grazing in a sparse meadow. Scattered on either side of the runway, disembodied tail-planes and fuselages of destroyed aircraft lay jumbled like a vast scrap - yard, a stark reminder of Taliban attacks. The dull whirr of the undercarriage exiting the bay eased his mind as the wheels locked into position, followed by the sudden screech of tyres making contact with the tarmac runway. The roar of reversing engines filled the cabin. For the second time within months he set foot in the Islamic Republic of Afghanistan, a landlocked country in central Asia, bordered by Pakistan in the south and east, and China in the far north-east. Today it remains the second least-developed country in the world, its main export the opium poppy, responsible for 93 per cent of the opiates on the world market.

Free from the bone-melting heat, he entered the air-conditioned terminus. Shortly security police would appear from nowhere, demanding money to fast-track passengers through airport customs. Refusal to pay the going rate would lead to complications, and disregarding the bitter taste of intimidation, he handed over a fistful of Afghanis. The luggage check consisted of a perfunctory shake down with the electric baton. Armed with a Foreigner's Registration Card, he exited the airport, climbed into a taxi and told the driver to take him to the Mustafa Hotel.

Ill at ease, by the window of his hotel room he watched the sun drop behind the mountains, adrenaline coursed through his veins making sleep impossible. Wait until you are contacted, Tubeh had said. Waiting wasn't Gillet's game. A cool shower put him in a better frame of mind, and barefoot, in chinos and a T-shirt, he swung open the glass doors leading to the balcony overlooking the bustling city. A muffled knock distracted him and he looked at the man carrying a tray of coffee. Gillet smiled. The coffee, he assumed, a welcoming gesture from the hotel management.

"Leave it on the table, please."

"Yes, sir. Please, you are to go to the Share Naw Park tonight at eight o'clock and wait outside the cinema." he said, disappearing into the corridor, and not bothering to wait for the customary tip.

Gillet felt as if he lay on a bed of needles in a city he didn't care about. Kabul was a place where death and misery lingered, more commonplace than a breath of cool wind. He felt alone, trapped in a world vague and transparent, smeared by the occasional sense of reality. In the cramped bathroom he swilled his face with cold water and gazed into the mirror. They were still there, like a permanent fixture, the tension lines clamped on his brow. A premonition that no good would come from him being here entered his bones. Everything was different. No battle orders, no Intel, no Captain Frome, no Sergeant Pink, no company or platoon. He was alone.

Pushing his spectacles up over the bridge of his nose the receptionist raised a pair of dark bushy eyebrows. His rheumy eyes stared at Gillet as if he were a ghost. Eleven years he'd spent working at the hotel, and during that time no European had ever asked for directions to the Share Naw Park cinema.

"The films are not in English, sir," he said. "And it is most unwise to go unaccompanied."

"Cinemas fascinate me and I want to see the building from the outside," Gillet lied. "I'll be fine on my own."

The receptionist sucked in a deep breath, wiped a hand across his nose, and looked over Gillet's shoulder.

"Ah, you are fortunate. Najib has finished his work for the day; he will be happy to show you the way."

Outside, the evening lay heavy, the air sluggish and oppressive. Accompanied by Najib, he stepped into the thronging street greeted by the discordant sound of Bollywood music competing with gritty repetitive American rap. A cacophony of traditional music mixed with modernity hung harsh on the ear. On either side of the bustling Chicken Street rows of brightly lit open-front shops, each crammed full of photographic equipment, computer discs, DVDs, garish and exotic clothing, leatherworks and jewellery. Vainly competing with the musky aroma of spices, the odours of blocked drains with the stench of humanity brought breathing to a minimum. On both sides of the street a small army of clerks sat at rickety tables, charging a small fee to fill in visa applications and official documents for the milling queues of illiterates. The inevitable occurred and their passage became blocked by the onslaught of shopkeepers intent on selling him an Eastern carpet or at least a rug at a bargain price. Like bees in a beehive they swarmed around, begging and pleading. Najib berated them, gesticulating like a windmill in a gale. *Baksheesh boys*, faces covered in flies, attempted to make a living selling old maps or copies of the Kabul Weekly, tugged at his clothing, eager to practice their English in the hope of making a sale. Gillet's eyes flickered, scanning each face, hopeful he might catch a glimpse of Shafiq.

At the end of the street, Najib lost his patience and his body went into a manic dance, screaming abuse at women clad in filthy burkhas waving prescriptions for drugs and begging for money to buy them.

"Ignore them, they are the daughters of whores," he ranted, gasping for breath.

His remark carried, and beneath a hail of abuse from the maligned ladies they made their way to safety. Away from the teeming horde, the heaving mass of traffic weaved its way through the city centre like a huge metal snake. Najib grabbed Gillet's arm, and they entered Flower Street. Moment later they entered the park. Long queues thronged outside the Chief Burger Bar offering kebabs, pizzas and snacks beneath a colourful spread of multicoloured lights. Najib pointed through the crowds to the cinema and, without a word, disappeared. People stared through slitted eyes. A few slowed and muttered words out loud that he didn't understand, but knew their meaning. On the opposite side of the road, groups of old men with wild grey beards below black and white turbans sat drinking tea and smoking hand-rolled cigarettes. Other men, younger men, with dark suspicious eyes filled with hostility, pushed the numbers on their mobile phones. His apprehension ratcheted up a notch. He was being 'dicked', an expression soldiers used in Northern Ireland when locals kept tabs on patrols and reported their movements to the IRA. He'd been a fool to come alone and unarmed. Close by a man dressed in a pale blue *shalwar kameez* and white turban with a mobile phone pressed to his ear watched his every move. Small beads of sweat formed on his brow. Fear sucked at his strength, and with his arms dangling loose by his sides he moved backwards until he felt the cinema wall against his back. A hand gripped his elbow and he turned with clenched fists. A small man with a wizened face, like an aged monkey, quizzed him through thin wire spectacles hooked over large stick-out ears.

"Salaam Aleikum, Mr Gillet?" he said with a downward nod.

Gillet swore a stream of quiet intense obscenities, blinked and expelled a sigh of relief.

"My name is Bashir. Follow me, please," the man said.

The route they took was the exact reverse that he and Najib had taken from the hotel earlier. Bashir slowed in Chicken Street and glanced over his shoulder. Satisfied they weren't followed, he indicated to a narrow alley festooned with bright coloured lights; lanterns suspended by rusting chains hung unmoving in the still night air. At the bottom, a stall littered with fruit and vegetables, the kind of which Gillet had never set eyes on. Crowds of shoppers thronged around bartering over prices, each bemoaning their discontent until the right bargain was struck to satisfy all parties.

"Welcome to my father's house, Mr Gillet," Bashir said, pride edging his voice as he pushed open a heavy wooden door with peeling blue paint.

A small boy approached carrying an earthenware bowl of water. In spite of personal feelings during his time in Afghanistan, Gillet had found it good sense to familiarise himself with a smattering of local customs during the occasional hearts and minds exercises. Smiling, he doused his hands and wiped his face with the cool water. The boy nodded; the *Pashtunwali* code of *Melmastia*, the traditional display of hospitality, had been satisfied. Bashir beamed his pleasure, adjusted his spectacles and introduced Gillet to his father, Abbas, who insisted he stay for the evening meal. No wish to offend the people trying to help him, Gillet sat cross-legged over a palatable meal of beef kebab, Kabuli rice, naan and green *chai*. The conversation was staggered, small and meaningless – the weather, price of corn – politics was off the agenda. With the meal over Abbas leaned back, and amid much sucking and puffing, lit a rolled cigarette that left a sweet sickly smell hovering in the air. Women and children rose and left together. Gillet waited to hear the reason why he'd been brought to the elderly man's house. Abbas spoke first.

"You are a brave man Mr Gillet, to attempt a foolhardy venture, Mr Gillet."

"I do as my conscience tells me; a man can do no more," Gillet responded, hoping his words would meet with the old man's approval.

"A conscience, my friend, is a luxury few men can afford in the present climate, especially a soldier. We know the reason you are here and have given our word to help you as much as we dare. *Bacha Bazi* is a scar on the heart of the people of Afghanistan, the sooner it is healed, the better. Act with haste if you wish to achieve your purpose, word moves quickly in Kabul, should my family be discovered assisting you, our punishment will be rapid and harsh," Abbas said, staring at the glowing end of his cigarette as if it might hold the answer to his problems. "Tomorrow, go to the park. There you will see boys flying kites. It is a very popular pastime amongst both the young and old. Sometimes dancing boys are present with their masters; maybe there you will find the boy you seek."

"And then?"

"If you are successful in removing this boy from his owner, bring him here and leave; you will be contacted when necessary. Go now. May Allah keep you safe."

*

Gillet's hotel room faced south-east, towards the distant mountains of the Hindu Kush split by the Khyber Pass. At three forty-five a.m. the first glow of the sun had become evident. By four thirty a.m. the room shone as if bathed in a multitude of arc-lights. Relinquishing the opportunity of sleep he stared up at the ceiling and contemplated the day ahead. Excited by the proposition of making contact with Shafiq his feelings stirred of success. A handful of painkillers eased the perpetual hammering in his head to a dull, bearable throb. His thoughts bordered on complete success and shortly he'd be on his way home. At the same time, he knew this wasn't the time to soften his stance; this was just the opening gambit with his life, the endgame. Undiminished, he listened to the sound of the city waken from its feverish slumber. Dressed, he swilled his face in cold water, and drifted his fingers through his cropped hair. Kabul was a city gripped with a reluctance to wake each morning, afraid to face another day of misery and turmoil. Modern buildings, war torn and empty, nuzzled side by side with traditional covered bazaars surrounded by a labyrinth of narrow streets, with room for nothing more than a laden donkey to negotiate. An American armoured personnel carrier careered into view, followed by two Humvees crowded with stone-faced American soldiers. The British Army's role in Kabul was to act as peacekeepers, Americans, better equipped and better armed were keen to flex their muscles, ready to engage in large-scale confrontation followed by the inevitability of combat. Contrary to worldwide belief, the oil and gas reserves in Afghanistan are minimal. Nevertheless, it was common knowledge that the country offered an attractive route for pipelines into Pakistan and India, along with other oil-producing Middle Eastern countries. The complexity of it all was lost on him. Politics was of no importance to him. He was a soldier, a simple man with a common rattle who obeyed orders and never questioned their validity. Contrary to others thoughts, he would never profess to be an action man. Battle orders, commands, deployment, sweat and blood, these things he understood. Analysis, he did not, and this is where his predicament lay. Time approached when he would need a detailed plan if he were to extract Shafiq from the depraved individuals who held him in the grip of sexual slavery. For all the humanitarian thought processes that manifested in the cells of his brain, he still didn't have the faintest idea how to proceed.

Unable to dismiss his frustration, he made his way to the dining room. Coffee made with boiling water would help soothe his nerves, that and naan bread fired in the ferocious heat of a baker's oven to neutralise the swarm of antigens itching to turn somersaults in the confines of his bowels.

Frustration soared at his failure to come up with a reasonable plan and he stretched his legs, one foot over the other, as he sipped hot black coffee. Leaning back, he surveyed those around him. To his right, two tables away, his gaze fell on three swarthy Afghans dressed in tailored green military uniforms, dark glasses and turbans, and sporting thick black beards. His lips twisted, another bunch of posturing tribal warlords. One turned and faced him with a stony stare, he feigned a smile. His efforts reciprocated by a cold stony glare.

"Hey, mind if I join you?"

Startled, he looked up into the intruder's podgy tanned face and shrugged.

"Suit yourself."

"I guess you were about to add, it's a free country, but we both know that isn't true, don't we? Anything free in this world isn't worth jackshit. Dan Riley, CNN news."

"Tom Gillet, tourist."

"Tourist my arse. I followed you to the park last night, and then to Chicken Street."

If Gillet had been a different man, he might have got to his feet and walked away, or at least have the sense to ignore the remark.

But because he was what he was, he thought of none of these things and stared hard into Riley's face.

"Oh yeah, and why would you want to do that?"

"Got a nose for a story, and things round here are getting boring. The world's tired of this goddam war, along with all the shit that goes with it; they want something else to sit and slurp their coffee over each morning."

Gillet's temper rose. He didn't need a hard-nosed Yank newsman sticking his snout into something that might wind up getting him killed.

"You can always go back to America and learn to mind your own fucking business."

"I'm Canadian, pal, big difference. And you know what, buddy? I reckon you're looking for someone or something. Maybe I can help. I've been here long enough to know this city back to front."

Gillet studied Riley's face. Mid-forties, tired eyes, a sagging jaw and a body past the ability to cope with the natural attrition of time. Three months previous he'd failed the strict medical on which his position as head reporter in the Middle East depended. It had cost him the price of a week in a top New York hotel for the shyster of a doctor to alter his report. His demeanour resembled a cock in a hen run. Gillet needed time to think; maybe the newsman could be useful; God knows he needed all the help he could muster. Riley held Gillet's gaze, searching for a sign of weakness. He read faces like a priest reads a Bible. Gillet remained stone-faced. Time lapsed and conversation halted, they were no more than strangers in all but flesh and blood. Gillet's first reaction had been to play down his movements the previous night, make up a tale of becoming lost in the maze of alleys. Instead, with abrasive honesty he went for the jugular.

"Ever heard the expression, *Bacha Bazi*?"

Riley's eyes narrowed, and reaching into his jacket pocket he pulled out a packet of menthol cigarettes.

"I'd keep your voice down if I were you, buddy. Buggering little kids doesn't go down too well in places," he grunted, inhaling. "Say, you're not looking for a kid for the night are you?"

"If I were, would you know where to look?"

"Sure I would, but you can go screw yourself, you limey bastard."

Gillet smiled.

"Loosen up, I was only kidding."

Riley stuffed his forefinger up his bulbous nose, inspected the result and glanced around the room.

"Yeah, well everybody has their share of depravity and perversions; some just don't like to talk about it."

"I'm searching for a kid caught up in this *Bacha Bazi* racket. I want to get him out of Afghanistan to somewhere where he'll have a chance of a better life."

"Any kid?"

"No, one in particular. He saved my life, and I owe him."

"How very noble," Riley said. "Also very stupid."

"So everybody tells me," Gillet said, getting to his feet and walking away. "From the time I set on eyes on you, I thought you were full of shit."

"Whoa there, just a minute," Riley called.

"Room twenty-one," Gillet called over his shoulder.

*

He came as Gillet knew he would, like a hungry donkey chasing a carrot, his gaze a pair of laser beams penetrating his brain. Pulling up a chair, he mopped the fine beads of perspiration popping from his forehead with a large white handkerchief, lit a menthol cigarette and listened to as much as Gillet chose to tell him.

"Better get one thing straight, buddy, you won't last five minutes wandering round parks staring at kids flying kites. I've got a cameraman, Mike Fisher, working with me. Find a diversion, something to draw their attention so Mike can sweep the park. Later, we can check the film to see whether or not the kid shows up," Riley said. "If he does, perhaps I can help you locate him."

"Sounds good, but what's in it for you?"

"Me? Hell, I'm calling this story through to my editor. No names mind you, and you can trust me on that. Do we have a deal?"

Gillet wrestled with his feelings without jumping for joy.

"Yeah, why not. It's a deal."

When Gillet left, Riley made his way to Fisher's room.

"He's one crazy bastard. As sure as shit he's gonna get himself killed, you can bet on that," Riley said, shaking his head.

"That's his problem. What about the park tomorrow?" Fisher grunted.

"Wouldn't miss it for the world. My nose tells me we are going to get a good story out of this."

It had become something of a habit of necessity to Gillet, standing at the window staring up at the Hindu Kush whenever he needed to think. Like cleaning your teeth each morning, or putting your pants on the right way round before stepping out into the world. Cause a diversion, Riley said. He could whip his flies open and stand with his dick hanging out, that would cause a diversion. Or better still rip the burkha from a passing young woman and expose whatever she wore beneath the garment, which would in all probability be a mini-skirt, sheer black stockings and suspenders complete with a pair of crotchless panties.

In an unfamiliar light-hearted mood, he made his way down to reception. With no thought for the unknown hazards that might lurk in the crowded surroundings, in broad daylight he made his way to the park. Halting by the entrance, out of loose respect he listened to the strain of the centuries-old call to prayer, *Azan*, hanging over the city like a religious blanket. Five times each day – dawn, noon, afternoon, sunset and night – activities ceased as devout Muslims faced Mecca on their hands and knees. Medieval in tone and tempo, it hailed as a testament to faith and suffering in the name of Allah. Gillet found no compassion for those who prayed, or what it was they prayed for. Not even the faintest prick of regard touched his heart for the way they honoured what he considered a barbaric religion. When at last meditation came to an end, as one they rose and went about their business, apart from those that lingered to glare with open hostility. Throwing caution to the wind, he curled his lips and stared back, oblivious to the consequences. Then a sweeping hush, all eyes turned to the black 4x4 with tinted windows pulling to a halt. Riley stepped out first, followed by a tall spindly man hefting a camera. Gillet turned his back on the ill-disposed crowd and made his way towards the vehicle.

"Don't you have any brains, Gillet?" Riley nodded. "Hanging around in the park like a jockey's whip at a wedding while they pray is just asking for trouble."

Mike Fisher, the cameraman, glared with open disgust, reached into the car and produced a square metre of red and white chequered cloth.

"It helps keep prying eyes away."

Gillet sucked his teeth; he'd seen a *shemagh* many times. Used by desert dwellers to cover the head and face to prevent the sun melting the brain. Favoured as a precaution against sunstroke, it was popular with Special Forces on covert desert missions. Folded and tucked onto his head, he pushed his shades over his eyes. He had no intention of assuming their character, but at least he could conceal his own and pass unnoticed.

Riley ambled towards the crowd in a cool display of defiance, returning their threatening looks with a nod and a warm smile. Fisher followed, camera perched on his shoulder. Gillet smiled with a grudging admiration as Riley salaamed his way into the centre of the ring of kite runners preparing for the morning sport. Tension eased, and Fisher panned the camera across the excited faces of the competitors. Gillet moved closer and halted beneath the overhanging branches of a gnarled olive tree. In the coolness of the shadow, he trained his gaze on the rows of boys tugging and loosening the kite strings as they battled for supremacy of the sky. Working in pairs, one controlled the length of string with a spool, the other manipulated the kite into a series of dives and complicated manoeuvres to gain the upper hand by sending their opponent's kite plunging shattered to the ground. Voices became louder and, incensed with fierce encouragement, urged the kites higher into a cloudless blue sky. Gillet watched, unaware each kite string had been impregnated with glue and powdered glass. Once two strings crossed, the operators loosed off a length of string attempting to cut his opponent's string, forcing him to retire from the competition. His eyes focused on the animated crowd, hoping for a glimpse of Shafiq.

Time passed as the fire in his eyes dimmed to a weary wisdom. The victorious team basked in their hard-fought victory. The crowd dispersed, People went about their business of the day, while others with nothing better to do sought the welcome comfort of the shade.

"Hello, Mister Sergeant."

He frozee, afraid to turn; afraid he might be hearing things that should not be present in his mind he remained still, waiting.

"Are you well, Mister Sergeant?"

Another voice stabbed out words he didn't understand. His fists clenched ivory white and he turned in time to see Shafiq bundled into the back of a long black Mercedes. The door slammed shut, Shafiq's face pressed tight against the tinted window, his hand raised in a plaintiff wave as the car pulled away. Gillet unclenched his fists and shook his head with frustration. He cursed for not reacting sooner, for standing there like a tailor's dummy, and with inconsolable grief watched the car disappear in a cloud of dust. Level with him, Riley spoke, he didn't catch the words. His anger festered into rage, racking up until the familiar hammering struck into his brain. Trapped in a fit of temper, he ripped the *shemagh* from his head and made his way back to the hotel. How he found the way to his room, or how he came to be sitting in a chair by the window overlooking the Hindu Kush he couldn't remember. Eventually time allowed the wash of conformity to restore him to his old self. He breathed out a long breath. Shafiq was in Kabul.

*

Riley had never overcome the habit of failing to knock before opening a door; it wasn't his way of doing things. Knocking on doors was synonymous with waiting for a response and that took something newsmen didn't have – time, he argued. Deadlines didn't wait for knocks on doors, he expounded, nor did the heaving presses waiting to spew out the scoop of the hour.

Fisher followed him into the room.

"Is this the kid you are looking for?" Riley grunted.

Gillet peered at the small camera screen.

"Yes, that's him; how did you know?"

"I didn't, but I know of the man with him, Mirza Khan, an ex-Mujahidin commander from the Soviet conflict. A real evil son-of-a-bitch, his party piece consisted of crushing captured Soviets feet first under the tracks of a Russian BMP light tank. Today, he runs the Afghan National Police force. He's also the godfather of *Bacha Bazi* here in Kabul, so you'll have your work cut out to get your hands on the kid and stay in one piece," Riley said, drawing on a freshly lit cigarette.

"Do you know where he lives?"

"Sure, who doesn't?"

"Show me, now, today."

Riley stared, cataloguing every aspect of him. The dark, determined brown eyes, the jutting jaw, the thick muscled arms. Gillet waited, his expression unflinching. Something was about to begin and he didn't know how it would end.

"No problem, but you're off to a bad start if you cross Mirza Khan. Don't say you haven't been warned."

*

It is often said a man's stature can be measured by the size of the property he owns. On the northern outskirts of Kabul, Mirza Khan's palatial residence nestled inside a thick whitewashed mortar wall isolated from all other forms of dwelling. Flat-roofed, it sprawled like a diamond in the desert over two acres of manicured scrubland. Tended gardens contained vivid displays of greyish silvery-blue violets separated by paths of wide crazy paving and terracing. In the centre, separated by a host of olive and orange trees, mingling with towering pomegranate trees adorned with bright red flowers, an ostentatious fountain manufactured from white marble threw a cascade of glistening water into the air. Each droplet pattered down onto large green lily pads like falling spring rain. Away in the south-eastern corner of the complex, set in a grove of protective pines, a small mosque awaited man's veneration towards his chosen god. Entrance to the main building was through a pair of ornamental metal gates guarded by tall Corinthian fluted marble pillars surrounded by papaya trees. Dotted around in casual array, solitary groups of uniformed guards armed with AK47s watched anything out of the ordinary. Some astride powerful motorbikes, others on more sedate mopeds, a few watched on foot, occasionally pulling high-powered antenna from mobile phones to report the existence of a 4x4 slowing as it passed the entrance to the property for the third time.

"The guards sleep in the building on the left; behind that is the dog pen where they keep the Dobermans," Fisher said. "If you manage to get in there, you sure as hell won't come out alive."

"What about the boy?" Gillet murmured.

"If the Khan's in there, then the boy is probably there too; he'll keep him close."

"Is that where the dancing takes place?"

"Sometimes, it depends. For security reasons the Khan doesn't allow too many people at one time into his home. Anyway, this kid

Shafiq won't be involved in the dancing just yet; it takes anything up to a year to train them properly, get them used to the way of things, almost like brainwashing."

"You mentioned you know of other venues where dancing takes place; have you ever witnessed it for yourself?"

"Sure, a couple of times. Not really my scene, but it happens pretty regular."

"Weren't you questioned? Surely you didn't just walk in unannounced?"

"The stench of money gets you anything in Afghanistan. The whole structure of the country depends on corruption; without it they'd be back in the hills living in tents and eating goat shit three times a day to stay alive."

Gillet dismissed Riley's rhetorical outburst. Maybe corruption wasn't a bad thing. It beat piles of time-consuming red tape beloved by Western civilisation. Common sense prevailed, and he relinquished the idea of risking entry into the Khan's home to snatch Shafiq.

In the air-conditioned coolness of the hotel, he crossed the room to the window and squinted out over the bustling street below while Riley lit another cigarette. Fisher took his time inspecting his camera. With thumbs hooked into his back pockets, his view swept over the shops selling traditional handcrafted goods, mingling side by side with those that sold modern cameras and radios. Afraid of Taliban repercussions, women no longer walked the streets unveiled. An old man astride a dirty grey donkey with split hooves added a much-needed touch of authenticity to the scene. It had been a long day, a breakfast of lukewarm coffee and soft naan never a match for his ravenous appetite. It was time for the customary meal of beef kebabs accompanied by rice cooked in the clay ovens dotted along the dusty streets. He tried to think of an alternative, something different to tempt the palate. He couldn't, not unless he wanted to spend the next five days shitting through the eye of a needle. It was beef kebabs or nothing.

"Can you get me into one of these dancing sessions?" he said, glancing across at Riley.

"Maybe, but it will cost you."

"Why doesn't that come as a surprise?"

*

Mike Fisher spent the best part of the morning cleaning his camera with a small horsehair brush. With painstaking precision he removed the residue from the lens and various compartments that had failed to resist the invasive fine talcum-like dust that hovered over the city. Educated in Melbourne, a camera had been his only source of income since leaving school, and he cared for it in much the same way a hunter might care for his rifle, as if his life depended on it. He spent a minute or two longer than he needed when he should have obeyed his instincts and walked out the door with the camera tucked under his arm. Instead, he stayed, shaking his head, and listened to Dan Riley promise Gillet the near impossible – entrance into the realms of *Bacha Bazi*. Riley sat on the balcony, the inevitable cigarette dangling from his mouth, aware he'd need the morals of an over-sexed buck rabbit during rutting season to get what he wanted. Consequence never existed in his way of thinking, only the story, everything else incidental and unimportant. Nor did he purport to be a man endowed with virtues, even less ethics that counted as unwanted baggage taking up precious room. In spite of what might level as his failings, he lived with his ego, all else a means to an end. He knew his cameraman's thoughts and glared back. He needed no lectures on his professionalism. Or the methods he used to keep his ex-wife in the luxury she had never been accustomed to before he'd been fool enough to take her for his wife. If she had her way, he'd spend the rest of his life searching for King Solomon's lost mines just to keep her in with polo ponies.

"Holy shit, it's Thursday already," Riley said out loud. "Tonight, Gillet, we'll show you the real Kabul. Do you good to get your ass away from that damn window, and be ready for a hell of a big surprise."

Weekends start on a Thursday in the Muslim world, and Kabul is no different. When the sun goes down the international crowd of diplomats, journalists, NGO workers and mercenaries put down their tools and get fuelled. Although the selling of alcohol is illegal, so were many other things that were subject to a blind eye. At the first venue Riley and Fisher introduced him to a small dumpy Filipino woman, wearing a pair of skin-tight gold pants and a black T-shirt three times too small. Her name was Valerie, and she was employed to stand by a door leading to a room blasting out music, flicking the light switch on and off to simulate a disco.

Later, inside a newly opened dance club called Martinis he encountered the darker side of Kabul. Guns, like the sands of the desert, were easily obtainable and in evidence everywhere. Most bars kept metal detectors by the entrances ready to scan patrons for weapons. Notices stated that if you drink alcohol, weapons are prohibited. Hidden from prying eyes up a short flight of stairs were private rooms that catered for Taliban warlords from the tribal areas making up Afghanistan. Integrated with the political elite, they mixed freely with girls of all denominations and religions, blowing the rants from the Koran into oblivion. Sex was always close by and never off the agenda, and with the men outnumbering the women the multinational promiscuous ladies revelled in the attention. Some, blessed with the attributes of gargoyles, shamelessly strutted their ample without embarrassment. Fascinated by the women gyrating on the dance floor, Gillet leaned on the bar. Bumping and grinding in their miniskirts and figure-hugging dresses, the women drew the drunk, yet willing men with their come-ons.

"I've had enough of this shit, I'm out of here," Gillet said, washing the single malt down his throat.

"Hold on, for Chrissake, you ain't seen nothing yet. We're heading for the French Embassy next," Riley said, winking at Fisher.

Fifteen minutes later, Gillet gaped as the 'Taliban and Tarts' themed party revved up into full swing inside the French Embassy. French, German, American, Australian, even British diplomats paraded around dressed as Taliban. Female embassy staff – the tarts – wearing next to nothing, flaunted their bodies as if they were born to lurk in the darkened corners of a dingy bordello. Woman of all sizes and shapes writhed in figure-hugging Gucci dresses hitched up around their waists. Sexual acts between high-ranking personnel from foreign embassies openly took place to the delight of those who chose to watch and scream drunken encouragement. Gillet cast his mind back to the serving soldiers. To those with limbs blown off by IEDs (Improvised Explosive Devices), or traumatised by fear and the incessant threat of death lingering around every corner of a city which, a few years ago, hardly anybody had ever heard of.

Unable to contain his temper, he pushed his way through the drunken crowd and stepped out into the cool night air. There were few things he disliked in life more than those who looked down on others. But that night he wished his time away for a handful of fragment grenades to blow the degenerates that dwelled in the safety of the embassies into tiny pieces. When a taxi full of revellers turned up he heaved them to one side, insisting the driver take him to his hotel. One reveller, a large man with a guttural accent and an alcohol-bloated face, told him to learn some manners. Gillet's fist slammed into his mouth, leaving him on all fours spitting blood and searching for his teeth.

In the sanctuary of his hotel room, he sat by the window and found it impossible to stop his brain rattling against his skull. His eyes gleamed with a feral light. Undressed, he stepped into the shower and scrubbed himself clean until his skin bled. Politics and power held few charms for him, but he knew no faith in any form could stand against money and pleasure. Out on the balcony, the noise and stink of the traffic merged with the chaos and clamour of the unholy city clouded his thoughts. It seemed to overwhelm him, occupy him, and he sensed a form of sympathy he'd never experienced. He felt a growing pity for the people of Afghanistan.

CHAPTER THREE

If it wasn't the relentless vision of Amy that kept him from sleep, it was the woman holding the baby that left him in a sombre mood the moment he pulled himself from the bed. Breakfast – a solitary cup of coffee – did little to raise his flagging spirits, and scraping away the chair he stood and made his way past the reception desk to the main doors. It was hot, hotter than usual, and drawing in a lungful of choking air he glanced at his watch. It wasn't far from the park, just a short walk, and who knows; maybe he might get lucky and catch a glimpse of Shafiq. A cool wind from the mountains fanned his face allaying the searing heat burning into his neck, and he regretted tossing Fisher's *shemagh* away in his temper.

Close to the park he skirted the decomposing carcass of a dead dog covered in swarming flies. A group of excited children kicked a deflated plastic football over in the far corner. The elder locals had more sense than to move around in the forty degrees of sweltering heat sat in the shade laughing, and hurling advice at would-be Lionel Messi's. The sun rose from the east bathing the open park in a carpet of unbearable heat. The patrol of British soldiers attached to the International Security Assistance Force (ISAF), weren't permitted the luxury of choice. In the shade of the swaying olive tree branches he watched them move along the road in single file, weapons tucked into their shoulders in the 'watch and shoot' alert position. Children crowded round, offering high fives in the hope of chocolate, or maybe a cigarette. The soldiers slowed. Some turned in a slow, deliberate 360-degree circular motion, their red-rimmed eyes scanning for anything out of the norm. A sudden movement, a man with a phone pressed to his ear, someone astride a moped counting their strength. The lead soldier, a fresh-faced lieutenant, stopped and leaned against a wall, raised his rifle and scanned the buildings through his telescopic rifle sight. His comrades dropped to a crouch, waiting for the all-clear. Gillet remembered the feeling. The everlasting itch lodged between the shoulder blades; the itch that could never be remedied, not even with long raking fingernails. The stinging sweat that threatened to blur the sight, obliterate the position from where the random shot came, and then the agony when the bullet buried itself into the unyielding flesh, smashing nerves and bones into pulp. It wasn't the pain; that was bearable. It was the shock of dying like a dog in a dusty street, miles from home and away from those he loved. Gillet headed in their direction with his arms hanging loose by his sides, a sign he carried no weapon. The fresh-faced lieutenant saw him approach, stopped and raised his hand. A few steps behind a staff sergeant signalled his men to take up position against the safety of a low whitewashed mud wall. Gillet slowed, the sergeant's finger curled around the trigger, the safety catch already turned to 'off'.

"Careful that doesn't go off and do someone a mischief, you scouse bastard," Gillet called.

Staff Sergeant Morton pushed back his helmet and allowed the air to circulate around his sweat-plastered head.

"Tommo, what the hell are you doing here?" he said, lowering his weapon.

"It's a long story."

The young lieutenant brought the meeting to an abrupt end.

"Okay, sergeant, break it up and move on." His deep voice belied his boyish face. "We're sitting targets here."

"Come to the camp tonight, I'll let them know you are coming," Morton said, signalling to his men to move out.

Gillet stepped aside and watched the young soldiers continue their patrol, tension strapped taut across their faces. Mouths set grim, most just boys yet to break out of their teens. His memory stretched and he recalled his days in Iraq, the days when he'd walked with the cheeks of his arse pinched tight together, fearful that at any moment his bowels would explode with fear. Others, glad they weren't alone, admitted they felt the same, yet it did little to help relieve the speculative feeling when the insides turned to water. In a momentary stillness beneath the hot sun, the weary grey faces passed him by, hazed in tiny clouds of dust thrown up with each step.

In the hotel, showered, he gave the window a miss and instead flopped onto his bed. It would be good to be among his kind once more, among the sweat and banter. Feel the exhilaration that had once intoxicated his mind on the killing plains of Afghanistan and Iraq. Casually opening a magazine he'd taken from a pile scattered across a table by the hotel entrance, he flicked through the pages. He didn't bother to raise his head at the *patter-patter-patter* of the helicopter passing overhead; it was just another one of those everyday occurrences accepted by all as normal in the battle-scarred city. Then a different sound, familiar Warning bells echoed through his head, rolling off the bed he pressed his body down onto the floor and clasped his hands over his head, listening to the rushing roar of the rocket drawing closer. A blinding flash stung his eyes and a force hurled him across the room in a hail of shattered bricks and masonry. Dust clogged his nostrils and blinded his sight. Trapped in the vacuous trail left by the missile, he gasped for breath. Habit forced him to perform the customary 'immediate fingers and toes check' in case of injury. On his feet, he staggered to the gaping hole in the wall as the US Army helicopter wheeled away to the south. Somewhere within a two-kilometre range, someone had the chopper in mind as a target, and using a crude launching pad the missile had missed the chopper and struck the hotel without exploding. What remained of his possessions he packed in his travelling bag and, pushing his way through the gathering crowd eager for the sight of blood, hailed a cab.

*

Camp Souter acted as the UK's main military base in Kabul. A converted fertiliser plant on the edge of the city, it served as the HQ of the British Peacekeeping mission in Afghanistan. A force of three hundred troops handled the engineering tasks for the ISAF, its prime responsibilities the order and protection of Kabul's interim government. Allied soldiers reckoned compared to other compounds it's about as comfortable as it gets for the British forces in Afghanistan. A coffee bar, gym and weights room, even paradigm communication satellite phones and Internet suites, where troops could talk face-to-face with their families and loved ones back home. Gillet sneered at the overweight pen-pushers and logistic guys walking around in tailored combat fatigues. Maybe their input was important, but it didn't lead to sleepless nights or extended periods of anxiety. Most couldn't find Helmand district on a map with the aid of a magnifying glass. Although loath to admit it, he knew the armed forces were littered with its share of hitch-hikers looking for an easy ride in life.

Morton waited for him like he said he would, showered, his lean body dressed in camouflage trousers and a black tight-fitting cotton T-shirt. He was army; fit, reliable and good at his job. In this theatre of war, nothing much else mattered. Gillet felt it come to life again. What he had thought erased from his memory in a short time, lingered when it should have been reduced by degrees until it no longer existed. In the past, during times of deep solitude, he'd had cause to draw on past times for the sake of his fading sanity. Now the undeniable reek of military fired his memory as if it were yesterday.

"How are you managing minus your foot? I hear they can do wonders today," were the first words Morton said in the cold light of the day, bringing Gillet down to earth.

An icy shaft of reality slithered into Gillet's spine. He didn't answer at first, just pursed his lips and followed the tall staff sergeant to his quarters. It was the usual military-styled room, small and furnished with nothing that wasn't necessary to the objectives of the day (if you excluded the poster of a naked woman lying with her legs wide open). Littered with that and the accoutrements of war, it was a testimony to a fighting soldier.

"I manage. There's plenty worse off than me."

"True enough, but the thing is, Tommo, what in God's name are you doing here?"

By the time Gillet finished relating his story, Morton's creased brow had turned to deep furrows.

"Bloody hell, have you gone crazy or something? What do you intend to do with him if you manage to get him back to Blighty? What about the welfare, child agencies and the social security when word gets out? He'll be classed as an illegal immigrant. The authorities will probably throw the book at you for kidnapping under-age kids."

"That's all sorted."

"Come on, Tommo, get fucking real and do yourself a favour, go home; the only sorting you need to do is with Amy and Luke. And stay away from that bloody CNN reporter. He won't give a monkey's shit for you or the kid; he's just on the lookout for a story."

Morton's evaluation of the situation might have been spot on, but not to Gillet. He'd never expected love and kisses, but hoped Morton might have provided him with a shoulder to lean on. Standing up, he made his way to the door.

"Hang on, for fuck sake! Don't you ever change? Always going off half-cocked. Get your head down here for a couple of nights, I'll clear it with the C/O," Morton said. "I don't suppose you have heard about Pinkie?"

Gillet wheeled round to face Morton.

"Heard what about Pinkie?"

"Poor bastard's back in Blighty. His nerve's gone, blamed the army for refusing him permission to be with his mother before she died. When he returned from her funeral he was   sent on patrol. They stopped by a village for a bit of hearts and minds, you know the score. Couple of kids came out to see what was on offer for free, the rest stayed indoors, so Pinkie, being the kind old soul he is, stopped to give the kids a few sweets. On the way back they found the kids lying in a pool of blood with their throats slit for talking to the enemy. He reckoned it was all his fault, threw his weapons on the ground and told the captain he was finished with the army, and bollocks to the war."

"Then what happened?"

"He went missing for a couple of days. They found him out on the desert sniffing lines of coke in the middle of a poppy field. Of course they placed him under arrest and banged him up. When they searched his room they found five kilos of pure cocaine at the bottom of his kitbag. Seems he'd been taking the stuff home on leave and selling it; must have made a small fortune. Word is he's being treated for Post Traumatic Stress Disorder," Morton said, glancing at Gillet. "Good soldier Mickey, I liked him a lot. Fucking war."

*

The news of Pinkie shook Gillet, but why he'd kicked off over a couple of kids was a mystery. All the time he'd known him, Pinkie had established a reputation for remaining detached from all the shit that happened around them day after day. Washed and shaved, at eight o'clock that night he sat and picked over a plate of scrambled eggs and baked beans. There was no rule book for this war. Nothing printed in chapters and paragraphs. Soldiers, like ordinary folk back home, found it difficult to grasp what they were doing in Afghanistan in the first place. No real directive existed, no solid reason anyone could put their finger on, no far-reaching solution. His eyes flashed, and cradling his head in his hands he recalled past stories of men stressed out of their minds and on the verge of breaking point. Those that drank a litre of vodka each night so they could sleep. Men who sat at home all day with a loaded gun pointed at their head, afraid to pull the trigger that would release them from their torture. Perhaps he was the same, heading for a breakdown. He considered going home, calling off the whole crazy affair. His mind cleared. He could handle it stress; his training made sure he could handle anything the world threw at him. Then, instead of admitting to the truth, he laughed off the whole ridiculous idea and centred his mind on Shafiq. Nothing had changed, except that now he was the instigator giving life, instead of the perpetrator ending it violently.

Outside, he gulped in the fresh air. A warm breeze separating the clouds into dark patchy woollen shrouds brushed his face. The moon appeared, bright as though dipped in fresh paint. Staying at Camp Souter wasn't a good idea; it brought back memories he might do better to forget. Anyway, he needed to keep Riley close if he wanted to find Shafiq.

"Mustafa Hotel," he said to the taxi driver, tossing his bag in the back.

*

Gillet glanced up at the wrecked hotel. The rocket had passed through the corner of the building, failed to explode and exited the other side. Damage was negligible and repairs were already in process. He saw Fisher first.

"Hey, we thought you were dead."

"Not yet. Where's Riley?"

"Scraping the shit out of his pants. Boy, did that rocket put the fear up him. You'll find him in his room. Don't knock too hard, though, there's no saying what he might do."

Gillet grinned. Content with Riley's way of things he didn't bother to knock, instead walked in unannounced. Riley stood rigid, looking old and weak, as if ready to collapse with a coronary.

"Hey, I've got good news for you. There's a gig going down and Mirza Khan is expected to show," he said in a hoarse voice.

"Yeah, can you get me in?"

"You are one goddam stubborn bastard, Gillet; cost you one thousand dollars, US."

"Bollocks! You want the story, I go free."

Riley heaved a sigh and slicked down his wispy hair as if it might help improve his shabby appearance, fired a cigarette and sucked noisily. Why did life have to be so complicated, with every issue clouding the bigger picture? Why couldn't the boundaries be more defined like they were with his wife, Sandra? She wanted every cent he earned, and she wasn't going to get it; simple as shit from a horse's arse.

"Be here tomorrow night at nine o'clock, and try and look the part – you'll never get in dressed like that. Find a shop and ask for a *perahan tunban*; it's the traditional dress. Plus you'll need a black jacket and a *shemagh* to cover your face."

"Will you be there?"

"You're a funny guy at times, Gillet. I'll show you the venue, after that you are on your own."

The silence in the room was almost tangible, the odour of stale smoke crushing.

"No deal, Riley; you said you would help me," Gillet said, watching Fisher enter the room. "If the kid shows with Mirza Khan, I want you waiting outside with a vehicle to get us out of there. Fisher shouldn't have a problem finding a safe spot to film those entering and leaving. It should be quite a show if the Afghan National Police turn out looking for us. Just think of it, Riley, CNN will have the biggest story since the Yanks found Saddam living like a rat in a hole."

"He's right," Fisher chipped in. "The venue is surrounded by flat-top buildings. I could film from a roof and cover half of Kabul without touching the ground."

Riley nerve ends wriggled like a can of maggots. Far too old for Hollywood-style car chases, he felt uneasy.

"Yeah, and if the kid shows, how do you intend to get him and yourself out in one piece? Kill every arsehole in the place?" he grunted.

"Leave that to me."

*

Even with his brusque manner synonymous with the regular soldier, Sergeant Morton had the respect of his men. Easy on their minds they expected no more from him than clear commands and complete trust. Wild rumours persisted that while serving in Helmand, he'd found a Holy Bible lying in the dust after a fierce small arms fight with the Taliban. Under the impression it might be important to someone, he took it upon himself to make extensive enquiries as to who the owner might be. All he received for his troubles were vacant stares, so he visited the wounded; still no one admitted to ownership. A fearless leader attuned to killing, those who knew him reckoned he took it as a sign of godliness, and kept it with him at all times.

The following morning he gazed into Gillet's face like he was the devil.

"Did I hear right? Stun grenades, you want deep-fire stun grenades, and sonic earplugs to help steal the kid from under their noses? Bloody hell, Tommo, it's treatment you need!"

"Tell me about it." Gillet shrugged. "Well, do I get them or not?"

Morton sighed. "Yeah," he said, screwing up his face, "I suppose so."

*

Darkness came and scourged away the daylight. Jumpy, like old times, Gillet sensed the thrill of nervous excitement. At eight thirty he tapped on Riley's door and stepped inside. Riley turned off the shower and walked, dripping wet, from the bathroom. Gillet grimaced, the sight of Riley in the altogether enough to make a blind man wince twice.

"You're early."

Allowing the remark to pass, Gillet unpacked a small holdall and changed into the *perahan tunban*. He'd pass as a local, though Fisher advised it would be wise to keep his pale hands out of sight.

"Hey, pretty damn good," Riley said with unveiled admiration. "Still can't make up my mind whether you are a brave bastard or a complete prick to think you can walk into this place, then walk out with the kid."

Gillet rummaged in the holdall.

"See these little beauties? Stun grenades timed to go off two seconds after pulling the pin, and these are sonic earplugs, the kind pop groups use on stage to block out the backing soundtracks. And this, my insurance," he said, pulling out the double-edged knife. "Once I'm outside, take me and the boy to Chicken Street, then leave. I'll make my own way back. Is that clear?"

"Yeah, but you had better remember that if you get caught, you are on your own. Your Embassy won't help you," Fisher said.

"Who said anything about getting caught?"

Riley fumbled in the pocket of his jacket hooked over the back of a wicker chair.

"An elderly man with a grey beard will be on the door. Hold this in the palm of your hand, but don't flash it around. Show it to the man and you'll be allowed to enter. Rumour has it Mirza Khan will be present. Whether or not he has the kid with him, your guess is as good as mine."

Gillet slipped the small metal disc into his pocket.

It was an easy drive to the eastern side of Kabul, no more than twenty minutes beneath the blood-red streaked evening sky. A perfumed air-freshener dangling on a chain from the rear-view mirror helped to dispel the stale smell of Riley's menthol cigarette. Gillet slipped his hands into his pockets and fingered the two stun grenades nestled next to the cold steel blade of the knife. He had considered carrying a handgun as extra insurance, but decided it best not to get involved in any needless killing. Stun grenades would give him the edge he needed. Riley feathered the brakes and slowed. Winking brake lights from the vehicles in front swung left and disappeared between a petrol station and a bomb-wrecked building with rows of shattered windows. Buckled metal window frames swayed in the light warm evening breeze, clattering and banging against the smoke-scarred building.

"Okay, stop here," Fisher said. "Good luck, Gillet."

Fisher disappeared, swallowed up by long dark shadows. Riley eased the gearstick into gear, moving down the narrow alley they reached a large unlit square lined with vehicles.

"That's the place, there on the right," Riley said. "Get out the car and watch where I park. That way you won't need to run around looking for me."

Gillet pulled the *shemagh* tight round his mouth, slipped his shades over his eyes and glanced across the square. The venue was a large nondescript mud-brick building with a flat roof. At the front, two double ornate wooden doors hung open, throwing a square patch of light across the dirt entrance. An elderly man with the grey beard and bent with age touched his chest with the fingers of his right hand, and then held it out palm upwards in a form of greeting as men filed past into the building. Satisfied he knew Riley's location, Gillet sucked in a deep breath and made his way towards the building. Now, in the realms of the unknown, only fate held the answer to the outcome. For some obscure reason he found it necessary to understand the process that had brought him to this moment. What it was that drove him to choose between a violent death, and the opportunity of a peaceful, harmonious life. The unparalleled raw beauty of the north Norfolk coast seemed far away in another world. All around men spoke in a tongue he didn't understand, low, a cross between a murmur and a whisper, lengthening his stride, the soft dust gave way beneath his footsteps. The elderly man seemed a million miles away as he fought to retain his composure, forcing his breathing slow and even. Then, at last, he was there.

The elderly man stared at him. His wrinkled face burned tobacco brown and creased like worn leather. The hairs on Gillet's neck stood on end. Unclenching his fist, he exposed the metal disc. The elderly man stared into his face, his expression unchanged. Beads of sweat sprouted on Gillet's top lip. His tongue thickened, an expression of bewilderment stretched across his face and he struggled to swallow. The elderly man reached down and closed Gillet's fist. He was in.

It was a spacious room, the size of a tennis court. Heavy patterned drapes suspended from the walls muted the sound of expectant voices to a dull mumble. Across the floor, oriental carpets of all colours lay scattered in no specific order. Men of all ages sat with their legs crossed, chatting with animated fervour like children awaiting entry into a birthday party. Every now and then heads turned to stare with nervous anticipation at the closed door to the left. From the door and leading to a small square in the centre of the room, a pathway lit with flickering candles like an airport runway emitted the sweet pungent aroma of jasmine. Gillet peered over the top of his shades and ran his eyes over the clientele. The majority bedecked in traditional dress. Others, politicians, rich businessmen or high-ranking government officials, dressed in expensive suits sat segregated from the lower classes. In one corner three men in military uniforms were bent head to head in heated conversation. Whoever they were, whatever their creed, they were all here for one thing – to drool with debauched minds at the sight of a male child dancing like a girl. On the perimeter of the small square a man sat holding an elaborate long-necked lute, the surface inlaid with mother of pearl. When he tapped the instrument with his fingers, instant silence descended over the gathering. Men swarmed closer, huddling shoulder to shoulder, straining for a better view. The murmur of blurred voices rose to a hum, filling the room.

Gillet shivered, unaware of what might happen next. A man next to him wearing a bright red turban nudged his shoulder and spoke. Gillet's heart leapt and thumped in panic. Then at last the long-awaited spectacle began, as if from nowhere a shape fluttered in the semi-darkness of flickering candles. Like something from a past Arabian night, a haunting tune floated across the room. Gillet riveted his gaze on a young boy, no more than fifteen years of age, swaying and writhing in time with the music. White flimsy, baggy transparent harem pants covered the bottom half of his body. His black shirt, unbuttoned to his waist, exposed his milky white skin. In his hand a tambourine rattled in unison with the soft sound of the lute. Gillet saw the eye - shadow used to accentuate the dancer's large brown eyes, a splash of bright red lipstick on his pouting lips. The moment he began singing a tuneless melody in a high falsetto voice, Gillet felt the bile rise in his mouth. His chest tightened as if trapped in a skin-tight iron cage. He gasped, reaching for his breath as a tall, lean man dressed in white traditional clothes, his face hidden by a cotton *shemagh*, emerged from the door, followed by Shafiq. Squatting on the front row the man swayed in rhythm to the lilting music, his arm resting on Shafiq's slim shoulders. The atmosphere thickened as men moaned and sighed in ecstasy, clapping their approval as the dancer moved faster, gyrating and twisting. An old wizened man seated in the front row, overcome by the occasion, reached out and lunged for the boy. Overpowered by two burly men, after a stern rebuke he sat in shame with his face buried in his hands.

Transfixed, Gillet felt himself caught up in the increasing fervour as the music became louder, pressing against his eardrums. His shoulders moved in unison with the baying crowd. Seized by a burning shame, he massaged his neck and stared up into the roof of the building. It was time. He pressed in the earplugs and released the pins from the grenades, and clasped his hands over his ears. After the explosion he pulled the knife from his belt. Naked fear brought him to full alert, his senses heightened. He'd faced risks before, but never in a room of writhing bodies with only a knife for protection. Trampling over the mass of stunned bodies, he swept Shafiq into his arms and headed for the door. A man dressed in military uniform fumbled with a leather holster. Gillet lashed out with the knife, the man staggered back, attempting to prevent the blood pouring from his neck.

Outside, the night air cooled the sweat leaking from his brow, sandy gravel sucked at his feet as if it were a swamp. If he lost his nerve now he'd be finished. There was no reason to relax; not now he was so close to achieving his objective. His pace quickened, his mind trembled with apprehension; one slip and he was a dead man. From nowhere a man dressed in a dark grey suit appeared and barred his way. Gillet raised the knife and sliced open his face, exposing a jaw full of white even teeth. The man screamed in pain and fell to his knees. Reaching the 4x4, he crammed the dazed Shafiq into the rear. Riley stared dead ahead and gunned the engine for Chicken Street. Fifteen minutes later, Shafiq, unable to comprehend what the situation, felt himself pushed inside a small windowless room. Gillet, for the sake of safety, dropped the idea of returning to the hotel and made his way by taxi to Camp Souter, ordered a beer and brought his nerves to order.

*

The next morning Abdul al-Hashmi opened the door to the windowless room and, placing a bowl of water on the floor told Shafiq to wash. He did not leave straight away, but hesitated, and calculated Shafiq's size and stature. His job was to purchase clothing to help the boy pass through customs at Kabul Airport dressed as a young woman. He felt nervous; should anything go wrong, he would pay with his life.

Shafiq stirred from the single mattress on the floor and stared at him in bewilderment.

"You must trust me, no harm will come to you," Abdul said.

"Why have you brought me to this place? Don't you know my master, Mirza Khan, will kill you when he discovers my whereabouts, which he surely will?"

Abdul rolled his eyes. He wanted to flee, to anywhere, even the hills where he might find safety with those he hated most, the Taliban. But first he must attend to more important things.

"Someone will come later, someone who wants to help you."

"Help me, help me from what? Do I not have everything I need? A kind master, food in my belly, nice clothes, all this and my master pays a man to teach me to dance," Shafiq said. "Allah in his wisdom has blessed me. My life is good. Now release me and I will say nothing of this foolishness, this I swear."

Abdul blinked and ran his eyes over the boy to make certain of his calculations, then left. Allah had indeed been kind. Shafiq was much the same size as his eldest sister, Aaqila, the intelligent one. It would make good sense if she were the one to select the best burkha money could buy as a disguise for Shafiq, he thought. It wouldn't seem right for a boy to be seen buying women's clothes; the ridicule from the shop owner would be harsh and uncompromising. Anyway, known for her impeccable taste he was certain she would choose wisely. A fine blue burkha edged in gold, complete with golden slippers befitting a woman of high birth to stem the unwanted flow of corrupt airport officials.

Gillet left the comfort of Camp Souter to the rear-line soldiers. Most of whom seemed to have nothing better to do than spend time chatting up female soldiers. Back at the hotel reception, because of the incident with the rocket, they offered him a ten per cent discount on an upgraded room. He laughed. Fifty per cent of the going rate or he'd find somewhere else. A fierce argument followed, and after a barrage of rushed words intermingled with curses, accompanied with the obligatory hand wringing, they accepted. Agreeing to move into a ground-floor room, he left the window open in case the helicopter returned. That night he didn't ready himself for bed; instead, he lay dressed, staring up at the ceiling. He thought of those things he had no real knowledge of, things he might live to regret, like smuggling a boy out of Afghanistan into Pakistan, and from there into the UK. The presumptuousness of what he intended to carry out sat as though it had been forced upon him against his will. But there were issues he needed to face, what if Shafiq failed to respond to a new life in England? What if the harsh difference in cultures left him bewildered and shaken? He knew from experience that for each law in the simplistic nature of Afghanistan, a hundred existed back home. Beads of sweat gathering on his brow went unnoticed as he wrestled with his conscience. There were many things to consider, things he had given no thought. Like in what manner would the boy react when he cast off the shackles of childhood and reached out into the realms of manhood?

Refraining from the habit of staring from the window at the distant mountains, instead he lay on his bed until nightfall. Amy failed to appear, but the woman holding a baby in one hand and a grenade in the other did.

At last daylight broke and when he woke, drenched in sweat. A cool shower did little to cast away the doubts of the previous night. Tired, and without energy, he cursed his lethargy. A knock on the door separated him from his thoughts, with his languor replaced by a soaring temper he wrenched open the door and stared at the elderly man with the stoop.

"Please, you must go to Chicken Street," he said, and left.

Gillet slumped onto the edge of his bed and raked his fingers through his cropped hair, giving scant consideration to anything other than his crushing headache. Unable to believe his eyes, he stared where his false foot should be. It had gone, replaced by flesh and bone. Through disbelieving eyes he saw movement, as if he had clenched his toes. Coldness entered his body and he felt as though he was floating, drifting upwards towards the ceiling. Wide awake in the middle of the day, he was having a nightmare. Panic replaced reason and he snatched at the edge of the bed with both hands to prevent himself from floating higher. His face pinched, his eyes blinked as the blurred walls returned to normal, and struggling for his senses he breathed out through his mouth with great gasps. Life had become a patchwork quilt, each patch different from the next resembling a mood – anger, sullenness and discontent – each waiting to leap out and stifle reality.

Dressed, at the entrance to Chicken Street, he probed his memory trying to recall where he was. His mind remained blank. Tormented by the ceaseless crowd of shopkeepers tugging at his clothing, he fought to free himself.

"Please, mister, you come, Shafiq has the best carpets in all Kabul. Please, follow me."

Shafiq, the name had a familiar ring. He gazed at the youth's pleading eyes; one of his ears was missing, a stump where his right hand should be. The youth moved away, glancing over his shoulder checking if Gillet followed. Gillet lurched forward until they reached the rear of a shop selling perfume and men's aftershave. At the bottom of the stairs leading to the room where Shafiq waited, the youth stopped and pointed to the top.

"I am Abdul al-Hashmi. The boy you seek is in the room at the top of the stairs. I fear he has no great desire to see you. Your time is short. Already we are great danger; it is good you understand this."

Gillet shook his head. He felt like shit; his eyelids fluttered and his vision blurred. Ignoring his throbbing head, he gazed up to the top of the stairs at the wooden door. Shafiq, yes, the name was familiar and then he remembered.

"I'll be as quick as I can," he said.

At the top of the stairs he pushed open the door. Shafiq's eyebrows leapt.

"Mister Sergeant, you have come to return me to my master, is this not so?"

"No, Shafiq, I've come to take you away from the man you refer to as your master," he said, "before it is too late; trust me."

Shafiq frowned, his eyes vague, and Gillet struggled to explain the consequences if he chose to stay with the man he referred as his master.

"Why should I believe these things you speak of, and why would my master want to do bad things to me against Allah's will?" Shafiq insisted with childish simplicity. "What would I do in your country? I am Afghan."

Gillet sighed as Abdul al-Hashmi entered the room and hunched down in front of Shafiq.

"Tell me what you see," he said.

Shafiq's eyes fluttered with mild embarrassment.

"Do not be afraid, tell me."

"I see a boy with one ear who does not hear what others hear. I see a boy with his left hand missing to suffer the shame that comes from using one hand for all things." Shafiq shrugged. "It is unfortunate."

"Hah, you call it unfortunate, then you are a fool. It is more; this is the mark of an outcast, the mark of one who will live his life in the gutters, begging to survive. I shall never know a woman or raise children, and who will be my friend? Answer me that."

"This I do not know; perhaps you will allow *me* to be your friend."

"Impossible."

"Why should it be impossible? I don't understand your questions. Why do you talk to me like this?"

Abdul al-Hashmi stared at him, his wide brown eyes bursting with pity and loathing.

"It was the man you call your master that did these things to me, Mirza Khan. Like you, I was also trained to dance. Later, in the eyes of Allah, I refused to bow to the foul deeds he ordered me to do to him and his friends. You are foolish, Shafiq, you know of *Bacha Bazi* like all boys do. Go with this man to a new country where you can live in peace like all men, before it is too late. You have been away from Mirza Khan throughout the night, now he will lose face. If you stay here, you too will end up like me. If you are lucky, and if Allah wills it, you will die."

Shafiq's eyes fluttered. Everyone knew of *Bacha Bazi*. He was no one's fool. Many times in the past he'd seen men enticing young boys from their families with offers of large sums of money. The boys, from poor families, led to believe they were about to enter a better life and at the same time help to provide for their kin, went willingly. Later, most would fear for their lives when they refused to commit to the disgusting sexual acts thrust upon them by men old enough to be their grandparents. Dismissive of Gillet and Abdul's presence, he shuddered; their words were words of truth. Plucked from the streets orphans like him were like fallen fruit not yet ripened. He knew those foolish enough to disobey their master's wishes would learn that no one cared whether they lived or died.

"What must I do, Mister Sergeant?" he said.

Gillet heaved a sigh of relief.

"Trust these people, do as they ask without question. Above all, you must be strong, understand?"

Shafiq nodded.

"Good. Everything will be explained later. Next time you see me will be at the airport. Do not approach me or attempt to speak with me, regardless of what happens."

Abdul al-Hashmi's smile was slow and sly. When the coast was clear, he'd make his way to Mirza Khan's home on the outskirts of the city, tell him that Shafiq had taken the bait and that he and the Englishman called Gillet will leave for Pakistan as planned. For his part in betraying Shafiq and the man called Gillet, Khan promised to forget the past and promote him to keeper of the mosque beneath the pines, a position close to Allah, and three square meals a day.

*

It was almost done. In the cool of his hotel room he closed his eyes and tried to understand why his moods changed so rapidly. Maybe he should have stayed at Camp Souter. At least that way he'd be away from Riley's constant attention. Afraid of losing his story, he followed him around like a scented bloodhound, refusing to allow him out of his sight. Casting his mind back to the first time he'd met the newsman, he had every reason to show his gratitude. In search of a story, Riley had offered his full support, even helping in the abduction of Shafiq. The pungent odour of his body fouled his nostrils. His shirt wet with sweat and the hairs on his chest matted to his skin. To side to ease the tension he rolled his head from side to side and then tore off his shirt. About to turn on the shower, he tensed at the sound of footsteps, and pressing his back tight against the wall he made his way towards the door leading out into the corridor. The footsteps grew fainter. When he jerked open the door, the corridor was empty; a large brown envelope lay by his feet. Inside, two air tickets, one to Peshawar leaving at six o'clock that night, and the other from Peshawar to Heathrow the next morning.

*

Riley lit another menthol cigarette, and leaving it dangling from his lips stared down at his laptop. This was it, his finale, the big story, the one that would send him out in a blaze of glory. Time to throw away the pencil and notebook. For too long he'd borne the constant worry of not hitting deadlines; sucked dry of all enthusiasm from his once fervent endeavours to unearth the big story that made the wires sing.

"Fuck the alimony, and fuck Sandra," he muttered, smoke drifting into his eyes.

He'd had enough of shelling out every cent he earned to keep the idle bitch sitting on her skinny backside, posing with the other jumped-up wonders at the local country club. Sarah, his younger sister, lived on the outskirts of Sioux City, Iowa, a stone's throw from a river full of fish and a short drive from the state golf course. She'd welcome him with open arms, she'd told him enough times since her husband died fighting with the marines in Vietnam.

When the phone rang, jolting him from his quiescence, he stubbed out the cigarette and thumbed the green button.

"Yeah?" he grunted.

"You'd better come to my room," Gillet said.

*

Abbas sat with his legs crossed, twirling multicoloured beads and gazed at Shafiq. His stubby finger rubbed his twitching eye; had he not seen it for himself, he would never have believed it. Shafiq was pretty enough to pass as a young woman. Squaring his shoulders, he pushed the distraction from his mind. It was of no consequence to him; he had other thoughts swirling through his brain. His eyes drooped.

"You are indeed fortunate to start a new life in a country full of many opportunities. Take the time to learn to embrace this country and its ways, yet never forget who you are and the country of your birth. Above all, give thanks to Allah for his mercy," he said.

"I will, and I shall remember your words, this I promise."

"Then take this and keep it safe. It will help you in times of doubt and confusion."

Shafiq frowned at the small bottle filled with dirt and tied to a loop of cord.

"It is dust from the Shamali plains of Afghanistan, the country of your birthright. When your mind is troubled, look inside and you will see into the heart of Allah and that which is written."

Shafiq nodded and slipped the loop over his head.

*

Fisher trailed in Riley's wake as he pushed his way into Gillet's room, his face flushed. The unrelenting flourish of excitement of a new story about to break held him in a grip of euphoria.

"Okay, buddy, spill the beans," he said, sinking into the soft sofa.

"We leave tonight, six o'clock, overnight stop at Peshawar and then on to Heathrow in the morning."

"Give me your home address, in case we get separated."

Gillet smiled. "No chance. If anything goes wrong we don't know each other, keep up, Riley, or lose your story."

"Bastard," Riley grunted.

Gillet listened to their muffled voices diminishing as they made their way down the corridor. He had much to do, and began packing his travelling bag.

At four thirty in the evening he approached the Kam-Air check-in at the airport. One hour later in the departure lounge everything had gone smoothly. No PAT checks, no waving of the electric detector, not even the customary menace of security guards sniffing around for the chance of a bribe. A flashing glance saw Riley, followed by Fisher, entering the lounge. His gaze settled his gaze on the three Afghan women dressed in the traditional pale blue burkha. Then his shoulders tightened. The hairs on his neck pulled taut against his skin as four members of the Afghan National Police marched through the lounge heading towards Riley and Fisher. Gillet caught the remonstrative voice of Riley shouting over the call to board. A policeman unzipped the case carrying Fisher's camera equipment and held the camera aloft as though it were a trophy. Fisher lunged for the camera as the metallic crash of automatic weapons cocking echoed throughout the lounge. People turned their backs breathing a sigh of relief it wasn't them the police searched for. Seconds later, arguing and shouting both men were escorted from the departure lounge.

Aboard the airbus, he prayed to the God he'd refused to recognise for the aircraft to become airborne.

At Peshawar it was a different story; one of hold-ups, shortened tempers and tight security. Long crocodile queues formed as disgruntled passengers waited, too afraid to complain, for the completion of everlasting security checks by overzealous Pakistani security staff. For a further hour the carousel remained empty, unmoving, and as passengers began to raise their objections, police tugged their weapons from their shoulders. Complaints were pushed aside and replaced by a sudden hush. Three long hours dragged by before at last he managed to negotiate his way out of the airport. He had hoped that someone might contact him, but wasn't too disappointed when they didn't. On the way to a small hotel recommended by the taxi driver on B Y Jang Road, the police stopped them twice and carried out spot checks. Peshawar, once known as the City of Flowers, had been gifted with a new name, the City of Blood. A popular haven for sanguinary terrorists, a target for indiscriminate suicide bombers and the reluctant object of rocket attacks. Civil aircrew flying in remained in the airport waiting for a fast turnaround, prepared to fly out as soon as possible after the Grand Hotel, a well-known venue for aircrew, had been bombed, injuring several stewardesses.

Curbing his impatience and damping down a hankering to check out the city, he decided it a good idea to stay put in the hotel until morning. So close to his objective, the less people that saw him the better. A smile of circumspect touched his lips and his mind dwelled on Riley and Fisher. Whatever had become of them after the ruckus at the airport, he neither knew nor cared. For the time being, they were out of his hair. Sure, they had been more than helpful, he wouldn't deny that, but this was war, his war, a matter of life or death. In Kabul he'd seen the three burkha-clad women embark on the airbus, certain one was Shafiq, he felt at peace.

In the small dining room, he took the time to study the menu. Unused to foreign guests due to the dangerous nature of the city, staff fussed around him, eager to please. His mind divided by the least of a host of evils, he took a chance and chose the chicken curry. After the first mouthful he lunged for the glass of water to stop his eyes slipping from their sockets.

"You like, sir?" the waiter smiled.

"Bloody hell," Gillet whispered, trying to catch his breath. "What the hell's it made from, blasting powder and sulphuric acid?"

"Oh yes, sir, plenty blasting powder, no sulphuric acid, not good for digestion," the waiter gushed.

When he'd eaten his fill he decided to take an early night. It was a simple room suited to his purpose, nothing dignified – a single bed below a revolving fan sending a gentle stream of cooling air. Preferring to be ready for any unseen event he remained dressed. Sleep didn't come easy; outside, the nerve-stretching cacophony of car horns, interspersed with the roar of aircraft taking off and landing from the nearby airport, made it near impossible to doze for more than a few minutes at a time. Not that he was worried; he was becoming an expert in the art of existing without sleep, and for once his recurring nightmares would have to forego their nightly torment. Even with the overhead fan the heat was stifling and wished he'd taken more care choosing a hotel. Covered by a thin cotton sheet he dozed and waited for morning.

In the beginning he thought the noise came from outside. Then it came again, like a drawer pulled open and slid shut. Out of the gloom the outline of a crouching figure approached his bed, the handle of the raised knife covered by a bony hand. The figure turned and started to rifle through his jacket pockets. Keeping his eyes anchored on the knife, he rolled from the bed and sprang to his feet. The figure swivelled, the blade arced down, hissing for his neck. Gillet gripped the thin wrist and, bringing to bear all his unarmed combat training, blocked the thrust and twisted. The man grunted in pain and, riding the twist like a trained acrobat, landed on his feet. Gillet sneered into his assailant's face. Slitted eyes and pendulous ears, his breath reeked of rotting teeth, and unwashed sweat oozed from every pore in his body. Gillet snapped his head forward and smashed his forehead between the man's eyes. He screamed in agony as Gillet's knee cannoned into his groin. With one final explosive gesture, the knife thrust upwards, slashing across Gillet's chest. He swayed back in pain. Then a blinding flash followed by the bark of a handgun reverberated in his ears. The man groaned, his legs buckled and he slumped to the floor. Gillet looked up at the waiter holding a gun.

"Are you all right, Mr Gillet, thank goodness I came in time," the waiter said. "We must inform the police immediately."

Gillet glanced down at his chest; the cut wasn't so deep it would need stitches. The last thing he needed was contact with the local police.

"My flight leaves in a few hours and it's vital I board. Maybe we can dispose of the body, somewhere it won't be found for a few days?"

"No, sir, that would be a very bad thing to do indeed. The police must be informed. We do not know who this man is."

"Does it matter who he is? He's dead."

The sound of a slamming door, the room bathed in brilliance as lights flashed. Gillet groaned.

"Mohammed, what is happening? I heard the sound of a gunshot."

Gillet stared at the soldier's uniform.

"We are most fortunate. Mr Gillet, this man is my brother, Ahmed. He will call the Chief Inspector of Police. Soon they will be here and the matter cleared," the waiter said.

Gillet considered his chances of walking away from the scene and searching for another hotel closer to the airport. They were slim, left with no choice he'd have to brazen his way out during the meeting with the Chief of Police.

There were three uniformed armed policemen, accompanied by a chief inspector wearing a peak cap above a neatly pressed suit. The inspector straightened his cap, clasped his hands around his back and glared up and down at Gillet like he was conducting a military inspection. Gillet did his best to make light of the occurrence while the inspector, with great deliberation and aplomb, took notes. When he'd finished, Mohammed, the waiter, backed Gillet's story, explaining it was an open-and-shut case of self-defence.

"Have you seen this man before, Mr Gillet?" the inspector said, nodding at the body. "And may I enquire what you are doing in Peshawar?"

"No, of course I haven't seen him before; I'm en route to England, from Kabul."

"Strange, why didn't you leave direct from Kabul? You have business in Peshawar perhaps?"

"No."

"Perhaps you have come to Peshawar for other reasons, to buy drugs perhaps?" the inspector said.

"If I wanted drugs I'd have bought them in Kabul."

The inspector pocketed his notebook, his eyes triumphant and fixed on Gillet's face. Gillet fidgeted on the balls of his feet.

"Mr Gillet, I am holding you on suspicion of drug trafficking and murder. You will accompany us to the station for questioning. When we are satisfied you are telling the truth, you will be allowed to continue your journey."

The words pierced Gillet's brain and his eyes darted around like an animal trapped in a corner. To be hauled into a stinking Pakistani cell for a grilling was the last thing he wanted.

"Bollocks, that's rubbish! Show me your proof."

"Proof, Mr Gillet? Why should I need proof? I suggest you intended to smuggle drugs into Pakistan from Afghanistan and then on to London. You are not the first; it has been attempted by coalition soldiers on many occasions."

"I've never been into drugs, you can search my luggage. I'm here as a tourist, nothing else."

"A tourist, Mr Gillet? I think not."

"Yeah, a tourist, and you can think what you like. Now get me to the airport."

"Mr Gillet, I have a feeling that your stay with us might be a long one."

Gillet cursed his crass stupidity. He'd passed sentence upon himself. His only option would be to contact the British Embassy.

"I'm entitled to a phone call," he grunted.

"Maybe tomorrow. Perhaps by then you may feel like telling us why you are in Peshawar. Take him away."

That night Gillet lay in filth with six other prisoners in a communal cell. Without light or means of sanitation, the nauseating stench of human shit clogged his nostrils. When morning came they refused him his phone call, blindfolded he was taken to a small interrogation room. Stripped naked, for two hours they questioned him about his movements, afterwards they beat him with a rubber hosepipe. At night he sat in a corner with his head cradled between his knees, trying to block out the noise from other prisoners. Two days later they transferred him to a single cell. High in one corner and out of reach, a small grated window let in the sounds of the outside world, and fighting for his sanity, he paced the cell. For the next six days the interrogations ceased, and he believed his release imminent. On the seventh, dragged by his feet to a small room he received another beating. The beatings would continue until he confessed to being a drug trafficker, they told him. A further five more days passed, unable to stand and dragged from his cell by three guards they threw him into a bare room with a water tap in a corner. Two hours they subjected him to 'water-boarding'. Placed beneath the water tap with a cloth over his face, his tormentors turned the tap on and off at different intervals until the water soaked through the cloth. Eventually the water entered his nose and mouth, cutting off the supply of oxygen. In his mind he thought he was about to drown and gagged. That evening, gasping for breath, he lay in the cell, listening to the curses of a Frenchman as guards dragged him kicking and screaming along the corridor. Faced with the concept of death, he shivered on the cold stone cell floor and tried to find a semblance of sanity. In the days that followed he waited for the summons to more torture. After a further five more days had dragged by, his spirit curled and his mind started to sink into oblivion. Head to toe in blood and sores; thin and pale, he waited for his heart to cease. You won't leave here alive, drug traffickers never do, a bloated black African told him through torn gums after the guards had ripped out his gold teeth. As though the words were a challenge, pushing despair to one side with a pragmatic and logical concentration, he collected his thoughts.

A loud explosion followed by a blast hurled him like a rag doll against the cell wall. Fresh air buffeted his face and he inhaled. All around the cell block collapsed, bricks and mortar crashed around his head. Overhead, through the dust and falling masonry, stars shone in the cool night air. Prisoners, like foraging animals, climbed and pulled their way to freedom.

"You come now, mister, we go," the black African said, grabbing him under the armpits and dragging him over the rubble out into the fresh air.

"What happened?"

"Who cares? Just get out of here."

Dazed, he teetered on the edge of a road, hooting cars swung out to avoid knocking him down. He didn't care, he was free, free where the air smelled clean and fresh. People came from all directions, crowding round him, staring. Their faces blurred, their voices garbled. He fell, jarring his knees; something cut into the palms of his hands and he rolled over onto his back.

"British Embassy, take me to the British Embassy" he whispered through blood-caked lips.

Hands reached out and lifted him. Bundled in the rear of a car, overhead lights jumped and shuddered one by one in the darkness. Incessant honking and hooting blocked out all other sound. The sway of the car rocked his head from side to side and he reached out for something to grip. Minutes later the car screeched to a halt and a strong light shone in his face. Everything became cloudy. A stirring uncertainty allied with panic entered his stomach, twisting at his guts. He was back in the prison cell and singled out for further brutal treatment? He wanted to cry out, beg them to stop. He raised his hands to protect himself against the kicks and blows from the blurred shapes ready to take what remained of his life. A pricking sensation shot into his arm and everything turned to slow motion; his pain drifted away. Whoever they were, they had him to do with as they pleased.

*

When he woke, he thought he was dreaming. Her face portrayed the merest hint of a tan. She was the kind that took intelligent precautions against the sun's harmful rays, or her time in this country had been short. Her make-up was minimal, neither enhancing nor detracting from her beauty. Soft grey eyes, the colour of a pigeon's wing, and when her lips parted she displayed a row of teeth whiter than a penguin's bib. There was a heaven after all.

"Hi," a soft voice said. "You sure look a little better than a couple of days ago."

"Where am I?"

"You're in the American consulate."

"How long have I been here?"

"A couple of days and nights. The Taliban rammed a car full of explosives against the jail's perimeter wall hoping to release their buddies, blew half the police station to pieces along with the cell block. Stupid bastards even managed to destroy the mosque next door at the same time. Must be a few happy miscreants wandering around Peshawar. Why were you in there?"

"It's a long story."

"I've got plenty of time."

Gillet pulled himself into a sitting position and told her as much as he thought she needed to know. A long way from safety, he decided on caution. When he'd finished, she raised her eyebrows.

"Wow, some story. You took one hell of a chance with a kid already waiting at home for you. Can't say as I'd do the same under the circumstances. Guess you must have been pretty desperate. Still, I reckon by now you may have lost the kid, Shafiq you called him. Guess you are just in one big hurry to get home right now?" she said.

"Shafiq might have made the flight to the UK."

She shrugged and threw him a rueful look.

"Maybe, but it's a long shot. Thing is, what would he do if he did? I'll let my boss know you are awake. By the way, I'm Jo McKenzie, assistant to the consul. He's a good guy and he'll help you all he can. In the meantime, if you feel up to it, get cleaned up; there's a set of clean clothes on the chair. Shower's down the hallway, someone will be along with some chow."

*

Two days later, Jake Linkletter, head of the American consulate, sat behind his vast desk staring through the window into the sunlit courtyard. At the far end, leading out onto the road, was a pair of rusting wrought-iron gates in dire need of a coat of paint. Trouble was, whoever had the nerve to paint them would more than likely end up with a bullet in his head before the paint had time to dry. Not that he gave a damn. For all he cared they could fall off the hinges and rust into oblivion. If he hadn't been caught with his dick in the mouth of the wife of one of the President's personal bodyguards, he'd still be in Washington playing the field instead of sweating his balls off in this dump.

Steve 'Buster' Matthews, head of security, wandered into sight, ready to share his first cigarette of the day with the two uniformed guards on the gate. Lighting his cigarette, he turned and waved a desultory salute. Linkletter raised his hand, noting he wasn't wearing his Dodger's baseball cap to prevent the sun peeling his balding head. In one simple depressing moment, leaning back, he ran his hand across his chin, feeling the stubble; should have wet shaved instead of using the electric razor. A wet shave left him feeling cleaner. Maybe if he hadn't spent the night screwing McKenzie he might have found the time to whip up a different kind of lather. God, she was one horny broad, always made him feel as if his veins had to grow to twice their size to cope with the rush of blood to his heart when she became aroused. The sharp rap on the door brought him back to earth.

"Mr Gillet, good morning. Good to see you up and about. You look a whole lot better after a good long rest. Guess they gave you a hard time in there. Miss McKenzie told me a little of your background, and I guess you want to get the hell out of here pretty damn quick. I can get you on one of our C130s tomorrow morning.

Afraid Berlin's the last stop before the good old US of A; from there you will have to find your own way home."

"What about the boy?"

"My advice would be to forget him. He'll be long gone by now, and anyway, I can't keep you here indefinitely. Sooner or later the local Gestapo will find out you are holed up here with us and we'll both be up to our necks in shit."

Gillet's face crinkled with disappointment. He'd failed. His eyes felt tired, heavy with dark circles. Yet in spite of the exhaustion his obstinate nature held sway; even though everything had gone wrong he refused to panic, defeat out of the question.

"Can you get me back into Afghanistan?"

The yellow sunrays piercing the window heightened the colour of Linkletter's short haircut. With his back to Gillet, he watched Steve Matthews grind out the cigarette with his heel.

"Berlin, you go to Berlin, or I'll have security leave you outside the gates of the consul, end of story," he said in an assured voice.

Gillet's shoulders dipped. There was nothing left. He couldn't go back and he couldn't go forward.

"I'll need money, and a passport."

"Money's no problem, a passport's out of the question. Of course you're welcome to contact the British Embassy here in Peshawar. No telling what they will do, probably hand you back to the Pakistan police to save themselves a pile of paperwork."

Gillet felt the urge to make a sour remark, tell him to go and fuck himself. Then changed his mind.

"What time does the C130 leave?"

"Four a.m. We'll get you out on the pan in one of our cars to avoid customs."

"Thanks, I appreciate all you have done for me."

"No problem," Linkletter said, extending his hand. "Good luck."

The following morning, at fifteen minutes before three o'clock, Gillet snapped the seatbelt round his waist and settled back in the Mercedes. Steve 'Buster' Matthews fired up his third cigarette of the hour and inhaled, started the engine, swung into Hospital Road and picked up the route for the airport. He never spoke, just stared straight ahead as if he were alone. Halfway down Airport Road he feathered the brakes, slowed, turned into a side road and killed the engine.

"Busting for a leak, won't be a second," he grunted.

Thankful to be rid of the stench of stale tobacco, Gillet wound down the window and sucked in the hot night air. He had no reason to pay any particular interest to the van pulling up behind, not even when the blinding headlights caused him to turn his head and squint. Seconds later, the door to the Mercedes swung open and strong hands pulled him from the vehicle. Something solid struck his head, bringing him to his knees. Plastic cable ties cut into his wrists, sticky tape sealed his mouth. Dragged towards a rusting Volkswagen van, his knees collided with the bumper as his captors shoved him into the rear. When he recovered, he looked up at a man dressed in a stained *shalwar kameez*. Dressed in filthy white trainers with no socks; the odour from his body smelled like a dead badger's arse. Above his deformed lips, a large hooked nose; blind in one eye, his good eye stared, grey and lifeless. Gillet winced at the pain. From the rear window he saw Steve 'Buster' Matthews watch the proceedings with a cigarette dangling from his lips. Gillet sneered. The Americans had handed him back, and he was heading back to the prison after all. Sweat poured from his face. Unable to move, for three long, uncomfortable hours the vehicle bumped and lurched over a dirt track until pulling to a halt. A slim man with an AK47 slung over his shoulder pulled open the doors.

"Drink," he said, cutting the plastic ties from Gillet's hands and handing him a bottle of warm spring water.

Gillet rolled his head and stretched his shoulders to relieve the knotted muscles, and took in the tight-fitting chinos, the dark blue polo shirt and *shemagh* wrapped around the slim man's head. When he spoke, it was with the clipped English accent of a man fortunate enough to have received a good education. A glance round showed no sign of buildings or civilisation, just bare open countryside as far as the eye could see. Ignoring the pain, Gillet tore the sticky tape from his lips and took a long swig from the bottle.

"Now what? You kill me and leave me here for the dogs?" he grunted.

"Drink, we have a long journey ahead of us," the slim man scowled. "And keep your mouth closed."

"Why waste water on the infidel pig? Kill him now and leave him to the jackals," the one-eyed man growled.

"Fool! Will you volunteer to tell the Khan and have your balls sliced off? Tie his hands and get in the front. I'll ride in the back."

Across to the east an orange sun rose over the horizon like a great ball of fire, sending long shadows racing for cover. Gillet turned away from the glare, and forcing a gob of saliva into his mouth licked his lips. Who these men were, he had no idea, but he knew sooner or later he'd find out. And why did the one-eyed man want to kill him?

"Okay, get in," the slim man said, nodding towards the rear of the van.

"Who the fuck are you?" Gillet grunted, standing his ground.

"In the back, Mr Gillet, or I'll blow your other foot off."

Gillet climbed in and settled in the rear. Certain that any form of protest was a waste of time, he sat, and stared at the man with the AK47 straddled across his lap.

"You're English?" he said.

The man raised his head and stared back with a practised detachment, and shrugged.

"My mother's English, my father Indian, and I'm from Luton. Satisfied?" he answered.

Distaste soured Gillet's mouth. Another home-bred idealist with romantic sensibilities, straight from Britain's conveyor belt of brainwashed Muslim militants. Yet he possessed an athletic grace about him, an air of social charm, and was strikingly handsome.

"Where are you taking me?"

"The Tora Bora caves in the White Mountains, to wait for someone very eager to make your acquaintance."

"Yeah, who might that be?"

"All in good time. In the meantime shut up and save your energy. Shortly we'll be leaving the van and crossing the Pakistan border into Afghanistan on foot. From there it's a hard five-hour walk up through the mountains to the caves."

Gillet slumped back. All coalition combatants knew of the Tora Bora caves. Constructed with the help of the Americans during Afghanistan's conflict with the Soviets, they were used to shelter the Taliban and store ammunition. Osama bin Laden was reputed to have used the caves as a refuge after 9/11, later making his way through the mountains to Pakistan and avoiding capture by American Special Forces by minutes.

"Do you have a name?"

"I am known as Jawad."

"So Jawad, what made you join up with the Taliban, apart from a shortage of brain cells?"

"I'm Al Qaeda, and your insults mean nothing to me. Soon you will learn to keep your mouth shut."

"Taliban, Al Qaeda, they're all the same, a bunch of murdering bastards."

Jawad took the bait.

"And the coalition forces, what are they, if not worse? You don't have the faintest idea why you are here, do you? Like morons you drop bombs like confetti at a wedding, then shake the hand of those who survived. Hearts and minds, you call it. Do you expect these people to grow wheat and corn at two hundred dollars a time, when the poppy earns tens of thousands? You are even more stupid than the Soviets."

"And that's why you are here, to help these people produce opium and heroin? Maybe even score a few lines for free?"

"I came to kill British soldiers, and soon I will add you to the list. Let me tell you a story. My younger brother, James, joined your army, the Royal Engineers," he said in a low voice. "From the moment he signed up to protect that shitty little island you call Great Britain they began bullying him, singled him out for being of mixed race, but they couldn't break him. Later he was sent here, to Afghanistan, they gave him a mine detector like something out of an Argos spring sale and told him to clear minefields."

"Banter is part and parcel of army life. All he had to do was rise above it and it would go away."

"Bullshit! Banter and bullying are poles apart, but arseholes like you don't have the intelligence to know the difference. Bullies hide behind their rank, pretending to be soldiers in the hope they won't be found out for the dumb shitheads they are. The day my brother died he halted a convoy of vehicles to check the road for IEDs, and guess what happened next? One of your half-witted squaddies thought it funny to throw a rock at him. Later, during his court martial, he described it as a joke, a childish prank. The rock set off a mine and that was the end of my brother. Accidental death, they called it, although I suppose a moron like you might refer to it as harmless banter."

Gillet ran his tongue over his lips. Jawad continued.

"My father burned every photograph of my brother dressed in the British uniform, and then wrote to the Ministry of Defence insisting his son's name be struck from their records. Later, in disgust he left the UK and moved back to India, where he worked as a heart surgeon. Now he works in a hospital saving the lives of ordinary decent people," Jawad continued. "He swears he will never lift a finger for any Brit for as long as he lives. As for me, I can't wait to see what Mirza Khan has in store for you."

Mirza Khan, the name jumped out at Gillet. The same man who had purchased Shafiq for a plaything, a sexual toy to pass the time at his pleasure. The reason for him to be here took on a new meaning. The reality was no longer fragile, but stark and laced with death. He had become trapped in a dangerous world of his own making, yet another part of him was a survivor that knew how to stay alive. The bumping and grinding stopped, and the van jerked to a halt. Doors slammed shut followed by the garbled sound of angry voices. The rear doors swung open. The one-eyed man reached in, and grabbing Gillet's shirt collar heaved him from the van and severed the plastic tie from his wrists.

"Okay, from here on we walk," Jawad said, nodding up at the mountains. "Up there, through the pass. It will be slow going, so conserve the water until we reach a stream. If you try to escape I will not hesitate to shoot you. Now move."

Gillet wiped away the sweat stinging his eyes and stared up at the craggy hills. Whether he had the strength to make the long climb he wouldn't hazard a guess. He had just two choices: complete the journey, or die trying.

Jawad took the lead, followed by the man with one eye; the driver of the van brought up the rear. Still sore and weak from the prison beatings, gritting his teeth Gillet picked each step as he went. Through a sparse forest of pines, the terrain spread out forming a barren flat plateau. His joy was short-lived, the gradient increased to a steep uphill climb. His efforts became laboured and his lungs seared as he gulped in the hot air. The scrubland rose steeper, occasionally levelling out into small even tracts littered with stones and large boulders. Dotted around growths of wild shrubs, stunted trees, alder ash. Thorny gorgora bushes barred their way, making their progress slow and tiring.

For two hours they cursed the rocky terrain as they continued up the mountain. At last, Jawad called a halt. Thankful for the respite, dropping to the ground each man rubbed cut hands and bleeding knees. Close by was a fast-running ice-cold shallow mountain stream, and they bathed their faces and wounds. Overhead the merciless sun strived to reach its zenith. Gillet filled the bottle and Jawad barked out orders to resume the journey. With no hint of wind to cool the scorching sun, the trek became more difficult, making it almost impossible to stand upright. Fatigue came without remorse. Earth, loose and treacherous, crumbled beneath his feet with every step until he lost his footing. Unable to stand he crashed to the ground, wincing at the sharp stones tearing the flesh from his hands and knees. The man with one eye sent his foot cannoning into his side and everything became etched with a red haze.

"Move, dog," he snarled.

Gillet's skin bristled, and he struggled to pull himself to his feet.

"Okay, we'll rest for a few minutes," Jawad said, slipping the AK47 from his shoulder.

Gillet's mind swirled, his breathing short gasping rasps; he gazed up into the sunlight sheering off the cliff face throwing a shadow up the craggy side of the mountain. Whatever lay in store for him the moment they reached the caves, he didn't know. Responsible for stealing Mirza Khan's dancing boy from under his nose, he had a good idea that nothing less than his death would satisfy the Khan's twisted mind. But why here, up in the mountains? Why drag him all this way? Summoning the last of his strength, he pulled himself to his feet. At first he'd been afraid, but now felt ready for whatever they had planned for him. He wouldn't go without a fight, and ignoring the others he rolled his weight onto the balls of his feet and started to make his way further up the mountain.

"Stay where you are, dog," the one-eyed man grunted, cocking his automatic rifle.

His finger tightened around the trigger. Gillet continued to move up the mountainside. The sound of a single shot echoed and re-echoed throughout the mountains. Squeezing his shoulder blades, Gillet waited for the bullet to smash his bones and the pain to flare through his body. He felt nothing, and waving his arms to keep his balance looked down the mountain. Jawad, with a 9mm handgun dangling from his hand, stared down at the one-eyed man's crumpled face on the rocky terrain. Blood drained thick like oil over the sun-bleached rocks. The body twitched and expired. Gillet's face remained expressionless, stubborn, one down and two to go.

"Lead the way," Jawad said, nodding to the driver.

"Inshallah," the man mumbled, pushing past Gillet.

*

Then, at last, it was over. Plastered in sweat and gasping with relief, he wiped the sweat blinding his eyes. Hot sun rays grilled everything in sight; shrubs, bushes and trees shimmered in the heat haze, making it impossible to see more than a few metres ahead. He swayed, and stared at the entrances to the caves. He'd made it, but what for what?

"Look around you, Gillet," Jawad said with a haughty wave, indicating at deep craters surrounded by charred trees blown out of the ground; twisted roots like grotesque crooked fingers pointed upwards towards the sky.

"This is where Bin Laden lived, until the Americans dropped their 500lb bombs and razed the place to the ground, killing women and children. But that is the way of the Americans is it not?."

Gillet hadn't the energy to argue, or even make an apt comment to even the status quo. His swollen joints ached. With his back against a jutting rock, he sat teasing out the shards of stone splintering his knees, wincing at the bubbles of blood sprouting from his wounds. The day wore on and night-time came, bringing the relief of cooler air. Like a gift from an invisible deity, he closed his eyes, his head slumped onto his chest and he lost consciousness.

When he woke, the pain in his head had returned. Under the cover of a fading dawn, he climbed to his feet and stretched. The roof of the cave was higher than he had expected, tall enough for a man to stand erect and reach up without touching the roof. Six by four metres, the floor consisted of loose dirt with scattered rubble. Discarded food boxes, once full of dates, and various empty fruit tins lay scattered around, rusting. By the far wall, empty American cigarette packets piled next to ammunition boxes with faded Russian words stencilled on all sides. Outside, he gazed up at the rising sun and shivered; the mountain air chilled his bones. The acrid smell of wood smoke drifted up his nostrils. Jawad glanced up and threw him a non-committal look, then continued to stir an iron pot of rice over a slow-burning fire. Twenty minutes later, he poured the lukewarm contents into three plastic bowls – one for the driver and one for Gillet. Jawad scooped out the contents of the third bowl with his fingers and sucked the rice into his mouth.

"Eat," he said. "You'll get nothing else until Mirza Khan arrives."

Gillet poured the contents down his throat. Then kicked a stone and watched it tumble and bounce down the rocky escarpment. Escape was impossible. He shrugged, and turned to Jawad.

"Why bring me all this way just to kill me, and what did the Americans expect to gain by handing me over to you?"

"Mr Gillet, your presence has been monitored since the first day you set foot in the Mustafa Hotel in Kabul. The Americans wanted you dead before you stirred up too much trouble with your ridiculous search for this boy. The Khan had paid a lot of money for the boy, and you have stained his reputation, most foolish. So, to get his hands on you, the Khan made a deal and exchanged you for two captive American pilots."

"Why, what do they expect from me, and what about the Pakistani police, and the prison?"

"Ah yes, that was unexpected. The police inspector has a reputation for being overzealous and almost ruined everything. We had to bribe the American consul and his Chief of Security to arrange to blow up the prison and get you out in one piece; the rest you know. The Americans got their two pilots and the Khan got you. Everybody's happy, except perhaps you." Jawad grinned.

Gillet licked the dryness from his lips. So that was it, the Americans had handed him over in exchange for two of their pilots. But still Jawad hadn't explained why the Khan wanted him so badly. He looked down the steep rugged slope of the mountain. Whichever way he looked at it, if he tried to escape he'd end up right back where he was, or dead. Apart from that he had no idea where he was, or where to go. The Pakistan police were looking for him, and if he set foot back in Kabul there was every chance the Americans would pick him up and finish him. During the climb to the caves he'd glimpsed hill tribesmen flitting from boulder to boulder, watching their progress.

"What about the boy?" Gillet asked.

"Shafiq? Boys like him are ten a penny, who cares?"

"I do, you sick bastard."

Jawad shrugged and walked away. The rest of the day Gillet sat alone, steeped in his own thoughts. Evening fell, and the driver disappeared. On his return, he carried an armful of kindling and lit a fire by the entrance to the cave.

"We sleep now," Jawad said.

Gillet eased his body onto the soft sandy floor, the relentless curse of fatigue bit into his flesh. The night was cold and unforgiving. The moment his eyes closed Amy entered into his dreams. Her corn-coloured hair tied in a ponytail exposed the gentle contours of her slender neck. She smiled; her eyes crinkled. By her side, Luke clutched her hand, his constant friendly grin splitting his face. He carried a blue mug with the word 'Dad' written on the side, a birthday present from happier times. Steam rose from the hot scalding tea and Gillet held out his hand. Then the dream turned into a nightmare and the image disappeared, replaced by a kaleidoscope of flashing colours forcing their way into his mind. Unimaginable noises mingled with screams of pain blocked his ears as a mass of unidentified bodies tumbled from nowhere onto the floor, blood spurting from gaping holes where their eyes should have been. Kicking and jerking, sweat poured from his body, matting his hair to his scalp. The nightmare went on until he didn't know whether he'd slept or remained awake, or if it was real. Jerking upright, eyes wide he stared into the dying fire, and shaking his head he cradled his face in his hands.

Soon another day dawned, and even though he had lain awake for the best part of the night, he felt refreshed. The sun wasn't so hot and the crisp mountain air cool.

Fifty yards away stripped to the waist, Jawad executed a series of martial arts movements. For the first time in weeks, Gillet raised a smile. He saw nothing to prevent a sharp kick to the balls, rendering the man useless. Loose stones bouncing down the shallow escarpment distracted his attention and he watched the driver make his way towards the cave. His hair lank and wet, raising a bony finger he rubbed his ear as if it might be blocked with water. Then lingered, sizing up Gillet with bird-like eyes, much in the way an undertaker might measure his next customer.

"Water; you wash." He shrugged, jerking his thumb towards a large escarpment behind an outcrop of boulders.

Gillet's spirits rose, passing a group of spruce trees made his way past the escarpment and stared at the fresh clean water bubbling down the mountain. The water glistened as it rippled over rocks and stones. Random swirling pools where he could sit and wash away the days-old dirt and sweat caked to his body. Removing his shirt and dipping it into the water he recoiled at the coldness. Then began to sponge away the grime, flinching each time the material made contact with the abrasions covering the upper part of his body. Dark bruises from the prison beatings had faded to a dull yellow, yet remained an incandescent reminder of his past allied with his present predicament. Other than an act of modesty, glancing over his shoulders he removed his trousers and, setting his teeth against the icy coldness, allowed the water to trickle over his legs. He felt strong and clear-headed, the pain singing out from his injured flesh eased and for the first time in weeks he wanted to call out in jubilation. Out in mid-stream the water covered him, leaving just his head above water.

At first the noise sounded like the barking of a crow. Distracted, he looked up, searching the clear sky. A speck at first, it drew closer and larger, more magnificent. The eagle beat her wings against the gentle thermals caressing the white peaks of the mountains. For a moment she hovered in regal grandeur merged with a graceful beauty, then descended onto a flat-topped rock jutting up into the sky. Unlaboured, she folded her wings and stood fierce and proud, defiant. Suddenly her solitary presence was interrupted by the intrusion of a lone male eagle, diving and gliding in the airspace over the jutting rock. With a wingspan more than the height of a grown man, he came swooping, riding the thermals, displaying his manliness as if to seek her acceptance. His piercing screech echoed through the mountains, and with drooping wings and hanging legs he settled beside her. In her acceptance she remained impassive by his side, and raising his golden beak he shrieked out a challenge to those who dared oppose his right. Gillet wrung the water from his clothes and dressed. It's never over until the fat lady sings, Dan Cook once said. On his way back, he stopped to gather dry wood for the fire.

"Is good," the driver said, glancing at the armful of kindling. "Drink tea; we have no food."

"You have weapons; there must be game in the mountains."

The driver turned, his hands sweeping in a forlorn manner with palms upturned.

"No game, no wildlife, no animals. When bombs fall people are not the only ones that die. Wildlife disappears forever; gazelle, bears, snow leopard, gone. In the sky we see birds no more, only the eagle remains; he is proud, like the people of this country," the driver said. "Once shepherds lived in these mountains, now they are no more. Forced to leave their villages and towns to escape bombs, the people take their animals to search for new grasslands. Soon no food left for animals and Afghan people die. Why you do this to us?"

Gillet looked away. No words of wisdom invented by Western civilisation could serve as an excuse. He wanted to tell the driver that like the eagles, they must be patient and wait for a better life to come to Afghanistan; instead, he remained silent, rubbing his damp palms on his knees. The surrounding countryside that had once flourished with life was now a cemetery.

*

For two days they survived on bitter-tasting roots the driver pulled from the woods. Interspersed with the occasional cup of hot water, Gillet feared dysentery. On the third day before the sun dropped, all eyes turned skyward at the fluttering helicopter rotors bending the treetops beneath the downdraft. A tall, lean man dressed in a tailored green US-style camouflaged uniform, with a black turban and dark shades above a stringy black beard, stepped out from the aircraft.

"Salaam Alaikum, Mirza Khan," Jawad said.

Mirza Khan wasn't an old man; he was tall, strong and nut brown. But soon he might be. The summer heat was oppressive to him where once he'd been used to it, and at times it made him do things he didn't want to do. His long handful of a beard, plastered tight to his face by sweat, irritated his skin. Long gone were the days when he'd been happy to lie with lions in comparative safety. Yet like all things they have a way of changing, taking different routes than those planned. Now, no matter how he valued his peace, he could not turn away from the needs of his country. Gone were the days when he brandished an AK47 above his head and cried for the blood of the Russian dogs. He ignored Jawad's greeting, instead stared long and hard at Gillet. Gillet blinked, noticing the shiny scar hidden by the black bushy beard, and stared back.

"So, Mr Gillet, at last we meet. Allah has been kind."

Gillet's bitter dislike for him was instant. If he was going to die, he would die like a soldier, cursing his enemy.

"Allah my arse, you came here in a Western helicopter wearing Western clothes; before you left, you probably ate a Western meal and screwed a Western whore. Your religion is no more than a fucking jack shit superstition."

Jawad sucked in a deep breath and fumbled with the AK47's cocking mechanism. The Khan raised his hand, staying Jawad's intention, his face white with fury.

"Go on, do it, pull the trigger and get it over with, you fucking wanker," Gillet sneered, waiting for Jawad to squeeze the trigger. "Or maybe you need to consult the Koran and find a chapter that condones murder. There must be one somewhere; if not you can always make one up."

"A quick death isn't something I have in mind for you, Mr Gillet, but I admire your courage," the Khan hissed between clenched teeth. "I have a surprise for you."

He snapped his fingers. The pilot slipped from the aircraft and opened the rear door. Shafiq stepped out with his raised hands against the receding sunlight. Stunned, Gillet balled his fists. At the sight of Gillet, Shafiq faltered, as if he was the last man on earth he wished to see. Face crestfallen, his shoulders sagged as if all hope had been dragged from him. Darkness closed over him, and remaining quiet, he stared down at his feet. The Khan's eyes darted from man to boy, expecting a reaction – an embrace, a gentle word of encouragement. When he received neither, his eyes narrowed.

"Unload the helicopter," he snapped at Jawad and the driver. "Hurry, I have to be in Kabul before nightfall."

Then it came, like Ahab's whale rising from the deep, and Gillet remembered where he had seen the Khan. It was in the Mustafa Hotel just minutes before Riley had forced his company on him. Three of them had sat at the same table in the dining room, bloated with their own self-importance. He recalled the Khan for the particular way he had stared at him, taking in every detail, as though one day they might meet and he needed to be certain of his identity. The muscles in his jaw twitched as the driver struggled to lift a heavy cine camera and tripod from the helicopter. He wasn't a man to brood, but he remembered the day he'd viewed the unedited version of Piotr Stanczak, a Polish geologist filmed having his head carved off by a Muslim militant in April of 2007 after the West refused to release captured militants. Shafiq stood pale-faced, and he reached out to pull him closer. Two and two made four, it always did.

"You bunch of sub-human bastards."

The Khan snaked out his fist, catching Gillet full in the face. He stumbled back, recovered his senses and dropped to a crouch, ready; hate flowed from every pore in his body. Swaying from side to side, he waited for the chance to strike back. A flicker of uneasiness crossed the Khan's face and he stumbled back, losing his balance; his arms grabbed at fresh air for support. In an instant the pilot stepped in between the two men, his pistol pointing at Gillet's brow.

"Step back, dog," he growled.

Gillet heard the metallic click of the hammer lock into position and stood his ground, aware that any moment he'd be just another rotting corpse in the sun charred mountains. He waited, erect, unafraid, staring down the barrel of the handgun. His breath ragged and the muscles in his face jerked. They had brought him to the mountains to kill him and he couldn't understand why they hesitated. Jawad was right; it was a set-up, the whole episode manufactured from the beginning. Then he remembered the camera. It wasn't courage or bravado that made him lean with his forehead pressed tight against the muzzle of the handgun; his thoughts precise, judicious. The day he died would be a time of his choosing. He wouldn't wait for them to film his head hacked off for all the world to see.

"Come on, you piece of shit, pull the trigger, if you've got the guts," he roared, pushing his head tighter against the pistol barrel, forcing the pilot to step back.

"Wait, we need him alive," the Khan said.

The pilot lowered the pistol. The Khan took Jawad roughly by the arm and whispered words that no one overheard, and then climbed into the helicopter.

The helicopter rose and disappeared over the pointed peaks of the Tora Bora Mountains.

Jawad stared in bewilderment. The intensity of the last few minutes had left him reeling. His mind blanked. It had all been a dream. Gillet's words pierced his confused thoughts.

"If anything happens to the boy, be assured I will kill you." Gillet spoke in a matter-of-fact voice.

Rattled, Jawad fumbled with the AK47; the feel of cold steel raised his flagging spirit. An image of his late brother lying blown to pieces sprang to mind and he felt his throat shrink. Gillet must be insane.

"Grab the cases of food and provisions and follow me, and that includes you too, dancing boy. We are moving higher up the mountain to a larger cave," he said, trying to add timbre to his voice. "Gillet, sooner or later your luck is going to run out."

Luck or no luck, Gillet knew the worst was yet to come, and to his way of thinking, that meant things could only get better. Sure, he was afraid, but he knew that fear heightens the senses, sharpens the mind, and for the time being he could live with that.

The narrow mountain path traversed from left to right as it slowly gained in height. Laden down with boxes of supplies, it took the best part of two hours to reach a height of sixty metres from the former cave, and half of the provisions still remained stacked below. There was food and drink enough for a month.

CHAPTER FOUR

The primitive fear of enclosed spaces had never been a factor during Gillet's life; just the same, he marvelled at the enormity of the cave. A dozen times larger than the first cave, it stood five metres high, with no sign of dampness. Next to the entrance, a small unused diesel-driven generator, large enough to power up a sequence of electric light bulbs and various domestic appliances, stood with the exhaust facing outwards. Jawad filled the fuel tank and cranked the generator into life. Seated on a wooden crate, he listened to the humming as energy fired into the bulbs, illuminating the cave.

"What happens now?" Gillet asked.

"We wait."

"Wait for what?"

"We wait."

"Twat."

Hunkered down, Gillet searched for moral insensibility to insulate himself against the ever-increasing fear for his future. It wasn't right that he should die and the bastards holding him survived. Jawad might run the show in the Khan's absence, but he detected an air of uncertainty in his character. His best bet, if he wanted to get out of the mountains alive, was to find a way of getting inside Jawad's mind, a way to unsettle him.

"What's your real name?" he said, not expecting an answer.

"Rupert Singh," Jawad answered, catching him by surprise.

"Did your friends call you Rupe, or Rupo, perhaps Rupers?"

"No, they called me Rupert. Were you known as Giblets, Gimpy, or just Gibberish?"

"No, just plain Gillet."

"I find that hard to believe."

Gillet smiled; Jawad had a sense of humour, a good sign. Jawad felt nothing but a faint impatience with Gillet's foolishness. As for himself, he was different, more focused, with a powerful grip on life, alert, vigorous in mind and soul. Within him the newly found joy of Islam lay in full blood and he revelled in the glorious experience, carrying it like a precious gift. Although his time on earth was short, he had glimpsed the good and bad of two worlds. Christianity he considered violent and angry, full of ugly passions, with habits that distorted life. But in Islam, he basked in the realms of purity, a freshness born of a simplistic calm. He looked across at Gillet like he was last week's pint of cream turned sour, and smirked. Gillet caught the look and, intent on prolonging the conversation to annoy Jawad, smirked back.

"Do you intend to remain a Muslim, or is it just your twisted way of seeking revenge for your brother's death?" he asked.

"What I do with my life is none of your concern, apart from the fact it will last a lot longer than yours."

Gillet snorted. Disenchanted with the response, he made his way outside into the night air. The wind came softly over the treetops, more coolly than usual. The yellow moon climbed until it hovered overhead and shadows moved and crept like living things. There were whisperings in the tall pines.

*

Night passed, and like always, dawn arrived on time, its gouging fingers seeking every crevice to chase away the shadows and worm out all that remained of unwanted darkness.

Shafiq rested with his head in the crook of his arm, woke and stretched with a near silent groan. He hadn't found the time to pray since Mirza Khan's men picked him up from Peshawar Airport. Whatever happened to those that accompanied him, he would never know, and daren't hazard a guess. On his knees facing towards Mecca, Jawad nodded his approval and, accompanied by the driver, knelt in the exaltation of Allah. Gillet watched, with his mouth twisted in disdain. Briskly making his way outside and glad to be away from the droning sound laying siege to his ears, he made his way to the stream. When at last the chanting ceased, Shafiq emerged from the cave and moved further downstream. Squatting, he gazed up into the sky. He didn't acknowledge Gillet; instead, looked in awe down the length of the great valley. Like Jawad, the love of Allah filled his heart. Each boulder, each dotted patch of greenery that lay beneath the silent swaying pines spread wild, a blessing from Allah. A sign to his followers that he loved them like a father loves his favourite son. He pressed his eyes shut, fearful he did not deserve to gaze upon that which his God had provided for him.

"*Allahu akbar*, God is great."

Gillet turned with a raised eyebrow, about to speak, he changed his mind. What did the kid know apart from the barren wastelands of the Afghan plains, where the only splash of greenery visible to his eye was the cultivated opium poppy fields?

"Don't you pray to your god, Mister Sergeant?" Shafiq said. "Or perhaps where you come from you do not need a god."

"I call on my god when I need him," Gillet grunted.

"He speaks the truth, Shafiq," Jawad interrupted with a wry smile. "His kind treat their god with words of profanity. They insult their god's son with blasphemous words such as Jesus fucking Christ; the list is endless. In Christian countries, the young pray because they are ordered to, and the elderly pray for fear there might be a heaven after spending a lifetime of abusing their god. Allah is the one true God. That is all you need to remember."

"So ends today's sermon," Gillet jeered. "And stuff Allah."

Shafiq bent to pick up a rock and hurled it at Gillet. Gillet staggered back, blood flowing from the wound on his temple.

"The words you speak are evil; perhaps it is better if we are no longer friends," Shafiq snorted.

Gillet took a step towards the boy.

"Stay where you are," Jawad said, pointing the AK47 at Gillet's knees. "Nothing would please me more than to pull the trigger."

The exchange was terse, intent etched on each man's face. Without speaking, Gillet moved to the edge of the stream. On his knees, he bathed the wound, waiting for the bleeding to stop. Anger burned in his eyes and he gazed thoughtfully at the stream's twisting path running down into the valley. He'd had enough, only the urge to flee filled his mind. Over the passing weeks his strength returned and he felt stronger. The time had come to make his bid for freedom, or die trying; anything was better than the cruel death he imagined was waiting for him. The muscles in his jaws twitched; a breeze darted across the cold water and he shivered. *Tonight*, he thought, *I shall go tonight.*

*

It was never dark at night in this part of the world, with stars slung low across a sapphire sky; unlike the north Norfolk coast, where they hid cloaked by dark low-lying clouds. Like a host of illuminated raindrops, they waited to fall to earth and form glittering puddles. Cautiously following the meandering stream running first one way and then the other he made his way down the mountainside. Beneath a ghostly moonlight glistening water splashed and rippled, surmounting each obstacle barring the way in turn. Pausing now and then he strained his ears above the tumbling water for any sound of pursuit. The rocky downward terrain became steeper, almost vertical. His lungs rasped for air. Unable to continue, he stopped, and clinging to a boulder waited for his heart to stop hammering against his ribs. Then stiffened, the roots of his hair tingled. Through the gloom, he saw them, moving figures darting from boulder to boulder like fleeting shadows. The figures drew closer and he felt bathed in the grip of a thousand searchlights. The harsh metallic rattle of cocking automatic weapons echoed through the barren hillside and his heart plummeted. It is said a man's of spirit is never aware of its presence until he has need of it, yet his vigour drained, leaving him devoid of energy. Upright, with arms dangling by his side, he stood like a trapped animal. Yet there was still a chance; he could run, risk being shot. His single-minded nature forbade it, instead he waited.

Hill tribesmen stepped from out of the gloom. The leader, a small man with a large mouth, walked towards him; his twisted lips resembled a buttoned-up overflowing pocket. From behind the boulders other tribesmen joined him, staring and jabbering. Jerking his head, the small man motioned to Gillet to retrace his steps. A sense of failure seeped through every pore of his body, and his shoulders sagged as though the lifeblood had been siphoned from his arteries. Twisted lips raised his weapon and fired a solitary shot, not as a warning but as a sign of victory. When Jawad appeared, his smile was smug and pretentious. Back in the cave, Gillet expected to be bound hand and foot; instead, they did worse – they wrestled him to the ground and removed his artificial foot.

That night, twisted lips and his companions remained in the cave, and he was subjected to their snoring and incoherent ramblings until his nerves jangled. Morning dawned, and he looked down at the bare stump where his foot should have been, loathing the fact he couldn't walk. Arms outstretched, he began a series of hops towards the stream. Three steps and he crashed to the ground, face contorted with agony he brushed away the stones penetrating his flesh. Small bubbles of blood sprang from his punctured skin, and unable to withstand the pain grinding into his knees, he groaned and rolled over onto his back. Like a crab he worked his way towards the stream, stopping to regain his breath and inspect the mangled stump oozing blood. From the entrance to the cave Jawad watched, pity remote from his heart. Metres behind, Shafiq's eyes welled and tears trickled down his face. He knew at times Mister Sergeant spoke blasphemous words with no consideration for those in earshot. But he was an honourable man, a warrior of great courage, not a crippled dog fit to crawl on his hands and knees for a drink of water. Squatted on his haunches, he poked the dry dust with his fingers, recalling the hot afternoon Mister Sergeant had entered his village. Three days before, a villager spotted an American armoured convoy lost out on the desert. For all their sophisticated equipment and navigational aids, the red-faced Americans asked directions to a village marked with a red cross on a large map. The youths of the village, young and sturdy, their hot flesh and blood heated at the sight of the hated Americans, began to jeer and hurl rocks. The Americans retaliated by laying down a short withering blanket of fire, almost destroying the village. Many villagers received wounds; one woman lay dead, shot through the head. Three days later Gillet sucked in his cheeks and spat in defiance when ordered by a British Commander to instigate a hearts and minds operation. Accompanied by British medics, he supervised medical treatment for the injured, growing angry when the men of the village queued for minor ailments, while forbidding the more seriously injured women to receive treatment. Aware women had no public role in Afghanistan, Gillet ordered the medics to halt treating the men and concentrate on the women and children first. The inevitable argument flared, weapons made ready to fire before the men of the village slunk away, angry and untreated. From the entire village, only four women possessed the courage to step forward; the first was Shafiq's mother, with festering wounds to her face from flying mortar chips. From that moment an easy relationship grew between Gillet and the boy. Later, Shafiq, for scraps of food fed them information on the whereabouts of the Taliban.

"It is not good you treat this man in this way, Mirza Khan will be angry," Shafiq said, glaring at Jawad.

"What do you know, dancing boy? You no longer hold the interests of the Khan," Jawad sneered.

"Then I will tell him of your words, and of the things I see."

Jawad shrugged. "Do as you please, soon I shall be gone from here."

Shafiq smiled, and tucking the false foot under his arm made his way across the escarpment. At the edge of the stream he stopped and watched Gillet ease his aching body into the ice-cold water, groaning as it closed over his open wounds.

"Mister Sergeant, I have brought your foot to help you walk," Shafiq said.

Gillet's stump leaked blood into the stream. It would be a long time before he would be able to walk, even with the help of the false foot.

"Thanks, but right now I need a crutch to support my weight."

"Jawad will not allow it," Shafiq said, shaking his head.

Gillet stared at the driver.

"You are a man of courage, Gillet, stupid maybe, but of great courage," the driver added. "I shall find a stick to help you walk"

Minutes later, Gillet hobbled across the escarpment with the makeshift crutch fixed under his armpit. Jawad eyes slitted.

"I gave no order to provide Gillet with a crutch," he sneered at the driver.

The driver's lips stretched tight over his teeth. Jawad hesitated, watching the mental manoeuvring behind the driver's cold piercing eyes.

"I need no order from you; you are a mongrel without a country. Curb your tongue, while you still have one," the driver spat.

Gillet's eyes darted to Jawad, then back to the driver. Up to now the driver had remained subservient to Jawad's wishes. Jawad's fingers gripped the AK47's trigger. The driver tensed, glanced at the AK47, then changed his grip on the knife nestling in his hand, the tip turned upward, ready to strike at Jawad's heart.

"Put the weapon down, dog."

Jawad's Adam's apple bobbed and his eyes widened. He looked across at Gillet as if seeking assurance of what to do next. Gillet raised an eyebrow.

"Your call, Rupes." He grinned.

The spell became fragmented by fluttering helicopter rotors. Mirza Khan stepped from the helicopter; gone the tailored military uniform, in its place a white *shappan*, the traditional robe. Perched square on his head a *karakul*, a soft oval-shaped hat made of sheepskin. Now he was the traditional warlord, the self-appointed aristocracy of Afghanistan, the man who provided a defence for the people of their ethnicity or tribe, the lord of the Panjishir Valley. Known as the Valley of Five Lions, it was a natural fortress with three hundred thousand inhabitants situated eighty miles north of Kabul, close to the Hindu Kush mountain range. The Americans, with his permission, had sparked a boom of development with the construction of roads. Even a radio tower capable of sending radio signals to and from Kabul. For allowing help to develop his country, the Americans had paid him inordinate sums of money, making him a wealthy man respected by his people. Deep in his heart the Khan hated the Taliban and anyone else who halted the progress of Afghanistan. Yet in fear of his life and for those he ruled, he obeyed their orders.

This time he and the pilot did not come alone. A huge man standing over six feet tall, his shaven head glistening with the fine sheen of sweat beneath the hot sun stepped from the helicopter. His eyes black and lifeless, like those of a dead fish. Gillet felt his gaze gauging him from head to foot and stared back. Then, with an air of satisfaction, the man turned to the helicopter and extracted a long polished mahogany box with brass hinges and a worn leather handle. Gillet's throat closed. Fear boiled in his gut. Shafiq's small fist forced its way into the palm of his hand, and he felt the boy tremble. He closed his hand as Shafiq pulled his body tight against his leg. The contents of the box were common enough in the bazaars of Kabul. Ceremonial swords used for execution could be bought for a handful of Afghanis.

*

An air of taciturnity hovered over the group as they ate the evening meal prepared by the driver.

"Tell me, Mr Gillet, for how long do you expect the coalition soldiers to stay in Afghanistan?" the Khan said, picking his teeth with a long fingernail.

Blessed with a certain amount of adroitness, Gillet smiled.

"They will leave when they have finished what they came to do."

"A wise answer, but can you tell me what it is they have come here to do?"

"If you don't know the answer to that by now, they have been wasting their time, and would be better employed developing the economy, security and government of other countries that understand the meaning of progress. Although I don't for one moment believe you haven't succeeded in filling your greedy pockets and profited from their presence."

Mirza Khan sniffed and pulled the back of his hand across his nose.

"You expect us to understand your reasons for being here when you yourselves do not? Is it not common knowledge that over three thousand coalition soldiers deserted last year, mostly Americans seeking citizenship in Canada who have no wish to return to their homeland?" the Khan said in an almost amiable voice. "War is the

American way of life; because of their paranoiac nature, they know no different. The wise Americans see this and convert to Islam. It is said at least one coalition soldier a week commits suicide in Afghanistan. Those who suffer stress from battle are ignored by their government and rely on anti-depressants and cheap medicines. But worst of all, you come to our country uninvited and tell us how to live our lives, deny us our right to grow the opium poppy which counts for one third of our economy, and you call this progress?"

"Those are questions for politicians, I am a soldier."

"Ah, yes of course, you are a soldier. Your work is to kill women and children indiscriminately, that is a soldier's job."

"Fuck you. We act as peacekeepers to keep the Taliban from taking over your country, to offer you the opportunity of democracy, yet you question our motives when it's you that sends suicide bombers into areas packed with innocent women and children who cannot fight back," Gillet said. "Civilians should never die during times of war; your ways are medieval and out of date."

It was there, in the Afghan's face, the anger.

"A war, you call it a war? Throughout history wars have been fought between armies alone; in your First World War ten per cent of the dead were civilians, the Second World War, fifty per cent, the Vietnam War, seventy per cent, and Iraq, ninety per cent. Perhaps in Afghanistan it will be one hundred per cent; do you think that possible?"

"Bollocks," Gillet snarled, losing his temper.

The Khan's taut smile never reached his eyes, his stare concealed any feeling. A shift of hopelessness shadowed Gillet's heart; sweat gathered in the small of his back and stuck like glue to his body. The chicken looked grey and inedible on his plate, the rice stodgy. His appetite waned and disappeared.

"We do not kill civilians," he said in an even voice. "That is your way, not ours."

"But it is," the Khan said. "The coalition army is prepared to destroy a whole village and its inhabitants to apprehend one man. That is murder, a war crime that will forever go unpunished. It is the Americans who make the rules. And you, the British, follow like puppy dogs on the word of fools like your prime ministers, shallow men of no standing to whom you gave a country and allowed them to play with it like it was a child's toy. A country once revered and respected throughout the world, now tottering on extinction because of ineffective leadership built on lies. You will never win a war with a handful of poorly equipped soldiers against the might of Islam."

"What would you prefer we do?"

"If you are wise you will leave Afghanistan before the day comes when we re-arm with nuclear weapons sophisticated enough to defeat the West. Your mere presence here is the biggest part of the problem; go away and take what is left of your soldiers with you. Speak with those who return in one piece and ask what they have accomplished in Afghanistan, and then ask the same question to those maimed by war. Their answer is always the same, nothing, apart from leaving my mind, or limbs behind."

"The Khan speaks the truth," Jawad said, leaping to his feet. "You erect memorials to your dead, but never to the innocent, the pregnant women, old men and young children slaughtered in cold blood. We fight a *jihad*, a holy war against the infidels and rid our country of the ungodly, like we did centuries ago in the crusades against your Richard the First, an English king who was no more than the Pope's assassin."

"*Allah akbar*, God is great," the driver shrieked in religious fervour.

Gillet sank back against the cold wall of the cave. "Why tell me these things? I've already told you, I'm just an ex-soldier injured from fighting the Taliban."

"You think we are stupid, Mr Gillet. You are more than an ex-soldier, you are here on a mission, sent to kidnap defenceless Afghan boys for pleasure." Mirza Khan's words sliced through the air like a hot blade through butter. "Perhaps you wish to introduce *Bacha Bazi* into your country, but you will not live long enough."

Gillet stared at Mirza Khan; the lump in his throat moved.

"Prepare yourself, Farzad, the time has come," the Khan said, turning to the huge man sitting in the background.

Farzad pulled himself to his feet and left the cave. Heads turned to Mirza Khan, then to Gillet. Time passed, Gillet raised his head and stared at the Khan. The Khan stared back, unflinching. Then from the inside of his robe he pulled out two postcard-size photographs. The first he dropped in front of Gillet.

"Tell me what you see, Mr Gillet," he said.

Gillet gazed at the photograph.

"It is a picture of you outside the Mustafa Hotel. So what?" He shrugged.

"And this, Mr Gillet, what do you see this time?" the Khan said, placing the second picture at the side of the first one.

Gillet sucked in a lung full of night air. The second photograph was identical to the first, apart from one small detail. Next to Khan was a small boy wearing faded denims and a white T-shirt – his son, Luke.

The atmosphere changed. His breath came in short pants like a thirsty dog. Unable to restrain himself, he lunged for the Khan with outstretched fingers, ready to gouge and claw the features from his face. Jawad plunged the butt of the AK47 into Gillet's temple, and then bound his wrists. When Gillet regained consciousness, he writhed on the ground trying to reach the Khan. Eyes veined blood-red. His lips stretched back, ready to tear the flesh from the Afghan's face with his bare teeth. The Khan flinched and moved out of reach. Again the butt of the AK47 smashed into Gillet's face; the sound of bones buckling and snapping filled the cave.

"Do as I tell you, Mr Gillet, after which your son will go free; however, if you refuse, you will never see him again."

"Fuck you," Gillet said, staring through unfocused eyes. "I don't know how you got your filthy hands on my son, but I promise you this, harm one hair on his body and you will wish you were never born."

The Khan rose, his smile mocking.

"Bring him and the boy to the lower cave."

Gillet winced as the driver, assisted by Jawad, dragged him down the steep pathway to the lower cave they had inhabited on the first day of their arrival. A frigid wind, cold and uncompromising, whipped at his face. Ignoring his pain, he hurled a tirade of obscenities at the Khan, at Allah and all the mindless termites that knelt before him.

The interior of the cave had been lit with rows of flickering candles, throwing a host of dancing shadows like agitated spirits across the walls. Gillet blinked, and peered through the smoky gloom. Pinned against the far wall, a black flag with bold words written in Arabic hung behind a wooden chair and table. In front of the table, a metre away, was a camera mounted on a heavy steel tripod. To the left, propped against the wall, a long curved sword glinted in the candlelight. Gillet stiffened, and moved as if he knew his fate in advance. Despair was mirrored in his posture. His time to die had arrived, and for the first time in his life he felt an urge to pray for the strength to destroy those around him, to kill and maim in a mad rage. Yet bound tight and useless through the red mists of hatred obstructing his sight, he visualised the image of his son. Luke, sweet, innocent Luke, the only thing on earth he knew for sure that was pure, innocent and without blemish. Farzad stood, his thick powerful legs apart like pillars, his bare chest rising and falling as he sucked in air through his nose and exhaled through his mouth. Jawad looped a small microphone around Gillet's neck and forced him down into the chair.

"Read the words written on the sheet of paper in front of you. After you have accomplished this simple task, you are free to go; you have my word," the Khan said, sliding the paper across the table. "If you refuse, you will not live to see your son die."

Gillet's chin slumped onto his chest and he strained to focus his eyes in the gloomy candlelight. Although the words printed in bold letters filled the whole of the page, he struggled to digest the meaning of the text. At last, mustering a small amount of reason, he read the words. Finished, and thinking he had somehow failed to understand their meaning, he read them again, one word at a time. Raising his head, he looked at the faces blurred by the gloom. Mirza Khan no longer looked tall and strong, but evil and rotten to the core. Behind his eyelids, his stare was cruel and malevolent. In contrast, Jawad stared, cocky, confident and unable to conceal his triumph. Gillet glanced at the paper one more time, praying he had been mistaken. He had never professed to be a disciple of education, a scholar, or a man of words, but the words he read and understood were the same words as those he'd read seconds ago. His brief was to admit to being a leading member of a paedophile ring, sent by members of the British and American governments to procure Afghan boys for the pleasure of high-ranking military commanders and politicians in the White House and Whitehall. His actions came with the full blessing of serving homosexual commanding officers in both Iraq and Afghanistan. With a deep-lying penchant for boys trained in *Bacha Bazi*, both Americans and the British were of the opinion that Afghan boys – orphans from war-torn areas – were the most subservient, the easiest to procure and prepared to do anything to please their masters.

"No one will believe this filth," Gillet mumbled.

"Read the words, Mr Gillet," the Khan said, switching on the camera.

"Fuck off."

Mirza Khan's face twisted with anger. Gillet's reaction had left him bewildered. Yet, being a man of a pragmatic nature, he had taken precautions to ensure his success in disposing of him and his son.

"Your puny attempts at heroics tire me, Mr Gillet. Perhaps you think I am making a joke," he said, turning to the driver. "Do you believe in Allah and the life hereafter, my brother?"

"Allah is everything; my life is his."

"What is your name?"

"Abdul-al Raheem."

"Show the infidel how a true Muslim dies, Abdul-al Raheem."

The driver hesitated and pulled in a deep breath. With sweat cascading down his face, he knelt before Mirza Khan and stared at the floor. Farzad raised the sword, laid the blade across the driver's neck and in one blurred movement leapt and spun in mid-air like a ballet dancer. With one blow, the hissing blade severed the driver's head from his body. The headless body slumped forward,

145

twitching, and blood erupted from the gaping neck. Eyes open and staring the head rolled to a stop. Spittle rattled through Gillet's congested throat, trapping the air. Shafiq stood rigid, pale as death; his lips, blue with shock, trembled while his mind fought to comprehend, to make sense of what his eyes had shown him. His right foot tapped on the floor and he urinated where he stood. Jawad staggered and felt his legs buckle as though punched by a heavyweight boxer.

"Now do you believe I am serious, Mr Gillet?" the Khan said. "Read the script, or the boy is next."

Gillet had had more than his share of near-death experiences in life. It came with his job – kill or be killed. But when he opened his mouth to protest, instead of words, streams of spittle ran over his lips and hung in long streamers from his chin. Fog clouded his mind, squeezing away all thoughts; his mouth opened and closed like a drowning fish as he watched the blood continue to gush from the headless body. It wasn't real, it couldn't be. He felt as if a ball had lodged in his throat; his chest rose and fell like a pump. He no longer felt connected to the world.

The Khan nodded. Farzad reached for Shafiq and clutched him by his throat. Shafiq's legs turned to air; already in a state of semi-consciousness he hung limp, powerless to prevent the executioner dragging him across the cave floor.

"Allah awaits you, little one." He smiled, raising the blade.

Gillet turned his head away, then curiosity ruled his mind and he turned, unsure if what he expected would happen. Seething with helplessness, he prayed to all the gods in the universe that wherever the next world might be, one day he would meet Mirza Khan face-to-face.

Jawad retched. An image of his brother manifested in his mind and he raised the AK47, squeezed the trigger and sent a hail of bullets ripping into the executioner's neck. To his left the pilot made a grab for the pistol tucked in his trouser top. Jawad squeezed the trigger one more time. The Khan darted to one side, screaming curses.

"You fool, you have ruined everything! The Iranians promised to supply us with missiles and rockets to fight the British and Americans if we delivered the film."

"Die, dog, you are no servant of Islam," Jawad spat, pointing the weapon towards the Khan's head.

"Wait, don't kill him, not until I know the whereabouts of my son," Gillet pleaded.

"Why should I listen to you? You too are unclean and unfit to be a father. I have read the paper on the table before you."

"If you believe that shit, why did you stop the Khan from forcing me to read the paper in front of the camera?"

"His way is wrong; it is not the way of Allah. Muslims do not kill Muslims or innocent children, we fight a *jihad*, against the infidel, and it must be fought with honour because right is on our side."

Gillet fought to stop the wrong words tumbling from his mouth.

"Does it not say in the Koran that Allah prevents the sky falling to earth because he is for mankind, full of pity, merciful?"

Jawad's head jerked up with surprise.

"Silence! You dare to quote the words of the prophet to suit your own ends?"

"No, Rupert, the Koran says be merciful. Let me and the boy go and search for my son. Go and fight your holy war, my war is over."

"Again you insult me. My name is Jawad the Generous, not Rupert. Many things in my life have changed over the years; I am no longer the same person."

"Men never change, they just pretend to be something."

"What makes you think I won't place you in front of the camera and force you to admit the truth? It would make for good reading throughout the world. I shall be the saviour of Islam and the coalition would be finished. All Islam would rise at the news that infidels kidnap Muslim boys orphaned by war for sex."

"Kill him, kill him, it is Allah's will!" the Khan raged, cowering in the corner of the cave.

Jawad turned and looked into the crazed eyes, squeezed the trigger, and blew the Khan's head from his shoulders.

"We return to the cave above. In the morning I will decide what must be done. Maybe I will kill you, Gillet; it would make my life easier if you were dead.

CHAPTER FIVE

It was morning when Jawad stepped from the cave into the bright daylight and stretched. A warm billowing wind swirled across his face as he looked down the sun-drenched valley as far as the shimmering heat haze would allow. He had decided to leave the bodies where they were, the hill tribesmen would strip them of their clothes and, for fear of reprisals, bury them where they'd never be found. For the best part of that morning he tried to forget the horrors of the night before. As hard as he tried, the memories remained. Kneeling by the stream, he dipped his *shemagh* in the cold water, bathed his face and then his feet and hands in accordance with *wudu*, the Muslim law for washing before prayer. On his knees, he shuffled until comfortable, then bared his soul and asked for extra guidance from Allah, the merciful one.

Gillet shaded his eyes against the rising sun. It wasn't from any form of respect that he stayed his time, waiting for Jawad to bond with his god, but fear. Jawad wanted him dead, he knew that, and would in all probability kill him to prevent him from finding Luke. With the makeshift crutch nestled under his armpit, he hobbled to the narrow pathway leading to the stream. Jawad finished praying and looked up at noting the uncertainty in Gillet's movements. He had given much thought to many things during the night, most of which concerned Gillet. Again, in his mind he ran through his plan. There were no obvious loopholes, or none that he could bring to mind; it was straightforward. He would spare Gillet's life, even help him to find his son, but there was a price to pay.

"Okay, so now what do we do?" Gillet said, interrupting his thoughts.

Jawad didn't answer. Instead, he picked up a stone and hurled it into the stream as if he hadn't heard Gillet's question. Contemplation is good for the soul, the holy book said, and it was important he make certain that what he was about to do was right. His mind dwelled on Allah's words, the words he had spoken to him while he had tossed in his sleep. His confidence had been dented by the savage incident in the cave and he needed time to recover his faith, to refresh his belief in all that was right. He must not turn from the teachings of the Prophet, yet felt certain he'd interpreted the dream correctly. The Koran states that Muslims may retaliate if attacked first, but must never bear a grudge or make to seek vengeance. It was this that had led him to contemplate whether or not he was correct in seeking to take his vengeance out on Gillet. Time spent in the great mosques with those who brimmed with wisdom, had taught him that many roads lead to the marketplace of fulfilment. In which case, it couldn't be counted a crime against Allah if he chose a different road to reach his goal. It takes one hand to wash the other, but two to wash the face, Allah told him in the dream. At first he didn't understand the meaning, but now he did and the time had come to find another route to eternal fulfilment. Satisfied, he congratulated himself on his good fortune, and tossed another stone into the water, hoping to stretch Gillet's anxiety.

Gillet shrugged, careful not to push his luck, he moved further upstream out of Jawad's sight.

For most of the day, tired and in need of sleep, he conducted a thorough search of the caves and surrounding woodlands for a sign of Shafiq. At the advent of dusk, he began to worry.

"The boy's missing," he grunted.

Jawad shrugged. "The boy? Who knows where he is, or cares? Maybe he came to his senses and left."

"Left, left for where? He wouldn't just leave without a word."

"Ha, what is there to keep him here; you, maybe? Why should he bother with you, Gillet? You brought him nothing but trouble. You should be more concerned with your son, Luke."

Gillet tensed. How could Jawad have known his son's name? And how had Mirza Khan managed to get Luke out of the UK, and last but not least, who had assisted him? The change within him wasn't subtle, it was instantaneous. He promised himself that when the time came he would wring the truth from Jawad, before he killed him.

Contrary to what Gillet believed, Jawad knew where Shafiq was. With his blessing and before first light, helped by the tribesmen, Shafiq had made his way down the valley to the Salang-Kabul Road. His mission was to return to Khan's palatial property on the outskirts of Kabul and confirm the whereabouts of Luke before the Khan's death became public knowledge.

Nestled next to the scrap of paper with the number of Jawad's cell phone in Shafiq's pocket was the small bottle of dust from the Shamali Plain, and a thick wad of Afghanis. As the sun rose over the mountains, he thumbed down a lorry and settled amongst a cargo of pomegranates bound for the markets of Kabul.

In the marketplace of Kabul, after a customary moment of heated bartering with a stallholder with one leg, who cursed him to hell for laughing when he lost his balance and toppled over, Shafiq left dressed in a new set of clothes. Next he purchased two roast chickens fired in a roadside clay oven, and, reluctant to arouse attention, he sat next to the beggars in the shade of the Great Mosque. There was much to think about, considering he wanted nothing more to do with Mister Sergeant. Had he not turned his life upside down when he'd grown used to a full belly each day? Not only that, he'd almost lost his head in the cave. Against his better judgment he had given his word to Jawad, in exchange for his freedom he would help find the boy called Luke. His immediate thought was to make his way back to Chicken Street and ask Abbas for help. Common sense told him that would place him and his family in danger, and make his own situation even more precarious. He liked Abbas, perhaps one day, when he was free from trouble, he would return to him and help to run the family business selling fruit and vegetables. Finishing the first chicken, with a wistful look he handed the second to the beggars to avoid their avaricious stares. Stretching out his legs and curling and uncurling his toes, he racked his brain for the best way out of his predicament. The odds were against him. Even so, it made good sense to assume the boy known as Luke would be at Mirza Khan's residence on the northern outskirts of the city.

Still hungry, moving away from the beggars he purchased another chicken and washed it down with a warm can of coke from a trader on a bicycle. Flagging a taxi down wasn't as easy as it looked, until he pulled out a handful of Afghanis, and the next one he beckoned screamed to a halt in a cloud of dust. Ignoring the driver's suspicious looks, he told him to wash the vehicle and send for a second driver to sit next to him in the rear. When he offered to pay double the fare, the two drivers mumbled between themselves, looked at him suspiciously and demanded the fare up front.

The taxi lurched to a stop outside Mirza Khan's home. The lounging guards came alive, fingering their weapons as Shafiq opened the rear door and stepped out into the sunlight.

"Hey, dancing boy, where's the Khan, and who is the man sitting next to the driver?" a guard called, cocking his automatic rifle.

"The Khan has been called away on important business. Beware of what you say, the man in the taxi is one of his personal bodyguards ordered to see me safely to my quarters and then return to the Khan. Not that it is any of your business, camel head."

"Ha, the beardless one has learned to insult his betters, or perhaps his arse is sore from last night and he has trouble sitting." The guard laughed, turning to the other guards for support. "On

153

your way, Farad awaits you with a new pair of golden slippers, beautiful dancing boy."

Shafiq shrugged off the mocking words; accepted by the guards as a freak, it would make matters worse should he be foolish enough to respond to their brashness.

With head high, he entered the grounds and made his way through the large twin cedar doors and into the house. Glossy pink marble Corinthian fluted columns supported the upper floor; in the centre a large mosaic courtyard. At neat intervals surrounding the courtyard, religious marble statues stood beside multicoloured cockatoos and screeching macaws perched on polished bamboo bird-stands. Weary, he climbed the ornate staircase to the upper floor, passing brass figurines clutching decorated tree branches. From the walls of the balcony huge mirrors hung amid exquisite ancient Persian tapestries, while the finest Italian majolica floor tiles from Naples cooled his tired feet. Chandeliers suspended by fine gold chains swayed and tinkled in a sleepy mistral wafting in from strategically placed openings concealed from the unwary eye. Although his body yearned for sleep, he paused to open the door next to his room and gave a small sigh of pleasure. The sunken pool had been filled with drawn spring water and smelled of jasmine. Stripped of his clothes and submerged, he allowed the soothing water to wash away his aches and pains. Refreshed and naked, he made his way along the balcony, listening to the faint chords of Farad strumming his lute from the outside veranda. He hesitated, and then changed his mind; Farad could wait, he was tired.

It was late when he woke. Shadows lengthened and disappeared into the gloom; the night warm and silent, as if only the breeze cooling the desert existed. Sat upright, he stretched, left his bed to open the window and frowned at the continual thumping interrupting the silence. Gazing from the curved window overlooking the cultivated courtyard, his lips parted and a smile sprang onto his face. The boy with corn-coloured hair kicking a football against the inner wall looked the same age as himself. Fascinated by his ability, he gasped as the boy trapped the ball beneath his foot before firing it back at the wall, all the time keeping control. His search had ended before it began. He had found the son of Mister Sergeant like Jawad had said he would; *inshallah*, it was Allah's will. Throwing on shorts and T-shirt he made his way down the stairs. Metres from Luke, he stood with a smile creasing his face. Luke returned the smile.

"Would you like to play? I'll go in goal, and you take shots?"

Shafiq hesitated, unsure.

"I am Shafiq," he said shyly.

"My father and Mister Khan told me of you. My name is Luke."

"You have seen your father and the Khan together?" Shafiq said, frowning. "I do not understand."

"No, a man came to my grandparents' house with an airline ticket and said my father wanted me to join him. At first my grandparents were angry, but later agreed to put me on the aircraft.

When Mister Khan met me at Kabul Airport he said my father had been called away on important military business and would be back in a few days, and I was welcome to stay in his house. I like it here, everybody is so friendly."

"Maybe we play later, first I have things I must do," Shafiq said, backing away.

The man in the small communication room leapt up from his chair, stubbing out his cigarette with one hand he waved with his other hand to rid the air of the billowing smoke.

"Do not be afraid, I must speak with the Khan. Please smoke your cigarette outside. I will call you when I have finished; my words are for his ears," Shafiq said, stifling a small smile.

Jawad thumbed the green button.

"You are sure it's him?"

"Yes, I am sure, he told me his name."

"You have done well, Shafiq. Resume your dancing lessons as if nothing has happened," Jawad said. "And don't use the communication room again. Buy a mobile phone and send me the number; when everything is in place I will contact you."

Shafiq replaced the phone; his job done. Still tired, he sat in his room wondering what life now held in store for him. Then, a great warmth filled his body, Allah, all knowing and merciful, would guide him along the path to eternal paradise. Ecstasy exploded within him, and with head bowed made his way to the small mosque, content in the knowledge his life was mapped out before him; he must thank his god.

*

Jawad sat cross-legged watching the glowing sparks from the fire dance into the air. The first part of his plan executed to perfection. Luke's whereabouts was no longer a secret. Happy, he experienced a vague morality by overcoming what could have been a long-term crisis. One problem still remained. Hidden from sight in the valley below, tribesmen lurked, watching his every move. Sooner or later their inquisitiveness would overcome their reticence to see a warlord as important as Mirza Khan. He hoped by the time the corpses were discovered, he'd be long gone. Satisfied all was as it should be, he closed his eyes and recalled the dream sent by Allah. No longer would he have to kill unbelievers, like a man trapped in a vortex of revenge. Long and hard he'd mulled over the words in case he might be wrong and Allah would vent his anger. Like most dreams, it never returned; not that it needed to, he felt certain his interpretation was correct. He felt like laughing, screaming out loud. Of all people, Gillet appeared as his saviour? He would use his son, Luke, as a bargaining tool in much the same way the Khan had intended. But he had a different ending in mind.

"I have a proposition for you," he said.

Gillet gazed into the fire, not bothering to answer. Caution came easily when dealing with Jawad. Jawad waited, aware delay would be asinine. Annoyed at Gillet's reticence, he poked the fire with a stick.

"Did you hear what I said?" Jawad said.

Gillet studied him, and then turned his attention back to the flickering flames. On the radio a woman expounded the ins and outs of global warming. A myth, she said, spread by politicians to cause unrest, to keep populations from finding out what was happening in a world on the brink of being ripped apart by war. Gillet ignored the words. He had his own predicaments to sort out; the rest of the world could go shit in a bucket full of lobsters. Steeped in the knowledge that he'd never find his way past the tribesmen alone was the one reason that prevented him from snapping Jawad's neck there and then. The time would come for him to make his move. As hard as he tried he couldn't dispel the thought he might never again set eyes on his son. He shut his eyes, knowing it would still be dark when he opened them and nothing would change. He tried to visualise summertime in his garden back home on the north Norfolk coast. The white cane garden chairs, butterflies, nettles stretched out on the small patch of lawn bordered by a dazzling display of summer blooms, the warm offshore breeze cooling the heat of the sun, and the sight of Amy's long, slender bronzed legs. She caught his glance, smiled, and reading his mind made her way to the bottom of the stairs and waited. When she saw Luke following she pouted and dashed up the stairs. In spite of her tantrum, he ruffled Luke's hair and smiled. Luke smiled, and didn't know why.

"Yeah," he said at last, facing Jawad, "what kind of proposition?"

"The kind of opposition that might offer you the opportunity to be reunited with your son, what do you say to that?"

"What do I say to what?"

Jawad gasped. He'd expected Gillet to show more interest, leap up and punch the air with jubilation.

"Do not play with me, Gillet, if you want to know where your son is," he said, battling to stay calm.

"Get to the point, you sick bastard."

Ruffled by his supercilious attitude, Jawad stared at Gillet, unshaven, thin and dirty.

"You remember I told you of my brother, James, how he died? I want you to find the man responsible, the man who threw the rock."

Gillet leaned and grabbed a handful of dust and watched it sift through his fingers into a neat pile. Christ, he could reel off a thousand names there and then.

"And then what?"

"I want you to kill him."

The words stung as if he'd been slapped around the face. He glared at Jawad, seeking an ounce of compassion, something to show that he was joking. Jawad lowered his eyes, unable to meet his raking stare.

"Is this the price Allah demands to free a defenceless child and return him to his father? Is this the figment of your imagination that you see as a god? Go home, Rupert, and get a job stacking shelves in Tesco's. Live your life away from all this shit."

Forced to admit Gillet's words held more than a hint of the truth, Jawad felt the heat of shame. He had done enough to atone for James' death and it was wrong to force a father to murder a stranger, even for the safety of his son. Then again, how could he tell when enough was enough? He'd forgotten how many times he'd risked his life ambushing British soldiers in a frenzied fit of revenge, and laughed out loud at the thought of killing more. How could anyone know what it was like under fire that hadn't been around to experience it, terrified one moment, paralysed with fear the next? Month after month he prayed he wouldn't be shot dead, or worse, wounded before he'd completed his personal vendetta against the British. Not that anything like that would ever apply to someone like Gillet; he liked to portray himself as an atheist, one who worshipped no god but himself. He cast his mind back to his childhood and the Sunday school teacher back home in Luton. There is no thing as a true atheist, he had told him. He went on to explain how his father had been present at the storming of the beaches at Normandy during D-Day, and came under withering fire from the Germans.

"Hear them all over the beach you could, my father said, called themselves atheists they did, liked to think it made them look tough, let me tell you, lad," he had said. "They cried louder than most for every god the world ever invented to come and save them when the Germans opened fire."

For a time Jawad had struggled to grasp the meaning of the words, but as he grew into adulthood he learned to understand their significance. As he stood watching the fire die, he knew there was purpose in the teacher's words, like there was in Gillet's.

"I must have your answer, now," he blurted out.

"How do I know I can trust you?"

"Because I am Muslim, and Muslims do not lie."

Gillet clenched his fist. He'd go along with Jawad's suggestion, for the time being.

*

The stump had all but healed, and offered neither pain, nor discomfort. In his mind Gillet counted the different ways in which he would dispose of Jawad when the opportunity arose. He didn't settle on any one particular method, God knows he knew enough, and when the time came he'd be ready with the one most appropriate. The spots were spasmodic at first, intermittent and small. Then the rain came as though God had lifted an ocean and poured it over the land. It came in sheets and torrents like no man since Noah could remember. Then, as quickly as it started, it finished. The landscape, touched brown by the hot June sun, lay fresh, glistening with raindrops like jewels caught in brilliant sunlight. Gillet's spirits ratcheted up another notch; it was a good day to contemplate murder.

"We leave tomorrow at dawn. You can't travel in those clothes; check the bodies in the cave and cover yourself best you can," Jawad said, interrupting his thoughts.

"Where are we going?"

"The Kabul River is less than thirty kilometres north of here. We'll hitch a lift to Jalalabad and then to Kabul by boat. The river will be high after the rains and we should have no trouble getting through in a flat-bottomed vessel."

"And then?" Gillet grunted.

"Then you find the man responsible for my brother's death."

Gillet pitied the man standing before him; he also pitied himself for having to bargain with him for his son's life. What did he know of compromise or concession? Jawad had become wearisome, when the day came, his punishment wouldn't be swift and lingering.

"What if he is dead, or has been repatriated back to the UK?"

"I think he is still here; if not, you must find him."

"Find him, back in the UK?"

"Yes."

"You must be joking, you dickhead."

"No, I don't do jokes, or banter, I thought you knew that."

"I want to see my son first."

"Impossible."

"Then it's no deal. My son first, then the man, or I'll kill you here and now. It makes no difference to me, I'll be doing the world a favour by getting rid of you," Gillet growled. "I'll take my chances on the mountain pass and then I'll track down your family and kill them one at a time."

"You will never get off this mountain alive without me, be assured of that."

Gillet reduced the space between them, backhanded Jawad across the face and wrenched the AK47 from his grasp. Jawad gazed down the barrel, listening to the safety catch release and the cocking mechanism slide into place. Gillet squeezed the trigger, sending bullets flying into the mountains. The heat singed Jawad's face and he rocked back as the strength trickled from his legs. Gillet pushed the weapon tight into Jawad's chest and sent him sprawling to the ground.

"You're an amateur, Rupert, but for the time being you hold all the cards. Pick up the weapon and remember, I can kill you any time I wish, understand? The sooner I know my son is safe, the sooner I will consider your offer."

Jawad's eyes were riveted on Gillet's back as he stalked away. Anger knotted his entrails. His finger curled round the trigger, and raising the rifle he aimed at Gillet's back, feeling the blood disperse from the artery as the finger paled beneath the pressure. Gillet turned; his eyes cold and malevolent. Jawad's blood froze in his veins, his grip loosened and his eyes brimmed with fear. Gillet smiled and turned away.

"Remember, Rupert, Allah is with those who restrain themselves, chapter sixteen verse one hundred and twenty-eight," he called over his shoulder.

Were Jawad's face constructed of porcelain it would have exploded into a thousand pieces as the frown ravaged his features. Who did Gillet think he was, hurling quotes by chapter and verse from the Koran? Grim-faced, he watched him disappear into the cave. Seething at Gillet's brusque manner, he made his way to the stream and washed his hands and feet, and climbed to the highest point of the escarpment. In plain view he faced Mecca, confident Allah would see him about to pray, he had much to ask. A fast fading light sent creeping dark shadows across the mountain by the time he had finished praying. For some reason unknown to him tt had been hard going, bonding with his God. No matter how skilfully he thought he had put his case he felt unfulfilled. He could kill Gillet anytime he wished, steeped in the knowledge that he had obeyed the words of Allah and destroyed one who didn't believe. Yet something gnawed at the back of his mind.

"I've decided on a change of plan," he told Gillet. "We leave after dark; it will be safer while the tribesmen sleep."

While Gillet made the best of the clothing available from the corpses, Jawad searched his backpack and produced a dark blue *shalwar kameez*. A further search revealed the absence of the English/Arabic Koran. Shaking his head, he sneered at Gillet's misguided attempts to express knowledge of the holy book.

They made their way down the treacherous terrain just after dark, taking care not to disturb the crumbling earth and send a shower of stones hurtling down the mountainside. Gillet winced at the pain shooting into his leg and trained his eyes on the rotting log barring his way. Unable to stand upright, his knees struck into the log and he toppled forward, his hands clawing the night air for support. No trees offered their branches as a handhold; no soft undergrowth cushioned his downward spiral as he plummeted through the air. Then a short termination of life the moment his head struck a boulder. When he regained consciousness, water blocked his nose and mouth, and he snorted to clear his airways.

"Get up," Jawad snapped, pulling the water bottle away.

"I can't move my leg."

Jawad peered towards a small wooded area of pine trees further down the mountain.

"I'll carry you; we need to be as far away from here as possible by morning."

Slinging Gillet across his shoulder fireman-style, Jawad began the dangerous descent to the pass. As time passed he gasped for breath.

"One more hour and we will be at the bottom of the pass, we'll rest until first light," Jawad grunted.

With a grudging admiration, Gillet doubted whether Jawad had the strength to carry him any further. Yet soon it became apparent Jawad possessed more resilience than Gillet had ever given him credit for, and without complaint he made his way down the sweeping valley until the landscape flattened out into a level plain. Just metres away the sight of the road sent a childish sense of joy leaping into his heart. They had done it. Jawad sank to his knees, fighting for breath; the mechanics of survival had brought him this far. Gillet lay with his back against a gnarled acacia tree, and for a brief moment considered congratulating Jawad on his courage. But he didn't. They needed each other. And they were not friends.

"I'll stop the next vehicle travelling to Kabul. I can't carry you any further, and your leg needs medical attention."

Gillet racked his brain for a response, something flippant. He thought of a few ignominious remarks that might suit his purpose, then changed his mind and stayed silent. Sometimes it wasn't wise to pay credit, even though it was due.

CHAPTER SIX

The bend angled at a sharp 90 degrees, making navigation worse than awkward, littered with stones from minor landfalls it made it easy for a vehicle to skid and overturn. Slowly the lopsided overloaded lorry approached. With the AK47 aloft, Jawad stepped into the middle of the road. The driver hit the brakes and leapt from the cab. Down on his knees, he mumbled his last testament to his time on earth. Gillet smiled; hitching a lift had its variations. After a brief conversation with Jawad, the driver ceased his trembling.

"Get in the back and keep your head down. The driver says ambushes are becoming more frequent, and a man with an AK47 might help keep him safe so long as we don't come across the Taliban," Jawad said, swinging open the rear doors.

It was hot, but bearable. The thick hessian sacks piled almost to the roof contained thousands of cotton turbans bound for Kabul's teeming bazaars. Known as *lungees*, of various lengths and patterns, the Afghans wore them with one end loose about the shoulders. Comfortably settled, Gillet drifted into a deep peaceful sleep, grateful for the respite from the gnawing pain in his leg. Three hours later, Jawad threw open the doors.

"We are on the outskirts of Kabul. Get in the front where I can see you," he snapped.

Gillet slithered down onto the road, feeling the pain shoot up his leg. Afraid Jawad might notice his discomfort, he stared out over the gorge and mountains, waiting for the agony to ease.

"Use my shoulder, we don't have all day," Jawad said.

"Rupert, I do believe you are starting to care."

Jawad pulled away, Gillet crashed groaning to the ground. Jawad watched fogged with hate as Gillet clutch his injured leg, and drawing back his foot he lashed out at Gillet's groin. Gillet reached down between his legs, his eyes bulging, a mewing sound slipped from his open mouth.

"I'm tired of your inane ramblings. You overrate yourself with your juvenile barrack room rhetoric. Now get up, or I'll leave you where you lay."

Gillet gazed through the red haze.

"Up! Last chance."

Gillet's face crumbled. For weeks Jawad had adopted a dogged refusal to be intimidated by his constant flow of sarcasm and scorn. On more than one occasion he had seethed with anger, his finger a degree from squeezing the trigger of the AK47.

"Start the engine, we'll leave the infidel here," he snapped at the driver. "Maybe the Taliban will find a use for him."

Gillet blinked, placed his palms flat on the ground and heaved himself onto his feet. The sound of grating gears added to his impetus as he swung into the passenger seat.

*

The slim, effeminate man who operated the cramped communication room in Mirza Khan's house on the outskirts of Kabul went by the name of Abdul-mateem – servant of the strong. That evening, he cursed his father for bestowing the name upon him as he quaked under Tariq's glaring eyes. Tariq was the Khan's second in command, master of the house and all things concerning security in his absence; and not a man to fool with. Abdul-mateem's demeanour wasn't helped by the fact he was an inveterate chain-smoker, and already he had stood for two hours outside Tariq's rooms before ordered to enter.

"Imbecile," Tariq ranted. "Why do you tell me you cannot raise the Khan? Have you sent a radio message via the helicopter?"

"I have done everything possible, master, and still no answer." Abdul cowered, his eyes fixed on the floor.

"Then try again, dog, and tell me the moment you succeed. Go now."

Abdul shuffled backwards. The sooner he was out of Tariq's sight, the better his chance of surviving the night. His mouth worked as if he might speak, yet no sound came as Tariq's withering stare grew colder than a dagger's blade. Rumours abounded while trapped in the mountains by the Soviets, he ate three mountain tribesmen to survive, and ever since had preferred human meat to that of animals. Abdul wasn't sure if the story was true, but it was said anger made Tariq hungry.

"The dancing boy says the Khan is not to be disturbed in the mountains while he prepares for his *hajj*," he mumbled.

Tariq pursed his lips. "*Hajj*? I know of no *hajj*. Send the dancing boy to me, now."

Abdul needed no second reminder. Seconds later, he made his way to the dancing master's rooms on the top floor as fast as his spindly legs would take him. Ignoring the nicotine craving threatening to close his throat, he tapped on the door. With his ear pressed tight to the door, he listened to the steady beat of the drum accompanied by the dulcet tone of the lute. His mouth dried. For all the time he'd known Farad he had always refused entry to anyone during the dancing boy's lessons. Afraid that Tariq's request would receive short thrift, he sucked in a great draught of air, closed his eyes and, tossing caution to one side, hammered on the door with his fists.

Inside the room, Shafiq's eyelashes fluttered as he swayed in time to the lilting music. Dancing in a circle, he shook his arms and, smiling, listened to the jingling bells around his wrists and ankles. Then, raising one leg, he leaned backwards and stretched out his arms, and sent a shudder through his body. Farad held his breath in wasted anticipation, his hands raised to stop the music. Then, as if by Allah's will, the door swung open and he stared into the frightened eyes of Abdul.

"Son of a three-legged camel, it is most fortunate for you we have finished. Abdul, what is it?" he said in a raised voice.

"Tariq desires to talk with the dancing boy, and his mood is black, like the dry wells of the deserts. It will be better if the boy hurries," Abdul said, and without waiting for an answer scurried back to the communication room, bolted the door and, fumbling for a cigarette, inhaled.

*

The sound of squealing brakes, and curses from irate drivers grated the ears as the overloaded lorry entered into the dust bowl of slow-moving traffic heading for the centre of Kabul. Jawad exchanged rapid words with the driver; the driver shrugged and cocked his head to one side as if nothing mattered.

"What's the problem?" Gillet asked.

Jawad stared dead ahead ignoring the question. Gillet, discomforted by his intense expression stared dead ahead, something wasn't right. Turning onto the Darul Aman Road, Jawad's eyes set hard. Gillet remained focused on the road, a thread of caution entered in his gut as a US military convoy came into view and made its way past the crumbling ruins of the Darul Aman Palace. A man dressed in a black *shalwar kameez* astride a 125cc motorbike pulled to a halt level to the open window where Gillet sat. Casually uncoiling a rolled-up carpet tied with cord across his back, the man hefted a rocket-propelled grenade launcher (RPG) onto his shoulder. As if he had all the time in the world, in full view of those around him, the man sent the missile snaking into the leading vehicle of the US convoy. From somewhere on the opposite side of the road a second missile struck into the fourth vehicle. Pandemonium broke loose as the vehicles exploded sending thick clouds of black smoke billowing into the sky. Gillet sat a witness to futile slaughter, absorbed in the horror, the screams of the dying and wounded pounding into his ears. From high on a rooftop a third missile pierced the vehicle bringing up the rear of the convoy. Unable to move forward or backwards, from the bowels of trapped vehicles US soldiers tumbled out firing into the crowd. A woman shielding her children with her body screamed as a hail of bullets ripped into her flesh; seconds later, her three children fell to the ground kicking and screaming. Women, children, the young and old fell like wheat before a harvester under a withering hail of bullets. A huge black African soldier wearing body armour ran at a crouch across the road towards the insurgent sitting on the motorcycle. On one knee, he emptied his M16A4 automatic assault rifle into the man's chest, sending pieces of flesh, bone and blood splattering over the lorry's windscreen. The driver, shrieking with fear, grappled with the door handle and fell into the road.

Jawad pressed his body tight back against the seat. Gillet kicked open the door and protecting his head with his hands rolled out into the road. Then, abrupt silence, as if nothing had ever happened. It was over; just another day in Kabul. The aftermath of carnage meant little to him; run-of-the-mill slaughter as Afghan murdered Afghan, he'd witnessed the same a dozen times. At times he had been the willing instigator, steady, disciplined, methodical. Who gives a fuck? All part of the job. It was war, and people died in wars. High-pitched wailing of women sent the hairs on his neck upright and tingling. Then it came, the agonising screams heralding a vacuum of hopelessness. It rent the air, testing his temper Cold shivers raked his spine as angry curses, followed by the anguished cries of men as they separated the contorted remains of the dead from the wounded. People looked up in shocked bewilderment through the pall of black smoke hovering like a menacing cloud over the burning vehicles, searching the sky, hoping for a sign from Allah. Others prayed for mercy. Neither prayer received an answer. Like all gods, Allah was always elsewhere when needed.

Pressed tight against the side of the lorry in case of another attack, he searched for a sign of Jawad. He had disappeared, and he felt a rising urge for violence. His body tensed with antipathy for the man who had brought him to this place to commit murder and then abandoned him. Startled by the crack of a handgun he glanced across the road at a wild dog tearing the flesh from a mutilated body; when the bullet pierced its brain it jerked and lay still. The throbbing pain in his leg increased and he shuffled towards the shade of a large tree opposite a shop selling wristwatches and mobile phones. His mental clarity dimmed, clamping his hands over his ears he tried to block out the sound of wailing, and sat with his back against the trunk. It would come soon enough, the time for contemplation; in the meantime, he treasured his hatred of Jawad like a gift from the gods. That could wait; right now he needed somewhere to stay, where he could rest his leg. Reaching down, blood stained his fingers. At least he was alive and immersed in a moment of triumph, he imagined the tilt of lunacy, and from the turmoil of his mind he sought order.

"Excuse me, sir, are you okay?"

He paused, opened his eyes and shook off sweat seeping from his brow. A brisk wind drifted the acrid stench of burning flesh into his nostrils. She looked in her mid-thirties, not much more, maybe less. He grinned; the sun's glare played tricks with his eyes. Honey-coloured hair man-short shaped into her slender neck. Small, firm breasts pushed against a black T-shirt with an imprint of 'Iron Man' emblazoned across the front. Her nipples, outlined by the tautness of the material, would have turned heads, and angered the religious zealots that inhabited the mosques of Kabul. His blurred mind cleared, she was real. Embarrassment swept through him; he hadn't washed or changed his clothes in days. The sudden need to appear appealing made him raise his hand in a futile attempt to push his cropped hair to one side. Her lips parted, revealing white even teeth, her green eyes widened. She couldn't be real. Too tired to care, he slumped back against the tree.

"You ought to go to the hospital with that leg," she said.

His stomach heaved and he shaded his eyes from the hot sun. Scented deodorant filled his nostrils, replacing the sweet sickly smell of dried blood.

"No, no hospital, I'm fine. Leave me alone, please," he muttered. "It's nothing, just an old wound reopened."

She knelt and pulled up his trouser leg. Around the stump blood had dried thick like black caked mud and she shuddered.

He wanted to smile at her reaction, but his cracked lips pained him.

"It's okay; it's a false foot, and a long story."

"Your leg needs attention now, is there somewhere I can drop you?"

"No, I'm fine, honest; don't waste time on me."

Uma Sorenson had worked for the Non-Governmental Organisation (NGO) for two years. A humanitarian group that worked independently of governments, she came under the banner of Afghans 4 Tomorrow. Dedicated to the reconstruction and development of Afghanistan, her job was to train Afghans to use burnable garbage as an alternative fuel source, or as a venerable colleague had once said, how to crap in a bucket, then set fire to it and save the world. During her time in and around Kabul she'd seen them all, thieves, murderers on the run from the law, drug barons, gun runners, along with the dregs that made Kabul a haven for those lacking in morals and a deep-rooted penchant to get rich, whatever the cost or circumstances.

"Are you a mercenary?" she asked.

"No."

"In that case I've a place not far from here and a certificate in first aid. I'll fix your leg and you can be on your way."

Across the road, a line of ambulances queued. Medical personnel worked in an organised manner, depositing the stretchered wounded into the back of vehicles ready for hospitalisation. Those laid in a neat line with their faces covered waited for transport to the mortuary and identification from despairing relatives. He'd never come to terms with the sight of

175

women and children ripped apart ever since he'd kicked down the door and forced to kill the woman holding the grenade. It was him or her, and he'd done the right thing. Yet here, amongst the death and misery, he felt like shit. All he wanted was somewhere he could rest, somewhere peaceful, where he couldn't feel the piercing pain in his leg.

"Thanks," he said.

Inside the 4x4, the air conditioning pimpled his skin.

"Phew, you smell like a fishmonger's arse. When was the last time you bathed?" she said, screwing up her nose.

He cleared his throat and remained silent.

Sparsely furnished, her rooms were suited to a person trapped in a busy work ethic with no time for the hallowed halls of domestic bliss. A table with four matching chairs sat in the middle of the largest room; in one corner a television offered a picture plagued by continual interference. In the opposite corner a desk littered with forms, sheets of blank paper mingled with out-of-date issues of *Time* and fashion magazines. Functional in the way he would have liked it to be. Dropping her shoulder bag to the floor she pointed to a small room, and told him to shower. He followed her directions. The thought of hot water threatened to deliver him into a state of euphoria and he struggled to remove his clothing. Beneath the soothing hot cascading flow, he sank to his knees and removed his false foot.

"Disposable razors and shaving cream in the cupboard," She called. "Take your time, there's no rush," she called.

It took fifteen long minutes for him to sponge and scraped the dirt and grime clinging to his body as if was part of his skin. When he'd finished, he wiped the steam from the portable mirror, and scraped the heavy beard from his face. Dried, he stepped back and stared at his reflection in the small mirror, his lean face worn and tired, almost unrecognisable. His eyes dark and sunken, black circles ringed the sockets, and his lips scabbed from Mirza Khan's blow. He blinked and stared at his cheeks, hollow they looked as if his cheekbones had been removed. Blood seeped from the stump of his leg and he debated whether or not to replace the false foot.

"Make yourself decent, I'm coming in to check your leg," she called.

Before he had time to snatch up the bath towel to cover his body, she appeared carrying a green plastic first aid case. His manner became mild, almost apologetic, as he covered his nakedness. She seemed unperturbed, her expression unwavering at the sight of his bloodied stump. With practised medical expertise she examined the stump, and then dressed the wounds in fresh bandages. He studied her profile, she had one of those pretty faces that either made you want to fuck her, or adopt her as the younger sister you never had.

"Best you don't walk on this leg for at least a week. If infection sets in there's a good chance you'll lose it," she said with abrasive honesty. "In the meantime, you can stay here until it heals, your choice. I'm not around much during the day so you will be able to rest. And call me Uma."

In light of his son's unknown whereabouts it would be logical to refuse the offer. No way could he afford to lose a week sitting on his arse waiting for his leg to heal. It was the same old story; it never takes long for trouble to turn to tragedy. But he knew his body couldn't tolerate much more punishment.

"Tom Gillet, and thanks, I'll try not to be too much trouble."

For a split second her eyebrows arched.

"You are a man, that's trouble enough. There's a home-made pizza in the fridge if you are hungry."

Opposite each other they sat and ate the makeshift meal in silence. Her eyes flickered to his face and then turned away. For the duration of the meal he attempted a stunted conversation; sensing that she wasn't bothering to respond, he remained quiet. As an intellect in the mysteries of womanhood he would be the first to admit he was a stunted weed in a flowerbed of exotic blooms. When she pushed away her empty plate she looked up and stared into his eyes.

"I know who you are," she said. "I recognised your name."

"What do you mean?"

"You're the Gillet that's been nosing around looking for a young Afghan boy, involved in *Bacha Bazi*. All of Kabul knows of you; most are convinced you are dead, and there are those who think you'd be better off if the rumours were true."

"I'll leave straight away." The words leaked from his mouth.

She leaned and laid her hand on his arm, cool, reassuring.

"Who said anything about leaving? For what it's worth I reckon you've got guts, and if I can help, just ask. Now you must rest, there's a spare room at the back," she said, dropping her gaze. "Right now I have to be somewhere; I'll see you later."

She never gave him the time to consider her offer, seconds later her 4x4 fired into life. By the window he watched her filter into the stream of traffic and remonstrate with the driver of a donkey cart slowing her progress. He replied with the international salute for fools, and jabbed his middle finger skywards. She hooted the horn and returned the gesture.

Like most days the inevitable clouds of dust hovered in and around Kabul. Hemmed in by the surrounding mountains, the ancient and the present, passed before his eyes like the turning pages of a history book. Men astride donkeys, mopeds, oxen carts and huge articulated lorries jostled with gas-guzzling 4x4s. A long, sleek Mercedes fought for a share of the thoroughfare with a haughty-looking camel ridden by a young boy. Through the cacophony of life came the sound the *Azan*, the call to prayer, and the world as he saw it came to a virtual standstill. Whatever the prayer there would be no bright, fresh tomorrow, only the usual misery and madness. A flag might change its colour, a pennant a different design, but everything would stay the same, it always did.

The spare bedroom felt comfortable. Suspended from the ceiling, a fan rotated, keeping the discomfort of continual perspiring to a minimum, for the first time in weeks he relaxed. Hhe still wore the bath towel around his body, and using the wall as a support hopped towards the shower room for his clothes. They were gone, too tired to care his eyelids drooped. Naked, he slipped between the sheets, and for the first time in weeks slept with an unfettered mind.

*

Dressed in a gold *pirhan tumban* edged in midnight blue, Shafiq faced Tariq. On his head a bright red turban woven from the finest yarn of silk. Head up and shoulders back, bold and unafraid, he looked at Tariq.

"When did you last see Mirza Khan? It is important you remember," Tariq said in a gentle tone.

"In the caves, master. He told me to return to my dancing lessons," Shafiq lied. "While he prepared for *zakat hajj*, to purify the body before pilgrimage to Mecca."

"Did he say how long this would take?"

"No, master."

Tariq edged closer and slipped his arm around Shafiq's shoulder.

"You are certain of this?" he said, sliding his hand down Shafiq's back and squeezing his buttocks.

Shafiq remained still; listening to Tariq's breathing increase.

"It is late, master; soon Farad will come looking for me."

"Go now," Tariq rasped, removing his hand. "Tomorrow I travel to the mountains to seek Mirza Khan."

"Alone?"

"No, I shall take a handful of guards."

Glad to be free from Tariq's unwanted attention, he left. Bypassing his room, he headed for the room where Luke slept, tapped on the door and stepped inside.

"We must leave this place, tonight," he said.

"Leave? Where will we go? What about my father, and Mister Khan?"

"The Khan is dead and your father searches for you, but he will never find you while you stay here. When darkness falls we go. I have friends in Kabul who will hide us, trust me."

"But how will my father know where to find me?"

"Do not be afraid, we shall find him, and I shall help you."

Darkness had fallen when Shafiq led the way to the south wall. Clambering up a stunted acacia tree the two boys straddled the wall, and dropping onto the other side they made their way to the outskirts of Kabul.

*

The pungent aroma of spices woke Gillet from his sleep. On a small table by the window lay a neat pile of clothes – grey chinos, and a couple of grey shirts – along with a pair of leather sandals. Dressed, he swilled his face in the chipped sink and finger-combed his hair. When he entered the sparsely furnished lounge, she smiled.

"The clothes are a good fit, good." She smiled. "Did you sleep well?"

"Yes. Thanks for the clothes, but I have no money to pay for them."

"No problem, call it a present. You're just in time to eat."

"Smells good."

"*Qabuli palaw*, my speciality – rice, meat, with carrots and sultanas."

"From your accent I'd guess you are Scandinavian, Swedish perhaps?"

"Swedish? No, Swedish women have big tits. I am Finnish. Our tits are smaller, but the good Lord compensates – Finnish men have big cocks."

Gillet smiled.

"How has your day been?" he said weakly.

"The usual, like banging my head against a brick wall. I spent the day trying to help the *kuchi* prepare for winter in the ruins of the Darul Aman Palace. They are nomads from the plains. The government confiscated their grazing lands eighteen months ago. After continual bombing by the Americans, they were accused of harbouring Taliban, and left homeless. The poor beggars have no electricity, no food, little water and no sanitation. Many will die of disease and starvation. For all the talk of progress and democracy, no one gives a damn."

"You care."

"There is so much to do and I can do so little; they are caged in by barbed wire. Afghanistan will take centuries to move forward. It is a country filled with a history of invasion, yet the invaders found little to interest them, apart from the poppy."

*

Close to the eastern edge of the city, Shafiq slid down into the wadi and called out a name. When he received no answer, he called again, this time louder, and from out of the gloom stepped a tall, slim youth.

"Who calls for Mahfouz when he breaks bread with his family?" the youth said.

"Shafiq."

"Ah, dancing boy, you come to entertain us, or perhaps you bring us food?"

"I have bread, meat and cheese from the goat; and this is my friend, Luke, the best footballer in all of Kabul."

Mahfouz stepped back, staring at Luke like a horse-trader purchasing a horse.

"You are welcome to share what little we have."

Shafiq gripped Luke's arm.

"Mahfouz is the leader of those without parents. In Kabul his skill with a football is unsurpassed. He will test your skills in and out of goal, and you must act wisely," Shafiq said in a serious voice. "Remember, we need him as a friend and not our enemy; he is *mohtaram*, respected."

"I shall try my hardest," Luke said.

Shafiq shrugged. "*Inshallah*, it is Allah's will."

They followed Mahfouz to a clearing lit by a large open fire. Around the licking flames sat at least sixty children, dressed in worn coats and tattered blankets pulled tight around their thin shoulders to keep out the cold night air their ages ranged from six

183

to eighteen years. Each the innocent victims of three decades of war. To live in peace and prosperity was something life had denied them, and the future offered no guarantee of change.

"These are the orphans Mahfouz calls his family, young people who try to make a living from nothing. Most have no education and cannot read and write; their only hope of survival is to beg from the rich and merciful," Shafiq whispered.

Luke's eyes flitted from face to face, expecting signs of misery; instead, smiles and the ring of boyish laughter recalled his comfortable life in north Norfolk.

Mahfouz shared the food taken from Shafiq between the youngest; the older boys nodded their agreement. After each boy had received his share, they approached Shafiq.

"*Tashakurr*, thank you," they said, nodding their heads.

With a serious look on his face, Shafiq returned the nod.

"Is this where they live?" Luke whispered.

"Most have no homes, no families. The NGO come with food and clothing; after they have left, grown-ups steal it to sell in the bazaar. No one cares."

Luke thought the boys might have looked down on him as an outsider, a foreigner, a white boy with smart clothes and new trainers. Instead, they smiled, nodding as if he was one of their own, a kindred spirit struggling to come to terms with life as it was. From a glass handed to him by one of the elder boys he sipped water, crossed his legs and returned the smiles.

Mahfouz rose to his feet and, raising his hand, signalled for silence. The buzz of conversation receded and their expectant eyes settled on their leader.

"Today, my family, my skills with a football have been challenged by our new friend, the pink boy," he called, a grin crossing his face. "Should I accept, or should I spare his shame?"

A roar erupted from the boys. As one they punched the air with puny fists, grateful for even the slightest diversion to detract them from their awful existence.

"Accept, accept."

Mahfouz smiled. "Penalties, we shall take penalties. Are they not the ultimate test of a man's nerve?"

Again the roar carried through the night air.

"Do you agree to this, pink boy?"

Luke laughed. "I agree."

Mahfouz elected to go in goal, the best of five penalties to decide the outcome. Luke stepped back, measured his run and planted the ball to Mahfouz's right before he had the chance to move. Minutes later he had scored three out of five; the last two shots struck Mahfouz's feet, rebounding to safety.

"You have done well, pink boy." Mahfouz smiled.

Luke crouched, his arms hanging loose by his sides, ready to throw himself either way to prevent Mahfouz from scoring. The first shot was soft and easily gathered. Mahfouz needed to score with each of the remaining four shots if he were to win the competition. Confident his superior goalkeeping would be too good for Mahfouz, Luke glanced across to Shafiq. The four following shots were as soft as the first, and like before he gathered the ball in his arms. Beaming with pride, he turned to Mahfouz. Instead of a congratulatory smile, Mahfouz turned and stalked away. The crowd of young boys leapt to their feet and raised Luke onto their shoulders. Luke smiled at Shafiq's serious face.

"It is most unfortunate." Shafiq shrugged. "Mahfouz will not thank you for shaming him in front of the boys."

*

Uma drummed a tattoo with her pen, at the same time taxing her brain to complete the list of things she needed to do the following day. By mid-morning the list would be worthless, not worth the paper on which it was written. Like those that she had slaved over in the past, it would become just another scrap of paper ready for the waste paper bin. Such was life in Kabul. It would have been rational to assume that whatever it was that held her there wasn't built on reason or sanity, maybe pity; then again, she wasn't too sure herself. Fidgeting with the pen, she looked up and studied Gillet struggling to hold his concentration leafing through the pile of age-old *Time* magazines. He had more pressing thoughts on his mind, not least the whereabouts of his son. Tortured by impatience, he cursed the long drawn-out process of healing. Fascinated, she studied his profile; washed and shaved, he was what she would describe as handsome, a little thin through wear and tear maybe, but handsome just the same.

She found herself wondering what he was like in bed – submissive, domineering or a crazed sex maniac. Quiet or noisy, or did he grunt and groan at every thrust? She felt separated from herself at her carnal thoughts. What man would leave his family to risk his life looking for an orphan in the middle of a war-torn country like Afghanistan? Or perhaps more to the point, why? One thing was for sure, he wasn't like the rest of the half-pissed coke heads that spent forever trying to get inside her knickers. That afternoon she had spoken with Riley, the Canadian news hog who spilled the beans to anyone that listened; that Gillet was responsible for his arrest at the airport.

"Goddamn fortune hunter, the son of a bitch used me so he could sell his story somewhere else. Can't get over being tossed out the British Army so he invents his own private war," he ranted. "You know what the Brits are like, an undernourished little nation full of shit-heads with rotting teeth. Goddamn dentists are as rare as an Irish snakebite, damn the whole goddam bunch of them."

She didn't tell him she knew Gillet's whereabouts; she had never liked him that much. He was coarse and arrogant. At the same time she didn't miss the look of suspicion dart into his eyes that told her to beat a hasty retreat after she had mentioned his name. As she pondered these things she failed to notice Gillet's gaze settle on her face. He didn't say anything, just watched her watching him. Her elbows twitched as if her inner feelings received a message telling her to stop staring, and she jerked her head away to hide her embarrassment. When she recovered her composure he still watched, his gaze unwavering. A thrill entered her stomach and dropped to her crotch; excitement ran through her body. The sensation in her groin made her sigh, her breathing became faster and her small firm breasts pushed against her T-shirt. Heat coloured her face, and she knew that he knew, and she didn't care. He got to his feet and held out his hands. She stood, her legs felt inflated with air, her feet no longer on the ground. In the bedroom she allowed him to remove her clothes and waited for the vitriol that men whispered in her ear of the things they wanted to do to her, as if it might raise her sexual desires. Instead, he was silent, gentle, demonstrative, and she was glad.

Relaxed, he listened to her easy breathing as she slept, her breasts rising and falling. Slipping from her bed, he made his way back to his bedroom. Sleep came, but not in the manner he desired. She was there again as if she'd never left, as if she wanted to punish him for his night of debauched pleasure – the woman with her baby in one hand and a grenade in the other. Even in his sleep he felt the pressure of his finger on the trigger and listened to the bullets ripping into her and the baby. The hot sweet smell of blood flooded his nostrils; he called out and sat up, drenched in sweat. Uma heard his cries, pulled the thin sheet up under her chin and closed her eyes. A man must learn to come to terms with his own devils.

CHAPTER SEVEN

In the dusty half-light of morning Shafiq nudged Luke from his sleep. Ashes from the dying fire glowed red, crackling like snapping twigs. A few boys stirred and turned over, unwilling to face another day, begging for survival in the crowded dusty streets of Kabul. Luke recalled the night before when Shafiq explained to him the truth of what had happened to his father in the Tora Bora caves. Unsure what to believe, he hadn't slept throughout the night. Now, in the cold light of dawn, he still didn't know what to believe. He looked at Shafiq with enquiring eyes. Shafiq saw the look and nodded.

In the early hours of the morning the orphaned boys of Kabul came. Most scarred, others minus an arm or foot from IEDs. Gripping home-made crutches, some hobbled on one leg, their heads tucked deep between their shoulder blades. Those without legs came assisted by the fit and healthy. The blind led by friends. Children of all ages, victims of a war they didn't understand. A generation robbed of their parents that would never know the stability of a normal childhood, a mother's love or a father's respect. Each one thrown without regard into the tribulations of manhood before they had reached their teens, yet they laughed as though it didn't matter, carefree.

"Good morning, I hope you slept well," Mahfouz called, walking towards them.

Shafiq turned his back and walked away.

*

With Uma away at work most days, Gillet had ample time to busy himself with simple exercises to hone his body. A semblance of vigour returned to his body, and restlessness set in. An inspection revealed the bruising had all but disappeared, the scab on his stump shiny and hardened, ready to fall away leaving new pink skin. In between the constant worry for the safety of his son, his flesh had weakened and he felt the cravings for her body whenever she was close. She had twisted away, touching his face with her fingers and kissing the corners of his mouth, and then pulled back when he reached out to take her in his arms. He didn't consider her to be the kind of woman who used men whenever it suited her, but as someone who had seen the hurt in his eyes and gave him comfort when there was nothing else to give. Out of respect he accepted the situation, deeply grateful for the kindness she had shown him. The time had come to concentrate on the whereabouts of his son. It is the duty of a soldier to maintain obedience, to carry out his orders to the best of his abilities and allow nothing to stand in the way, he reminded himself. His mind festered, and he became morose at the deal he'd cut with Jawad. Certain Jawad knew of the impending ambush he felt angry, and couldn't fathom out why he'd disappeared into thin air. Bewildered, he arrived at the conclusion it was time to leave. Two days later, he attached the foot to his stump and placed his weight on his injured leg. The pain was all but gone.

A little after ten o'clock in the morning, he slipped the money Uma had given him the night before into his pocket and left a brief note, including his telephone number on the north Norfolk coast. Bemusement crossed her face when he told her it was time for him to. She hated goodbyes she had told him, and he understood why she hadn't waited. Reflecting on her kindness during his hopeless position, he realised he owed her everything, his health, his escape from arrest. But most of all he owed her his sanity. In the rear of the red Corolla taxi, he told the driver to take him to Camp Souter.

*

"We leave now," Shafiq said in a quiet voice, watching Mahfouz poking the remains of the fire.

Luke rubbed the sleep from his eyes and stretched his arms upwards.

"Leave, why?"

"Mahfouz has betrayed us."

"Betrayed us? I don't know what you mean."

"Last night I followed him to the small bar where the police drink whisky after work; he is afraid you will become the new leader of the orphans and wants us gone."

Luke had come to look upon Shafiq like a brother, his faith in him unshakeable. It wasn't so odd that Mahfouz would want them out of the way; it stuck out a country mile that he revelled in the manner in which the boy's hero worshipped him.

Under a warming sun probing through shifting grey clouds, he followed Shafiq into the wadi, and kept pace until they emerged from behind a row of flat-roofed buildings separated by a maze of twisting alleys.

*

Staff Sergeant Morton leaned his back against the door leading to his room, his eyes screwed into a squint. He studied Gillet like he didn't know who he was, and at the same time tried to make sense of his words. Gillet, as bold as brass, insisted that he brief all patrols to be on the lookout for his son.

"No fucking chance," he said. "We've more than enough on our plate trying to stay alive without wet-nursing you and your hare-brained schemes. You got yourself into this mess, Tommo, now get yourself out. I've got my men to think of."

He waited, wondering which way Gillet would react. Instead of a tirade of abuse accompanied by the steely glare manufactured to turn lesser men into stone, Gillet sucked in his cheeks and shrugged.

"Look, if it's money you want…" he said.

Gillet shrugged and mouthed a silent obscenity.

"Do you remember the sapper that got killed diffusing IEDs? He was part-Indian. A soldier threw a rock at him and detonated a mine?" he said, changing the subject. "What happened to the soldier?"

"You mean Thorne, a trooper with the 1st Battalion Royal Welsh Guards? Yeah, I remember, why?"

"Still here in Afghanistan is he?"

"No, the army threw him out months ago. Came from Cardiff I think, best place for the stupid bastard, why?"

"No reason. Any spare beds going?"

*

In the ruined shop that once sold men's sandals, Shafiq raised his head and listened. Someone was pulling the sheet of charred plywood acting as a door away from the entrance. The chill night air fanned his face and he tugged at Luke's shoulder. Luke's eyes fluttered open. Shafiq raised his finger to his lips, signalling for silence. The stillness shattered at the sound of a torch clicking followed by a harsh beam of light spearing into his face. Blinded, he turned. A firm hand clamped on his shoulder. Shaking his shoulders, he tried to escape from the grip. Luke struggled to his feet, unsure what to do.

"Did I give you a fright?" Jawad grinned. "I've been watching you for the past few days; quite an interesting life you have been living."

Anger pushed the fear from Shafiq's legs.

"Son of a dog, may all your camels be born with three legs," he shrieked, balling his fists. "May Allah strike you dumb, like your brain."

"It is good to see you too, my little friend."

"You are not my friend," Shafiq spat, turning to Luke. "This is Jawad, the man I told you of at the camp of orphans. He is responsible for holding your father prisoner in the mountains."

Luke stood in a state of layered hatred.

"Where is my father, you bastard? What have you done with him?"

Jawad shrugged at the childish outburst. "I don't know. I was hoping you might tell me."

Shafiq's eyes latched onto Jawad's face, probing, assessing, trying to make up his mind if he spoke the truth.

"He was alive when I left the caves. Perhaps you killed him."

"On the contrary, he is more use to me alive than dead. We became separated when we reached Kabul."

Luke felt panic bubble up into his throat. Frightened for his father's safety, he clamped his hands over his ears to blot out the conversation. Was he dead? Had Jawad killed him? If he was alive, where was he? Had he given up and returned home alone? His slitted eyes filled with ferocity, and picking up a large rock, he hurled it at Jawad.

"Bastard!" Luke screamed. "You rotten fucking bastard, you've killed my dad."

Jawad wavered to catch his balance, his hands rubbing at his chest to alleviate the pain. Luke turned, searching the dimly lit room for another rock, one large enough to cave in Jawad's skull.

"You little fool, I haven't killed your father."

Luke picked up the rock, unsure of what to believe.

"Enough." Shafiq stepped between the two protagonists. "It is better we work as one if we are to find Mister Sergeant."

Luke took a deep breath and trembled.

Jawad shook his head from side to side in admonishment.

"Your father is a military man, therefore it would be reasonable to assume he will mix with the same. My guess is that sooner or later he'll end up at Camp Souter," he said. "As for you two, you can't sleep here, it's too dangerous." His words were softer, his voice held a kinder ring. "It is better you stay with me until this mess is sorted."

Luke faltered. He longed to feel his father's all-encompassing arms chase away his fears, to shield him from despair. Questions rose like dough in a baker's oven. What was happening, where was his father? What was the real reason for him being in Afghanistan?

The full moon hung high and bright. Below, the tightly knit buildings cloaked with long dark shadows made visibility uncertain. Jawad moved with ease, as if he knew every bend, twisting and turning his way through the tall pines and skirting juniper bushes. Throughout the next hour Luke followed, struggling to find the answers to the questions that might help to ease his wild imagination. At last they stopped and entered a large, brightly lit house. His mouth sagged below drooping eyelids as sleep overcame him. Jawad carried him to a bed in a darkened room and lay him down, his smile uninvited yet genuine. *Like father like son*, he mused.

CHAPTER EIGHT

According to Gillet, most things went from bad to worse and the unlikely turned into the impossible. That was the way it had been from the moment he returned to Afghanistan. Each time he climbed one obstacle, the next seemed higher, slipperier and more difficult than the last. Stretched out on the bed, he felt strong, clear-headed and ready to consider his few remaining options. It didn't take long to reach the conclusion that his options were less than a few. Ragged with frustration his mind refused to function in an orderly manner. He needed something to cling to, something he could control. He was used to that, controlling things, most things, not being up the creek without a paddle. Over and over he battled with the same question – where was Jawad? In a childish tantrum he remembered how many times he'd asked himself that question and had never yet come up with an adequate answer. In the past he hadn't been able to face the truth. Now, at last, he found the courage to admit he had fucked up big time, like a fresh-faced rookie with bum fluff where a beard should be. What made it worse was that it was his son's life that hung by a thread, Shafiq's welfare he pushed to the rear of his priorities. The piercing call of a bugle rent the still morning air, calling the day to order. They were about to raise the Union flag over Camp Souter, and with a grudging respect he drew himself to attention. As tradition demands, the duty officer stood at attention and threw the perfunctory salute. Then silence as the halyard was secured to the belaying cleat, leaving the flag waiting for a breath of air to justify its existence. A dull stir of activity interrupted the silence, signalling the end of the short ceremony. Hopeful of a lift into Kabul, he approached Morton.

"Not a chance," he said. "I've been ordered to wet-nurse a fat ex-soap actor making a documentary for a TV channel. He considers himself a real life hard-case. Heard he's a right pain in the arse that pisses his pants at the sound of gunshots. Grab a taxi from across the road."

A couple of well-aimed expletives made no secret of Gillet's feelings.

For a moment he thought his mind was playing tricks and stress had tipped him into insanity. On the opposite side of the road, stood Jawad with his hands pushed deep in his pockets and a supercilious smile etched across his face. .

"I guessed I'd find you here, Gillet. Still can't keep away from the spit and bullshit, eh? Left, right, left, right, three bags full, sir," Jawad mocked.

The word *bollocks* came to mind, but rather than start an argument he couldn't win, he turned his head away, stalling for time, waiting for the anger to lessen.

"Where's my son?" he hissed.

"Take it easy, Gillet. Your son and Shafiq are safe. We have a deal, remember?"

"The man you want is called Thorne. The army threw him out months ago. He lives in Cardiff. Now where's my son?"

Jawad tugged the phone from his pocket and thumbed a button.

"For the time being, this is as close as you get."

Gillet snatched the phone.

"Luke, is that you?"

It was a strange choice of words and he felt foolish. With his back to Jawad he stared up at the Hindu Kush mountain range shimmering in the hazy distance. He was fine, Luke told him, Shafiq the same. Then the line clicked dead, followed by the irritating buzz.

Gillet reached out and grabbed Jawad by the throat.

"Do not be foolish if you want to see your son again," Jawad wheezed. "We have a deal, remember, your son, for the man responsible for the death of my brother."

"I've told you his name and where you can find him," Gillet said, releasing his grip.

"I have always known his name and where he lives, I needed to be sure you took me seriously," Jawad scowled, rubbing his neck. "Find him and kill him, and then I'll make arrangements to bring Luke and Shafiq to England. The necessary papers are ready. When you have completed your side of the deal, they will be returned to you."

As if riddled with lice Gillet raked his fingers across his head. He had no choice but to go along with Jawad.

"One day, you fucking freak, I'm going to kill you with my bare hands. I don't have a passport or money, how am i supposed to leave the country?"

"You'll think of something, Gillet," Jawad smirked, stepping into the waiting taxi.

*

Gillet passed the day one moment in fretful depression, and the next in blind rage. A burgeoning sense of optimism changed his mood, the only thing on his mind the pending reunion with his son.

At mid-day Morton joined him in the coffee bar; he never spoke, just noted Gillet's jerky movements and drawn expression. He knew Gillet, and despite all reason and logic he would find a solution regardless of the consequences, it was his irrational behaviour that left him in grave doubt. He'd felt it before, here in Afghanistan, the times when he thought himself a victim, trembling, spasmodic loss of logic coupled with splitting headaches, nights spent tossing with nightmares. Stress did bad things to a soldier; it made him unreliable and unpredictable. He also knew that not in a million years, in the right frame of mind, would someone as strong willed as Gillet be as foolish as to rampage around a war-torn country looking for an orphaned kid. He was one of the finest soldiers he'd ever known, and wanted to think only good things of him.

"Your best chance of getting out the country without a passport is with the Americans at Kandahar; they can be lax at times, and you might be able to scrounge a lift on-board one of their C5 Galaxy transport aircraft," he said, pulling of wad of money from his pocket. "Take this cash and travel by taxi. A handful of Afghanis should get you through the roadblocks."

Gillet clicked his tongue, recalling the last time he accepted assistance from the Americans. But that was in Pakistan; he wouldn't be taken for a mug a second time.

*

Less than a hundred metres away from the transport aircraft, injured American soldiers were loaded on-board, some stretchered, others walking wounded. Gillet explained to the young American medical officer that his leg was in need of rapid specialist medical attention unavailable in Afghanistan. He had already lost a foot, and his leg was turning gangrenous. The young officer refused eye contact and hunched his shoulders; right now he had enough on his plate. Gillet tried again, wishing he had the smartness of words to convince the officer. The officer turned on his heel and stared at Gillet.

"Hey, man give me a break will you, I've a plane load of injured marines heading home for medical treatment," he said with an exaggerated air of disdain, then turned away and jerked his thumb. "Hot damn, guess one damn Brit won't make much difference. Climb aboard. We stop at Paris to refuel, and that's as far as you go, savvy?"

Gillet wanted to hug him. Instead, he offered his hand.

"Haul ass, fella," the officer grunted.

Ducking and weaving through a jungle of webbing and straps, Gillet made himself comfortable in the huge fuselage. Three times he moved without complaint to make room for the injured soldiers shuffling past, with lifeless eyes sunk inside dark sockets, faces sallow and expressionless. Others, looking as if they had just left high school, moved in a jerky fashion, eyes glittering, darting from object to object as if they concealed something that might leap out and attack them. A year ago a couple of SAS members had told him that American Seals had committed suicide rather than exist with the loss of a limb. At twenty-five thousand feet the huge aircraft straightened out and he shifted down the rows of injured stretchered American soldiers holding cigarettes to their lips, speaking words of encouragement to kids that didn't look much older than Luke. In a secluded spot, he swallowed his sadness and closed his eyes.

At Charles de Gaulle Airport, Paris, perched on the end of a KLM baggage train, he bypassed French customs and walked unchallenged from the airport; so far so good. From Paris to the UK was another kettle of fish. Mindful that to board the Eurostar to St Pancras without a passport was taking a big risk; instead he took a train to Calais and spent an hour trawling the hypermarket car parks until he found two coach-loads of day trippers on a day return to Norwich. The first driver told him in quaint old-fashioned English to go away. The second couldn't slip the two twenty-pound notes into his pocket fast enough before handing over his passport.

"When the French custom official comes on-board, just hold the passport up until he's taken a count. They never bother about the driver."

*

It was Sunday. From somewhere, a distant church bell tolled midnight when he stepped from the coach in Norwich. Unlike the thick cloying heat and dust of Afghanistan, the air felt crisp, fresh, like a typical early English summer morning, and he inhaled, filling his lungs as hunger prodded his stomach. Instead of continuing his journey to the north Norfolk coast, he sat by the window of an all-night café close to the station. Scrambled eggs on toast beneath a blanket of black pepper helped to ease his mood. Hunger satisfied, he lingered in the timeless realm of nothingness, trying to formulate a plan of what to do next. When nothing immediately sprang to mind, he left the warmth of the café and wandered through the city centre. Too tired to walk any farther, he entered a park and stretched out on a wooden slatted bench under the cover of a gazebo, and closed his eyes.

The next morning he shivered; dawn was breaking. The cold penetrated his bones and he made his way back to the café. Over a mug of tea he enquired about nearby B&B outlets. Two hours later, a flint-eyed woman snatched the money from his hand and handed him a key.

"No noise or floozies, or you'll be out on your ear," she said.

CHAPTER NINE

His room was light and airy, facing west free from the early morning sun. The comfortable double bed with matching furniture and portable TV suited his needs for the time he intended to stay in Norwich. Above the sink he studied his reflection in a small mirror; his face resembled an alien from another planet, come to whisk him away to an experimental laboratory on the far side of the galaxy. Thin, skull-like and lacking flesh, his skin was creased like grease paper, and his eyes stared, haunted, and almost frantic. Puzzled how he could look so bad, he flicked off the light and promised not to look in mirrors in future. Like always, nothing changes. And even now it didn't occur to him how tired he felt, how his body screamed for respite from the events of the past months. Outside his window, the bang of wings and the coo of a pigeon helped to remind him why he was here. The time had come to face the truth, but he would rest first, try to refresh his brain. The past few weeks had amounted to nothing, a complete waste of time and effort. Undressed and naked, he slipped between the cotton sheets, rejoicing at the coolness against his skin. Scarcely able to keep his eyes open, he fidgeted against his injuries, and seeking a position free from pain waited for sleep.

When he woke he was bathed in a hot sticky sweat, the new dawn still lay concealed beneath the darkness. The woman holding the baby had come again in the dark of night. A half-filled lukewarm bath offered small comfort. Desperate to be out of the room, once more, he walked the streets of Norwich. As he passed a chemist, he imagined the faint aroma of rosewater drifting into his nose, and his muscles sagged as if his bones might separate and fall apart within the confines of his body. He shivered and made his way back to the B&B, feeling worse than when he left.

Breakfast washed down with thick black coffee, followed by the sound of rain pinging off the window exaggerated the reality of his situation. Killing from a distance had been his way, not close up and premeditated. But it was different now. He had committed himself to coldblooded murder, and the harsh cut of uncertainty speared into his mind. Most of the eight hundred pounds that Morton had pushed into his hand at Camp Souter still sat in his pocket. Trouble was, he had no ID, no driving licence and no credit cards to fund his killing foray into the Welsh capital. Hopelessness shuddered down his spine, and he cursed the name Thorne. No matter how grotesque it was, if he wanted to see his son again he would have to keep his part of the bargain.

Next day he boarded a train to London, from Liverpool Street railway station he made his way to Paddington via the bustling London Underground. Aboard the rocking tube carriage he smiled at those clinging to the handrails, staring down at their feet. In contrast, those seated stared stony-faced up at the carriage roof, eye contact forbidden. At Paddington he purchased an evening paper, paid for coffee, pushed the soggy-looking roll away and wasted an hour reading the usual garbage. Aboard the train for Cardiff Central, he dozed, and tried not to think of the reason for his journey. Incarceration in a prison made him shiver. On top of that, how would Luke feel when the world discovered his father was a coldblooded murderer serving life behind bars? He had hoped to live until retirement to see the consummation of what he regarded as his life's work spent in Her Majesty's forces. But the pathway of fate had changed direction and his foolhardiness had forced him down a road he no longer recognised.

"Park Street?" the taxi driver said, pointing his nicotine-stained finger. "Straight ahead, second on the right it is, can't miss it."

It always rains in Wales, and it was raining when he entered the South Wales Echo offices and asked a pretty assistant for the archive section. Scrolling through the screens, he felt edgy and he glanced over his shoulder to make sure he wasn't watched. Private Derek Thorne, ex Royal Welsh Guards, had, for all the wrong reasons, made the headlines in his hometown. Further inspection had showed him to be a first-rate soldier; liked and trusted by everyone in his regiment, he was in line for promotion. At his court martial, his defence had pleaded a case of stress-related thoughtlessness having been responsible for his irregular conduct. Nevertheless, the man counted for nothing, only the honour of the regiment paramount. Dishonourably discharged, the court recommended psychiatric treatment. His address was listed as Branwen Close, close to the Culverhouse Retail Park, Cardiff.

*

Gillet stepped from the taxi, walked four doors up from the address written on a slip of paper and knocked twice on the door.

"You've got the wrong house, dear," the woman said. "Derek used to live further down the close, until he split from his wife. Threw him out she did, after what he did. Did you know him?"

"We served together in Afghanistan. I've got money I owe him," he lied.

"Lives in Ely he does. Works for the Salvation Army now, goodness knows why, guilty conscience I suppose. Somewhere on Aberthaw Road close to the old Ely hospital. Ask his wife, Rosemarie, she knows his where he lives. Shame really, he was a good lad, loved the army he did, don't know what came over him."

Fifteen minutes later, the cabbie dropped him off in Ely, outside a public house on Caerau Road.

"Just ask behind the bar, boyo, they'll fix you up with bed and breakfast somewhere in the area. Watch your back, though, gets a bit rough round here at times," the driver said, with a serious nod.

The cabbie was right. Twenty minutes later, Gillet waited for the landlady to answer his knock on the black door with a broken letterbox flap and peeling paint. A harpy of a woman with grey hair cut short and severe, she looked as if she had suffered an electric shock. Her suspicious eyes looked him up and down through a pair of plastic spectacles held together by a first aid plaster. Her voice was cutting, like a sharpened bayonet.

"Breakfast between seven and eight thirty," she rapped, counting the money in the palm of her hand. "After that you get nothing, so don't come begging, and don't leave hairs in the sink.

There's a two pound refundable deposit on a bath plug if you feel the need to use it."

He paid for three nights and kicked the door shut and sat on the bed. Killing an enemy in cold blood wasn't a problem, he'd done that a hundred times, all part of his duty as a soldier. But this wasn't soldiering, not real soldiering, it was different. To murder a soldier suffering from the stress of combat, one who walked on broken glass for months on end and slept on needles every night didn't sit easy on his mind. The newspaper report stated that Thorne had been remorseful over his moment of crass stupidity. He'd never have joined the Salvation Army if he felt some form of guilt. Somewhere outside in the world, quiet men, once soldiers, suffered from the same disease. He sighed and wondered what type of man Derek Thorne really was.

In a corner of the lounge in the Highfield Inn he sat with his drink pretending to mind his own business. The pub was the usual traditional run-down community watering hole surrounded by empty cans and polystyrene fish and chip containers. Inside, the obligatory pool table stood next to a fifties-style jukebox. Nearby, a money-grabbing one-arm bandit waited to ambush those blessed with a pocket full of cash and limited intelligence flashed a warm, inviting hello. It was the type of place found in the less desirable areas of cities steeped in crime caused by a low standard of living, and avoided like the plague by the local police. A handful of the local hard cases lingered around the bar, taking it in turns to give him the evil eye. He'd come across their type before; they all came from the same mould, shaven skulls, vacant eyes and beer-bloated bodies pierced with rows of cheap rings and safety pins, as if they might fall to pieces. Scribbled multicoloured tattoos adorned their arms and necks in a failed bid to make them look threatening. If he made enquiries about Thorne, they would want to know why and give him a hard time. That was the last thing he wanted. Thirty minutes to closing; perhaps Thorne didn't drink. He couldn't remember if he'd ever seen a member of the Sally Ann slurping pints while propped up against a bar. His everlasting tiredness helped him decide an early night would serve him well, and, draining his glass, he headed for the exit.

Cold driving rain merged with a chilled wind slapped his face and he jammed his hands deep into his pockets, and then hunched his shoulders up to his ears to stop the rai running down his neck. The unexpected bump jarred his arm and spun him round, and turned and looked into the saddest pair of eyes he'd ever seen.

"Sorry, I should look where I'm going."

"No harm done, pal," the man muttered.

Gillet took in the navy-blue peak cap edged in dark red. The writing on the shoulder flash said *Salvation Army*. Unable to believe his luck, he thought for a way to continue the brief conversation. If the man wasn't Thorne, he might know of him.

"I was just going in," he lied, jerking his head towards the door. "Let me buy you a drink."

"No need to b-bother, mate," the man stuttered. "I drink coke these days; been off the b-booze for months now, d-don't feel the need for it anymore."

"Coke it is then," he said, steering him towards the door.

Someone fed the jukebox. Rap shook the foundations until the rattling windows threatened to burst out into the street. Gillet pointed to an empty table in the corner.

"Grab a seat while I get the drinks."

The barman finished washing dirty glasses and sidled down the bar to serve him. Tall and blond, his receding hair tied in a tiny pigtail resembled a rat's arse. In the muted light his face looked mottled, and his beer belly stretched the buttons on his shirt to breaking point.

"Expecting the police?" Gillet asked.

The barman frowned, leaned over the bar and cupped his hand to his ear.

"I said, are you expecting the police?" Gillet said louder.

"The police, no, why?"

"Two marked cars outside full of old bill."

"Turn that jukebox down, now," he roared across the bar. "And if anyone is sniffing shit in the toilets, throw the bastards out the window."

Silence cloaked the pub. The barman waited, his hands resting on the bar, his eyes transfixed on the door.

"Give us a Pils and a glass of coke."

The barman reached for a couple of glasses.

"Friend of Rosie's, are you?"

"Sorry?"

"Rosie, the man you walked in with. Good lad he is; suppose you know all about his troubles?"

"Troubles, what troubles? I haven't known him long and he never told me about any troubles."

"He used to be in the army he did, Welsh Guards. Caused a soldier's death by accident he did, says he can't even remember it happening. On the verge of a nervous breakdown he was, stuck in the middle of that stupid war. Fucking politicians don't know their arses from their elbows, just a bunch of greedy bastards making a fortune flogging weapons and equipment. Joined the Salvation Army to make amends Rosie did, and attends church every day of the week, including Sunday. Wants God to forgive him he does. Shame really, he's a good lad, but he likes the odd line he does, can't say as I blame him."

"Line?"

"He's a druggie. You don't deal, do you?"

"No chance, but why do you call him Rosie?"

"His name's Thorne, you know how these nicknames start, thorn, rose. Always been known as Rosie he has. I thought you said you knew him."

Gillet opened his mouth to speak, changed his mind, paid for the drinks and made his way back to Rosie.

"There you go, my friend," he said, placing the drinks on the table.

"Cheers, mate."

"No problem. Live round here, do you?"

"Pyle Road, just a c-c-couple of minutes away," Thorne stuttered, placing his peak cap on the table.

Gillet's eyes flickered over Thorne's face. Hair cut short, military style, in his mid- twenties, with even features, at one time he might have been classed as a good-looking lad. A mother's pride and joy, and a young lady's fancy. His drug habit had made him otherwise. His self-control was spasmodic; assured one moment, and agitated the next. But it was the eyes that held Gillet's attention; deep brown, they brimmed with despair. They were impossible to look into and distinguish kindness from hopelessness.

"You're ex-forces, aren't you? Although you w-walk with a slight limp, I can tell by the w-way you hold yourself," he said, taking Gillet by surprise. "That or police."

Gillet squirmed and gripped his drink.

"No, I lost my foot when I was seventeen, motorcycle accident."

Irritated, he remained silent, ashamed of lying to a man he had to kill. He had to leave, get the job done and get away as soon as possible.

"Perhaps I'll see you again sometime," he said.

If Thorne offered any kind response, he never heard. Outside, the rain had stopped and the road glistened beneath a solitary streetlight. Gillet wiped away the perspiration rising on his face.

Back in his room, he filled the kettle and dropped a teabag into a mug. Impervious to the sound of the kettle boiling, he gripped the sink and stared from the window out into the darkness. He had learned the truth about Thorne's past. A passing second of foolishness had resulted in him taking a man's life, and without complaint, he had chosen to pay for his mistake with a lifetime of self-inflicted misery for something that could never be erased from his mind. Gillet had seen it in his eyes like he'd seen it in others', the faltering stutter, the abandonment of life. In the timeless realms of capability he was no different from Thorne, both prisoners of a dark past. Locked inside him he felt a rush of pity for the man. Then cursing his frailty poured the half-made cup of tea into the sink. No point in stretching out that which needed to be done. Now was as good a time as any to finish what had brought him here in the first place.

A few metres from the main door of the pub, he slowed and watched Thorne shuffle out into the street. His head hung so low it made it almost impossible for him to see where he was going, and his hands hung loose by his side. He staggered along the street as if drunk, drawing closer to Gillet. Gillet took cover in a garden littered with broken bottles and crushed beer cans. Concealed behind an overgrown hedge he steadied his nerve and prepared to confront the man who held the key to his son's safety. Waiting until Thorne was feet away he stepped out and grasped his head in his hands, ready to twist and snap his neck. Thorne looked up and offered no resistance. Despair fled from his eyes and the lines that traced the shape of a smile around his mouth softened as he waited for a quick release from his eternal torment. Gillet froze, let go of the head and stepped back. All self-respect washed away in a consuming tide of disgust. He wanted to apologise, get down on his knees and beg for forgiveness. To tell Thorne everything, of his son, of Shafiq, in the hope he might understand. The pub door swung open and the sound of loud music mingled with laughter burst into the street.

"Goodnight, Rosie," someone called.

Thorne's smile remained. His eyes fixed on Gillet's face with a look of expectancy that pleaded, *do it*. When he spoke, his voice was quiet, like a hoarse whisper, without stutter.

"Finish it, please, it doesn't matter."

Gillet gulped the acid taste in his mouth down his throat and backed away. The solitary street light seemed to shudder and jump in the darkness. As he turned and walked into the comfort of the all-consuming black of night, the soles of his trainers squeaked on the wet concrete pavement.

He didn't sleep that night, nor did he expect to; instead, instead he lay stretched out, wide awake until morning, waiting. At the end of the day, once again he had fucked up big time. He had signed Luke's death warrant. The strident sound of police sirens sent a shiver racing down his spine. Tensed, he sat up, expecting any minute for the sharp knock on the door, the feel of cold steel when they clamped the handcuffs over his wrists. The he-hawing of an ambulance grew louder and faded. He daren't relax; his mind turned over the manner in which he had handled the situation the previous night. Instinct told him he had done the right thing, yet he wished it were more than just instinct, a more solid reason.

At the breakfast table the next morning, instead of eating he chose to sip at the mug of tea. His nerves were jumping and his brain hammered against his skull, and he made a passing pretence of listening to the inane chatter and banter of the other guests, the majority East European labourers working for pennies on the closed Ely hospital nearby.

"I knew it, I knew it would happen sooner or later," the landlady stated, bursting through the door and replenishing the empty teapot with boiling water. "Disturbed, that's what he were, disturbed."

"What's happened, Mrs Palfrey?" someone asked.

"That fellow, Rosie Thorne, or whatever they called him, overdosed on drugs, fell down the stairs and broke his silly neck in the early hours of the morning, daft sod," she snapped, stirring the teapot with the wrong end of a table fork. "Knew it would happen I did, course no one ever listens."

It wasn't what she said, but the manner in which she said it that for an obscure reason made Gillet want to retch over the table. He should have been overjoyed at the demise of Thorne, grateful for the thankful release from his vow to commit murder. But he wasn't; instead, his anger festered and he left the dining room. Inside his room he stared out the window at the neglected garden and conjured up a mental picture of Private Thorne of the Royal

Welsh Guards. A proud soldier resplendent in scarlet tunic and bearskin, shoulders back at attention on Horse Guards to commemorate the Queen's birthday. The eyes of the world were upon him. At home his family crowded around the TV, hoping for a glimpse of one of their own. The stirring sounds of the massed bands rang out across London. To *Men of Harloch* they came, boots gleaming, bayonets glinting, arms swinging in precise formation, comrades shoulder to shoulder fit to burst and filled with pride – the world's finest at their best. Now he no longer existed, another unsung victim of a war no one understood. No drum beat the retreat, no bugle sounded last post at the going down of the sun, no Valkyries searched far-off battlefields for his soul waiting to be transported to the halls of Valhalla. Instead, he died unmourned and forgotten. Gillet's sniff turned to body-racking sobs, and his tears ran unchecked into the sink.

*

The taxi dropped him off at the railway station. He had fulfilled his side of the bargain, and without having to commit murder Jawad had what he wanted, the death of the man responsible for killing his brother. But he still felt the pangs of culpability. Mug of coffee in one hand, he sat drumming his fingers on the tabletop. Startled by a sudden tap on his shoulder, the mug slipped from his hand and with bunched fists he looked up.

"Whoa, easy boyo," the man said, stepping back. "Fellow back there handed me twenty quid to give you a message. Go to the mosque in Norwich, he said, nothing else, and disappeared."

Gooseflesh pimpled Gillet's arms. Jawad was the only person who knew he was in Wales, but what was his connection with the mosque?

The public address system announced the arrival of the train at Platform One for Paddington, and he glanced along the platform before boarding. He felt an overriding need to find somewhere quiet, secluded, somewhere he could think, anywhere he could avoid those irritating passengers in the habit of striking up a meaningless conversation about something and nothing. Somewhere that might act as a sanctuary where he could keep a grasp on his sanity. His disappointment was bitter as the carriage filled, surrounding him with rustling newspapers, crunching teeth working their way through endless packets of confectionary merged with the crackle of multi-flavoured crisps. The flick of a newspaper page sounded like a tumultuous clap of thunder, and peace and quiet became as rare as a priest without a Bible. To make matters worse, the train failed to stir until twenty minutes past departure time. When the train pulled away from the station, the pain in his head affected his sight, and he clutched at the armrest, afraid he was going blind.

*

In Norwich he purchased another packet of painkillers. With most of his remaining money he purchased a second-hand car from a side-street garage, a trade-in on its last legs, already three tyres into the scrapyard. It continually jumped out of gear, but would serve his purpose, and with his hand on the gearstick he made his way

216

through the busy rain lashed city centre. Parked outside the newsagents opposite the mosque, he shrugged at water trickling in through the windscreen. The bunch of Asian hoodies was nowhere to be seen. Tugging up his collar, he crossed the road and sheltered from the rain beneath the overhanging ledge of the doorway and shook the rain from his coat.

An elderly man with a handful of grey beard came out first, dressed in a suit that looked as if he'd slept in it.

"I need to speak with Tubeh," Gillet said.

The elderly man stared, expressionless.

"Tubeh, I want to speak to Tubeh," Gillet said, raising his voice.

His conversation was interrupted by two tall, skinny youths dressed in denims and sweatshirts. The elder of the two smiled briefly.

"He doesn't understand English, can I help?" he said.

"I need to speak with Tubeh. Tell him Tom Gillet's here."

"Oh yeah, what would Tubeh want with you?"

"That's my fucking business, arsehole."

"Enough, enough."

Gillet stared at Tubeh's pale face, his smile like someone had screwed it on seconds before.

"Mr Gillet, I didn't expect to see you so soon."

"Luke and Shafiq, where are they?"

"I'm afraid things have become a little complicated, please follow me."

Not in the mood to waste time with niceties, once inside the unfurnished room he grasped Tubeh by the neck.

"The only thing complicated around here is how long you can survive without breathing. Where are Luke and Shafiq?"

"*Luke*? I know nothing of anyone called Luke," he gasped.

If Karim hadn't appeared, Gillet might have strangled Tubeh where he stood. Karim moved into the centre of the room, perspiration glistening on his face.

"Is this behaviour necessary?"

Gillet eased his grip.

"I'm pissed off asking you two the same question; where are the boys?"

"I don't know what you are talking about, who is *Luke*?" Tubeh stammered, rubbing his neck.

Tension in Gillet's body rose. Patience hung in the air like a foul smell. His voice quiet and menacing.

"I'll ask you one more time, where is Jawad and the two boys?"

"I do not know these people you speak of," Karim mumbled, wiping his sweating palms down the side of his trousers. "Of Shafiq, yes."

The craving to kill the two men swelled to bursting point and, drawing back his fist, he drove it into Tubeh's face, grabbed him by his collar, dragged him outside and dumped him into the boot of his car. Karim followed, begging him to see reason.

"Give me your phone," Gillet sneered at Karim. "Call me when you have my son; until then this maggot stays with me. I'll send you a few reminders to help jog your memory."

On the outskirts of the city Gillet stamped on the brakes and pulled to a stop. In a DIY shop on a small shopping precinct he purchased a length of rope and four plastic one-litre bottles of white spirit, and then headed for the north Norfolk coast. An hour later, he pulled Tubeh from the boot of the car and pushed him towards a small grassy knoll overlooking the North Sea. An old Second World War bunker built to defend the nation from invasion remained full of human excrement from those driven by desperation. After tying Tubeh to a metal ring imbedded in the brickwork, he left. Two miles further down the coast he parked the car out of sight and made his way to his house. Stripped of his soiled clothes, he changed and stuffed a few spare items into his backpack. Concealed at the back of the bedroom wardrobe a cardboard box from which he took out five hundred pounds in cash, and a debit card in his name. Something for a rainy day, Amy said. Slipping out the rear door he made his way back to Norwich. His headache had eased and he felt prepared for all eventualities.

Emptying the four bottles of white spirit through the letter box, he struck a match and pushed it under the door of one of Karim's pound shops. Back at the car he watched the flames lick up to the ceiling. In a secluded spot by a slow-running river not too far from his home, he parked and sat in darkness on the bank. Careful not to disturb the swans, scrolling through the menu on Karim's phone until he found the word 'home', thumbed the green button and waited.

Karim answered.

"Things are going to get hotter unless you tell me what I want to know," he said, then pressed the red button.

Karim stared at the phone. The hammering on his front door distracted him.

"Mr Karim-al-Khattab?" the uniformed policeman said. "Are you the owner of the pound store on Castle Street?"

Karim paused. Already he was about to fall to pieces.

"Yes, that's one of my shops, why?" he stammered.

"It's been burned to the ground I'm afraid. The fire brigade's in attendance. May I step inside? Just a few routine questions, you understand, unless you'd rather come down the station?"

*

The night's excursions had left Gillet feeling content and he hunkered down on the back seat of the car. A decisive blow had been struck against those he felt certain knew the whereabouts of Luke and Shafiq. Their reluctance to tell him their whereabouts puzzled him. If they wanted to play hardball that was fine with him. Before he'd finished they would beg him on their hands and knees to take the boys.

The inclement weather had at last broken and sunshine streamed through the car windows. It was one of those days when all forms of employment should be banned, and people left to enjoy life as it should be. Settled, his strength returned and energy pumped through his veins. Yet still he couldn't rid the sneer that hung from his face as he stretched away the stiffness creasing his body. Armed with sandwiches and bottles of still water from the local garage, he entered the bunker. Tubeh watched, his eyes expressionless.

"You've got three minutes to get the food and water down your throat," Gillet said, loosening the rope. "In the meantime, start racking your brain for the whereabouts of my son and Shafiq."

"Mr Gillet, this is ridiculous, if I knew I would tell you. I have no reason to hold your son or the boy Shafiq."

"Your brother, Karim, said he'd never heard of Jawad, but you know him, don't you?"

Tubeh nodded and took a long drink from the bottle of water.

"It was a long time ago; he came to me from Luton to escape the attention of the local police."

"Out of the frying pan and into the fire; I bet that made your day. How long did it take to fill his head with shit and indoctrinate him into the world of Islam and fill him with a load of religious crap?" Gillet snarled. "What did you do, paint pictures of paradise on the mosque wall and beat the idiot senseless until he accepted it existed? That's what you do, isn't it, brainwash innocent kids into doing the dirty work people like you don't have the guts to do yourself?"

Tubeh's eyes flickered. Trapped in a loop of time, he remained silent.

"You know where he is, don't you?"

"No. Release me, perhaps I can help you."

The words challenged the limits of Gillet's reason, his eyes brimmed with hate and he forgot how angry he could be. The hammering in his skull started and as hard as he tried, he tried to find a form of respite. For the last few days he had managed to control his stress, keep it suppressed. He knew a long time ago he needed a doctor and medical treatment before his stress eroded his mind. But not just yet; he had to hold onto to the last of his sanity for a while longer. When the boys were safe, only then he would put an end to his problems.

"After I have finished with your brother you will tell me everything I want to know."

"My brother has nothing to do with this matter." Tubeh's voice notched up to a shriek. "How many times do I have to tell you?"

"Yeah, well that's tough. I've torched one of his shops and I'll do the same each night until his little empire is a pile of ashes. Then I'll start on the mosques and burn you and the rest of the termites like you into the ground."

Tubeh tipped the remaining water down his throat. The sudden change in his attitude caught Gillet by surprise. His lips quivered, and he made a mewing sound like an injured cat.

"Please, do not harm Karim, he knows nothing," he wailed.

Gillet's mood brightened; now he was getting somewhere, the Imam's eyes held his attention, cold and challenging.

*

Back at the river's edge, the swans waggled their tail feathers and with their heads high and regal patrolled their territory. A handful of painkillers offered him small relief from the mind-numbing headaches. The tremble in his hands almost permanent, like drawing breath. The harsh sound of the phone shook him from his lethargy and he looked at the number on the illuminated dial, wondering if he should thumb the green button. Taking a chance, he did and listened to the desperate voice of Karim.

"Mr Gillet, please believe me, I do not know the whereabouts of your son, and burning down my shops will not help you find him."

"Find my son and Shafiq," Gillet answered, cutting off the call.

On the far side of the river a brightly coloured butterfly flexed its wings in the shade of a rustling oak, then, spreading its multicoloured wings, skimmed like a coloured ribbon across the river's surface and disappeared. Gillet stared at his reflection gazing back from the water's surface. The bitter frustration on his face portrayed the anger fused into a sheer bloody determination. Tubeh and Karim were lying, and sooner rather than later they would feel the full force of his rancour. As for Jawad, one day he would discover that subtlety wasn't his way.

That night, gripping the gear lever he drove to the second shop on the outskirts of the town. Larger than the first shop, situated at the end of a small unlit shopping precinct it made an easy target. Certain he wouldn't be seen he left the car and made his way across the road. Unperturbed at the possibility of CCTV cameras, he unscrewed the caps from the bottles of white spirit and poured the contents through the letter box, lit the strip of cloth and returned to the car.

He felt buoyant; his grip on life tightened during the journey back to the north Norfolk coast. This time the house didn't feel the same; the smell of rosewater absent, everywhere empty and cold, as if she had never been there. Apart from the regular creaking he'd learned to live with over the years there were no other sounds. No blaring TV, Amy shouting for the third time at Luke to sit at the meal table and eat his food. Out of habit, he checked each room in turn with a mechanical thoroughness, rifling drawers, searching cupboards, looking behind doors, as if expecting to find visitors lurking uninvited. Old memories that should have long been forgotten returned thick and fast, and taking a deep breath he stopped to compose himself, then locked the front door in case someone should enter and discover him. Upstairs, in the bathroom he swallowed a handful of painkillers. Fully dressed, he climbed into the bed and straight away curses fell from his mouth. Cursing his foolishness; the smell of her freshness, not just the rosewater but her very being, smothered the room and he made his way to the spare room.

In the morning the luxury of a shower helped to begin the day. Feeling better than he had in weeks, via the back door he made his way back to the car.

*

It had occurred to him to release Tubeh, take a different direction. Try the soft approach, to coax the whereabouts of Luke and Shafiq from him instead of hurling threats. But deep down he didn't fancy running that gauntlet; the Imam was as slippery as a bucket full of eels and he didn't have time to waste.

Tubeh glared, his eyes red-rimmed, full of burning hate.

"Drink the water and finish the sandwiches," Gillet snapped.

"Surely I am permitted some clean clothes?"

"Bollocks. Until you tell me what I want to know, you stay here," Gillet grunted. "Where's my son and Shafiq?"

"I don't know."

Gillet's fist balled, ready to smash into Tubeh's face. Instead, holding his forearm across his throat, he pressed his head back against the bricks.

"You lying little prick," he hissed.

"You must understand that I do not know where your son is, and killing me will not make the slightest difference," Tubeh gasped.

Gillet released the pressure; the bastard could stew a little longer.

It rained again on the night the third shop erupted into flames. The people of Norwich drew their own conclusions. Riots broke out in Norwich city centre as Christian fought running battles with Muslim. The media took up the theme, blaming everybody from the BNP attempting to burn out Muslims, to Sainsbury's trying to burn down competitors. The Sunday rags took up the cry and ran with the headline that a racial war was about to break out and the government might have to recall the army from Afghanistan.

Two days later, Gillet drove through the winding road, parked and sat amid the grassy sand dunes watching the sun rise over the North Sea. The *Rooney*, one of the many crabbing boats, bobbed in the swell. A brisk wind penetrated his flesh and he tugged the coat tighter around his shoulders. Getting the truth out of Tubeh and Karim was like trying to change a fan belt with the engine running. Maybe it made sense not to risk destroying the rest of Karim's properties. Certain to be monitored by the police, Karim's people would be somewhere in attendance. Time was running out; he'd give Tubeh one final chance to answer his questions. A violent shiver sprung into his spine and he ran his tongue over his lips, tasting the salt whipped up from the sea by the gusting wind. Climbing to his feet, the phone vibrated and he thumbed the green button and listened.

Karim's voice sounded desperate as he struggled to get his words out.

"He's here, your son, he is here, in my house," Karim half shouted.

Gillet pulled the phone from his face and let out a long sigh. His body flooded with ecstasy.

"Is he injured?"

"He is fine. I answered a knock on the door and there he was, Allah be praised."

Gillet stared up at the sky in jubilation.

"What about Shafiq?"

"Your son is alone, says a man called Jawad dropped him outside my house, and then   drove off with Shafiq. That is all I know."

"Do you know where I live?" Gillet asked, sucking in his cheeks.

"Yes, Mr Gillet, I am aware of your address."

It sounded like a veiled threat, and Gillet pushed the phone closer to his ear.

"If you know what is good for you, bring my son home," he said, snapping the phone shut.

*

Tubeh smelled of shit, his eyes dull and lifeless; his mouth sagged open and he looked ten years older.

"You're a lucky man; your brother's found my son," Gillet said, screwing his nose up at the stench. "He says Jawad still has Shafiq and I think you know where he is going to take him."

"How would I know that? I don't know anything, I am a man of peace, I swear to Allah. Let me go and we will forget this foolishness. Speak with Karim; he will answer your questions."

"You're lying."

Then he saw it, the unmistakeable brief flash of light burning in the Imam's eyes. The black shadows that had lurked for so long in his heart over the disappearance of his son fled, replaced by a swelling anger. He'd been right in suspecting that Tubeh knew more than he wanted to reveal. Untying the rope, his fist sent Tubeh cannoning into the damp wall. The Imam groaned and slithered to the floor, his eyes staring like red-hot pokers into Gillet's face. Hostility replaced astonishment.

"Infidel pig," he spat through torn lips, his features distorted with hate.

The pain started, hammering in Gillet's head, and grabbing Tubeh's collar, he dragged him over the grassy dunes onto the beach. It was that time of day when the incoming tide made ready to recede and take all that dared stand in its way. Whatever the words Tubeh shrieked, Gillet had no idea, nor cared. Half pushing and half dragging him towards the retreating water, he waded out until the water lapped his waist.

"Right, you bastard, tell me what I want to know, now," he hissed. "Or I'll leave you here for the fishes."

"I don't know anything, and if I did I would never tell you," Tubeh shrieked.

Tubeh's words cut short as Gillet plunged his head beneath the water. He struggled at first as Gillet wrenched him to the surface, gasping and retching. Again, without pity, Gillet plunged his head beneath the cold salty water. This time he waited until Tubeh's struggles became feeble, and bubbles streamed to the surface. Loosening his grip, he watched the body face down and arms outstretched drift away with the outgoing tide. There was no sense of remorse, no feeling of loss or even wrongdoing at the Imam's demise, just the satisfaction that what he'd done he'd done as a favour to the world. On shore he shivered in the knowledge that rather than bringing an end to his torment, he had produced an escalation.

Concealed behind the tall hedgerow and no longer able to sustain the cold creeping into the marrow of his bones, he waited. Satisfied it was clear, he crept to the rear of the house, let himself in and made his way upstairs. The house felt oppressive, overbearing, as if he had no right to be there, and he pushed open the windows. Time was running out; his mood swings more frequent, the pain in his head more severe and affecting his vision. He couldn't stop, not when he was so close to everything he'd battled for over the past few months. Maybe later, when the two boys were safe, if things returned to normal perhaps Amy might come home and they could try for a brother or sister for Luke. Luke would like that; his was a caring nature. For what seemed an eternity he sat with his head cradled in his arms, thinking of the future. In his mind he searched for a form of guilt, culpability for the death of Tubeh. But felt nothing; nothing like the blackened sadness he felt over the death of Derek Thorne in Cardiff. Maybe that was because Thorne had once been a good soldier, a man who had served his country. The likes of Tubeh meant nothing to him, nor ever would; they had no country, and served nobody but themselves. A rare smile lit his face and he mused on the past, of the arguments he'd shared with fellow comrades-in-arms over the difference between patriotism and racism. What type of person could love a country where a loud sigh or a deep breath can be construed as an expression of racism or deemed politically incorrect? He tried to tell them the word racism in Britain amounted to no more than an expression used by a worthless government to hide the fact they had lost control of immigration along with everything else this country once held dear. A few sniggered, the ignorant ones, others were pressed to agree.

Then his thoughts changed, as the car pulled to a halt. Karim slipped from the driver's seat, opened the nearside rear door and waited for Luke to step onto the pavement. Gillet made his way down the stairs and flung open the front door.

Both men glared at each other. One dominated by anger, the other seeking a modicum of restraint, each waiting for the other to speak first.

Gillet experienced an emotional impotence, a lack of responsiveness, and struggled for something to say. Then felt infuriated at being unable to summon the correct words to suit the occasion.

"Hello, son, how have you been?" he managed.

"Hi, Dad."

"Hungry?" He cursed his lack of empathy.

"No, I'm just tired."

"Okay, get some sleep, we'll talk later," and then turned to Karim. "Where's Shafiq?"

"Where is my brother, Tubeh?"

Gillet hesitated. "Your brothers dead."

Karim's eyeballs swelled, and he stared into Gillet's face.

"Most men wish for life, Mr Gillet, you are the exception. Had I known, you would never have seen your son again. However, believe me, you will pay dearly for my brother's death."

"Don't threaten me, you bastard, it was you and your brother that arranged for Luke to be taken to Afghanistan to blackmail me into reading the crap about fucking Afghan boys," Gillet snarled. "That's how shit like you work. Tell me where Jawad is, or I promise I will bring you down piece by piece until you are back in Afghanistan shovelling camel shit for a living."

"You overrate yourself, Mr Gillet," Karim sneered. "You have knocked on life's door too many times and soon you will discover what lies on the other side. In the meantime, I suggest you keep your childish threats to yourself."

Karim's head exploded. Blood trickled from his nose. A stinging blow to the side of his head brought him to his knees. Gillet wrenched him to his feet, pushing his thumbs inside the corners of his mouth. Karim felt his face about to be ripped open from ear to ear.

"You have a wife called Mina," Gillet hissed. "And a beautiful ten-year-old daughter called Coco, after Coco Chanel I presume? Well, let me tell you a little joke, I'm on her scent. You have twenty-four hours to find Jawad and Shafiq, or I promise you will never see your wife or daughter again."

Karim scrambled to his feet and backed away. A black world of death and misery mirrored in Gillet's eyes and wanted to be gone, far from the lunacy. His bravado washed away like water down a drain. He sensed lightness in his head, a billowing wind that blew away any thoughts of reason. How could he tell all he knew to someone like as Gillet? It would serve no purpose other than to reveal a chain of events he wished to stay secret, and he had more to hide than most.

"Where would Jawad take Shafiq?"

Karim dabbed his nose with his handkerchief. "I don't know, perhaps he is considering indoctrinating Shafiq into the world of martyrs. There are people who know of these things, but beware, they are extremely cautious of anyone asking questions."

"Turn him into a suicide bomber you mean?"

"I know nothing of these things."

Gillet tried to think. Thorne was dead, that should satisfy Jawad's distorted religious views. Jawad had kept his promise and returned to the UK with Shafiq and Luke. But why allow Luke to go free and cling to Shafiq? The answers to all his questions floated face down in the North Sea.

CHAPTER TEN

At the bottom of the stairs, Gillet attempted to conjure up the best way to start a conversation with his son. Find a common denominator, or something that might induce words of comfort, like, what did you do in Afghanistan, did you like the people? Foolishness burned his face. Luke seemed thinner, tanned; maybe that would be worth a mention. On the edge of the bed he stroked a lock of corn-coloured hair from his sleeping son's eyes. Luke stirred, and his eyes flickered open. The smile softened his features, then his eyes drooped shut and he returned to the tranquillity of undisturbed sleep. Gillet stayed for a moment, grateful for the margin of time. He left none the wiser how to talk to his son.

For something other than his domestic problems to occupy his mind, Gillet stripped and ran the bath. Expelling a long drawn-out sigh, he sank down into the hot water and immersed his body in a hedonistic grip of luxury. The recent flood of memories he pushed to the back of his mind for another day, permitting time a free rein to pass unfettered. By the time he opened his eyes, the water had turned cold. The sound of shuffling came from Luke's room. Dressed and shaved, downstairs he rustled up two plates of beans on toast. Across the table they seemed wary, distant, no longer like father and son, as if the bond had been broken and in need of a wise man to broker the necessary repairs. Each alone with their thoughts, they ate as if a barrier existed between them, blocking off all further communication. Later, time reinvented itself and memories became jogged, Luke told his side of the story, omitting nothing. Gillet thought it wise to stay remiss, and told Luke the parts he thought he should know. Luke listened, aware his father hadn't told him the full story, but thought it best not to press the matter. Most important, they were as father and son. Shafiq had taught him many things, how to believe in himself and find a deep peace within his heart. In a boyish manner he felt that the past wasn't over, and one day he and Shafiq would meet under better circumstances. His father spoke.

"How did Shafiq react when Jawad dropped you off outside Karim's house?"

"He looked sad."

"Did Jawad mention where he was taking him?"

"No, we thought we were coming home to you. Are you going to try to find him, Dad?"

Gillet pulled his hand across his jaw trying to suppress his apprehension, and conjured up an image of Shafiq. The boy had risked his life to save him from a horrible death. His reward, to witness the horrific way in which his family died at the hands of the Taliban.

"Yes, son, I'll find him, if it's the last thing I ever do."

Luke looked up, his eyes bright. Whether with hope or fear Gillet could not tell, and looked away.

"You must find him, dad, he is my best friend, and has taught me much about Islam," Luke said, clutching his father's arm.

"Forget Islam Luke," Gillet grunted. "It has no place in our lives

*

Every nerve in Karims body tingled; three times he'd narrowly missed colliding with vehicles in front. After the fourth time, fearful for his safety, he pulled into a lay-by. Through the open window the cold breeze teased his damaged nose, and hurled a tirade of Islamic curses at the windscreen. What's good for the goose is good for the gander, he raged. His shops reduced to cinders was one thing; the death of his brother another. Those with suspicious minds in his community were busy at work connecting one to the other making his life even more difficult than it already was. Thumping the steering wheel, he mouthed another barrage of curses. Why hadn't Tubeh listened? Why did he meddle in things that didn't concern him? But Tubeh couldn't do that, no, not the great Tubeh, who revelled in his position as if he were the coming of the new prophet sent to save Islam from the infidel. He'd lost count of how many times he'd told Tubeh that Muslims didn't want the Islam of old. They wanted a new Islam, one of tolerance and understanding like it says in the holy book. But Tubeh, in his folly, allowed himself to become embroiled in the ways of the old Mullahs. Because of that, he had fallen foul of the self-seeking hate clerics that preached violence and unrest for fear of losing control of the world that had kept them in comfort for so long. Now he'd paid with his life. Seldom had he felt so angry. Closing his eyes, he attempted to keep his composure while sucking the salty blood where he'd bitten into his cheek. Hot tears blurred his vision. No matter how hard he tried he couldn't wrestle his uncertainties into submission. But at least he could reconcile himself with the knowledge his dead brother would never learn of the dark secret he'd harboured deep in his heart for so long. A secret so monstrous Tubeh would pray to Allah to strike him dead and cast him from the glory of Islam. He felt better, relieved. Then in desperation he threw his arms upwards and wailed.

"Why couldn't it have been Gillet's head and not his foot the Taliban separated from his body?"

Time cleared his mind, and he sat statue-like, his hands resting in his lap. The first signs of early evening shadows lengthened and the never-ending flow of traffic increased. Like spoiled children suffering a tantrum, impatient motorists honked as if in a hurry to reach the next traffic jam. Each was eager for a brief respite before the dawning of the following day, where once again they would be forced to relive it all over again. As a precaution he had sent his wife and daughter Coco to his mother-in-law in Bradford. Gillet's words were a live threat and he wanted to make certain he would never find them hidden away in the northern Asian community. He'd made sure of that by swearing his family and close friends to absolute silence, plus the bonus of brand new crinkly fifty-pound notes. Yet still his mind remained clouded with doubt. Gillet was like a boulder in a landslide, relentless and unstoppable. Pulling in a deep breath and pressing his head back into the headrest, he mulled over a host of alternatives that might serve to get Gillet off his back. Kill him; no, he hadn't the nerve for that. Assassination perhaps; who could he ask, and even more important, at what cost? He stiffened, arched a brow and expelled a long breath. Tomorrow he'd reopen an old acquaintance and visit Omar-al-Haddad, the radical Yemeni cleric rumoured to have links to Al Qaeda. He would know the whereabouts of Jawad, even better, know of a way to dispose of Gillet. It wouldn't be all plain sailing; Omar-al-Haddad knew of Karim's past and would exact a heavy price.

*

Karim gave his name to the surly black uniformed African security guard manning the gate leading to the mansion. Then waited as the guard made a brief phone call from his mobile phone then asked Karim to step from the car, conducting a thorough body check and raised the barrier. Karim gripped the steering wheel as he made his way through the fortified entrance of the exclusive estate and followed the narrow tree-lined avenue. Dead ahead and looming from the morning mist, a vast faux-Georgian pile, with grandiose pillars guarding either side of the shiny double oak doors.

In a small room overlooking the front gardens of the estate, a few miles east of Waterbeach, Cambridgeshire, close to the edge of the fens, Omar-al-Haddad stood short and frail, facing Mecca. Four times a day, seven days a week, he knelt and bowed his head, and prayed. He prayed for the earth, animals, mountains, forests and water sources, each entrusted to the human race with a moral responsibility to care for these breathtaking gifts from Allah. Of mankind there was no mention. In the past he preached of man's behavioural characteristics, a sign of God's love; all men cast in a different manner he stated. This parlance may have included a number of sins, but to Omar-al-Haddad it eased his conscience and allowed him the peace of mind to access a different side of his personality – his love of small boys, *Bacha Bazi*.

Surrounded by rustling elms standing at attention like shimmering sentinels, the mansion loomed into view. Time worn concrete steps led to the main doors. Omar watched from the top of the steps. Karim swallowed; his fear came like a habit.

"Salaam aleikum."

"Aleikum salaam," Karim answered.

"Allah is merciful."

Karim didn't miss the slow blink displaying an aloofness he hadn't seen since their first meeting in Kabul. He knew Omar was under surveillance from MI5. Yet, he never understood why a suspected terrorist could roam the country as he pleased. A case of better the devil you know perhaps. If the truth be known, Omar was neither temperamentally nor stylistically drawn to subtleties as missiles, strafing bomb runs, suicide bombings or minor open agitation, like setting fire to the Union flag. His war was more sophisticated, the kind that brings nations to the edge of damnation. Depriving them of their energy lifelines by crippling financial markets, weakening world leaders of their authority until the population capitulates into panic, and from panic comes chaos. By far the easiest, he could bankrupt a country by merely increasing the price of arms. Those same countries that pleaded with rich nations for aid while their people suffered famine and the lack of clean drinking water would pay any price for weapons enabling them to stay in power. Recent efforts to secure worldwide Islamic domination had been rewarded with major unrest and riots in the countries situated on the North African coast, along with Bahrain, the Yemen and even the despotic state of Iran. Raised by poor parents in the backwaters of Sanaa, the capital city of the Yemen, to sleep with goats and steal to survive, Omar had been born with a razor-sharp mind and had rapidly scaled the echelons of Al Qaeda.

Karim stood motionless, waiting for a man depositing a tray of *chai* and sliced lemon onto the table to leave the room. His mind shifted back in time. The first time he and Omar had met was the day he arranged for his younger brother, Aarash, to be taken from outside his home in Kabul and sold into sexual slavery. With the money received he moved to England, set up his chain of cut price shops and thrived. It was during this time that he procured young Asian boys from poor families in the north of England to satisfy Omar's insatiable appetite. Of course, like most nefarious illegalities, once in, the only way out was through death. Later, his brother Tubeh followed him using his position as an Imam to increase the child trafficking threefold.

"You wish to see your brother, Aarash?" Omar said with open contempt. "He has done well, he teaches the boys the way of *Bacha Bazi*."

The words didn't take Karim by surprise; he expected no less from Omar's twisted mind.

"What is done is done, it was Allah's will," he muttered.

The curl on Omar's thin lips stretched tighter. Karim's eyes flickered like a candle in a breeze. The last few days had been eventful and he cursed himself for contemplating Omar might help him. But he was here now and Omar was a dangerous man to fool with; even now it crossed his mind he might not leave the stately home alive after Omar had heard what he had to say. Too late to reflect on his stupidity, he waited for his flagging courage to return. The room was the same as the rest of the building. Where decadence once reigned, it stood bare, devoid of pictures, all forms of decoration, apart from the crystal chandelier suspended from the ceiling by gilded chains. Inner walls washed matt white with wooden chairs pushed beneath plain wooden desks in each room to represent a classroom. In the main hall, on the way in, he noted rows of prayer mats. Behind closed doors leading from the hall, the chanting of prayer; what was taking place at this moment might one day affect the world.

"I come to ask a favour," he said, "but I fear you have more important things to attend to than listen to my foolishness. Perhaps it is better I leave and come another time."

"Do we not share the love and trust of the same god?" Omar said in a disparaging voice.

Karim nodded.

"Then if you do not tell me of your troubles, how can we say we are brothers?"

Expressionless, he listened as Karim told him of Gillet and his son Luke. At the mentioned of Jawad, Omar fidgeted and his right forefinger beat a tuneless tattoo on the wooden arm of the chair.

"And what makes you think I know the whereabouts of this man Jawad, and the boy Shafiq?"

"You are blessed by Allah to know the movements of all the sons of Islam; you are Allah's font of everlasting hope, sent to spread the word of Islam to the infidels of this wicked country. Please help me," Karim whined. "Protect my family from this man Gillet."

The frail old man's self-esteem soared at the glowing accolade, and his beady eyes fluttered.

"In the past you have been a great servant to me, Karim," he said. "Tell me, if you were to find this man Jawad, what would you do?"

Karim's tongue searched for saliva to prize his lips apart. These were not the words he expected to hear. His mood changed, and his fear reduced to an abstract sense of futility. Adjusting his jacket, he gasped in astonishment at the sudden shift in bravado within him. His face wrapped in a bitter distaste stared at the wizened caricature of a man, gnarled like an old tree that should be hidden away in a thick wood. For a second he wondered if he possessed the courage to throttle the life from him right there and then. He wasn't a brave man, and his sudden thought no more than a fraction of his wild imagination.

"Tell me, master," what words can I use to make this man Jawad return the boy to Gillet?"

"It is simple, Karim, find him and tell him to do as you ask. If he refuses, you must rid yourself of him. Now go, I am a busy man."

Be rid of him, what sort of advice was that? Nonplussed, he backed away towards the door wishing he hadn't bothered to seek Omar's help. Fearful for his life, in a servile manner he nodded as if Omar and Allah were one. He had gone from nothing to nowhere. Outside, he wiped the pattering rain from his handsome face with a large pale blue handkerchief. He'd been a fool to expect Omar's help, and cursed his impetuousness. Paying no heed to the black glistening puddles barring his way, he sped past the gatehouse. Rows of concrete roadside lights reflected soda yellow on the wet road, passing cars hurled blankets of dirty brown water over his windscreen. Frustrations of the past few days had taken their toll and he needed narcotics to sooth his nerves; two lines should suffice. Parked on his drive, still feeling fraught, he stepped from the car and pushed his key into the front door. The first thing he saw was the silhouette of Gillet, the second, the gun pointing at his head. His mind blanked, he felt dizzy and clutched at his chest; he'd never suffered from heart trouble, until today.

*

Omar let the supercilious smile slip from his face. It was good to see the back of Karim along with his perpetual whining. The man was weak and infantile, of no use the day the crusade against the hated Christians began. Showered, he changed into a cream *chappan* with matching turban, with one end hanging loose over his shoulder, Afghan style, and spoke briefly into the phone. Minutes later, Jawad ushered the nervous young boy into the room.

"Red suits you, Shafiq," Omar said, appraising the tight-fitting *pirhan tunban*.

"Thank you, master, it is good it pleases you," Shafiq said, staring down at his feet.

"Learn to show respect and look at the master when he addresses you," Jawad snapped, slapping the back of Shafiq's head with his open hand.

Shafiq flinched and, raised his head to look into the frail old man's face. His insides turned cold. His fingers stiffened and he tapped his thighs, afraid of what would happen next. The sight of the mottled skin stretched tight across Omar's bony skull and the discharge of mucous reflecting in his rheumy eyes made him shudder.

"Wait outside, little one, I must speak with Jawad," Omar said.

When the door clicked shut, Omar spoke again.

"Kill Karim, tonight," he said, as if ordering coffee from a side-street restaurant.

"What of Gillet?" Jawad answered.

"We will deal with him later, perhaps teach his son the ways of *Bacha Bazi*."

Jawad forced a smile and adjusted his balance on the balls of his feet. To kill Karim face-to-face wasn't something he would relish. He wasn't a gangster, nor was he an assassin, or a man that lurks in dark alleys afraid to show his face. He was a freedom fighter, a man who fought to break the shackles from a world steeped in tyranny and injustice. Yet he dare not refuse the man before him waiting to slake his sexual needs on the innocent boy waiting outside.

"It shall be done, tonight," Jawad said.

Jawad left, and Shafiq entered the room. His eyes wide at Omar's beckoning finger.

"Do not be afraid, little one; show me what you have learned of dancing," Omar wheezed.

Shafiq gripped his bottom lip between his teeth. Without musical accompaniment, he began to move, swaying, shaking the tambourine in the hope of gaining rhythm. His steps were short, clumsy and lacking in confidence, and then he picked up the rhythm.

"Shafiq, Shafiq, you make my heart sing," Omar crooned, holding his clenched fists to his mouth. "Faster, faster."

Shafiq increased the tempo, the fine silk cloth pulled tight against his skin exhibiting the contours of his young, supple body. He danced like Farad had taught him in Mirza Khan's house, whirling, stretching and skipping. Bells attached to his wrists and ankles tinkled and flashed beneath the lights of the crystal chandelier illuminating the room. Omar's croons heightened to groans of sexual delight.

"Allah, Allah," he called out. "Why does this beautiful boy make my breast want to explode?"

Then he stood and hitched his *chappan* up over his waist to expose his nudity.

"Come, Shafiq, transport me to the edges of paradise," he shrieked.

Shafiq stared in muted horror at the frail old man's penis. Shrivelled like a dried walnut, it hung without form or shape.

"Oh, Shafiq, use your touch, as gentle as a dove's feather, to carry me to another world, a paradise made for you and I only."

Shafiq's mouth gaped open. He wanted to scream, to turn and run. But to where? Where would he go? The tambourine slipped from his grasp and he backed away towards the door. A snarl crossed Omar's thin lips, distorting his face

"Do as I tell you, bastard. You dare to disobey me?" he screeched, and approached Shafiq with his robe hoisted even higher, revealing his bony chest. "On your knees, you ill-bred dog."

Shafiq's spit of nausea gagged his throat, and with the old man's curses pressing against his ears, he ran shrieking from the room.

*

Downstairs, Jawad hesitated, listening to the sound of Omar's threats ringing throughout the building. He shuddered and pulled the doors of the stately home shut. The rain slowed, leaving a clear night. The last few weeks everything about his life had become confused and he felt no longer which road he should take. The night air smelled clean and he inhaled, as if the freshness might clear his mind. In the car he checked the time and fiddled with the radio. Tonight he would kill Karim, and after that Gillet, then return to Afghanistan to rejoin the *jihad*. By the time he had pulled himself together, a vague sense of morality entered his body. Listening to Adèle, he smiled and flipped open the glove compartment, the 9mm handgun nestled next to the silencer. Karim was a man of little dignity, a fool in the morning and a fool in the afternoon; he would make an easy target. Gillet was something else, tough and resilient, a man who looked down the barrel of a gun and smirked at the bullet. He would be difficult to dispose of, like an itch behind the eyeball. Prepared to give his life for Allah he would do his best, it was written. Past the gatehouse he headed across country to Norwich, his mind focused on Gillet. There was no way he would forgive him for breaking his promise to return both Luke and Shafiq to him. Thorne was dead, maybe not by Gillet's hand, but dead just the same. From the outset he didn't believe Gillet would kill him in cold blood, not even for the safety of his son. But things were different now and he no longer had a hold on Gillet's movements. He must find Gillet before he found him. He shifted in the driver's seat and felt uncomfortable.

*

Karim stared. Sweat trickled from beneath his collar and his bowels began to crumble. Both men eyed each other, silence broken by the ticking of the carriage clock on the mantelpiece.

"Time's up," Gillet said, dimming the lights.

"A few more days, that's all, these things cannot be hurried," he stammered. "Please, I feel unwell."

"Tough. Where's Shafiq?"

"Already I have spoken with a man who has promised to help. In a few days I will know the whereabouts of this man you call Jawad; after that you must promise never to contact me again." Karim cringed.

"Tell me about this man."

Karim hesitated and gripped the edge of the sofa for support. A man with the cunning of a fox, eager to never miss a golden opportunity a way out of his predicament manifested in his mind.

"The man I speak of is not a person you would wish to trifle with. He is a high-ranking leader in the Muslim community; however, he has a weakness for young boys," Karim said, keeping his eyes on the gun. "He knows of Jawad's whereabouts, and will learn the whereabouts of the boy, Shafiq. I will write down his address; it is secluded, but easy for a man such as you to find."

Gillet watched Karim. He was trickier than a sack of snakes.

"We'll go and see this man tonight, together."

Karim jerked and clutched at his chest; his breath came in spurts, laboured, as if they might be his last. His first reaction was

247

to make a bolt for the door, but he couldn't move and the pain in his chest increased. Instead, as a last resort and bolstered by fear, he lunged at Gillet. Taken by surprise, Gillet dropped the handgun and staggered back. Karim scooped up the weapon and levelled the barrel at Gillet's head, his hand unsteady, his finger curling round the trigger.

*

Jawad parked in a secluded cul-de-sac, surrounded by large private houses hidden from the road by tall mature pines. An easy five-minute walk halfway along the road, bordered by tall leylandii hedgerows on one side and open-plan gardens on the other brought him to Karim's house. The front lounge lit by a solitary dimmed light. Making his way down the drive, with his back tight against the house, he reached a hedge separating the garden from the house. A small shed with a sloping roof next to the garage served as a temporary refuge while he screwed the silencer onto the handgun and waited for his nerves to settle. Overhead a full moon; it was a time for madness, a time for doing things that shouldn't be done. In a crouch he reached out for the handle to the rear door. Locked, puffing out his cheeks, he cursed his luck, laid the silenced pistol on the step and fumbled in his pocket for a thin strip of plastic. Pushing it between the door and frame, he winced at the metallic ping of the latch relocating. From somewhere behind him a dog barked and another joined in, baying at the moon. He froze, blinked away the sweat from his eyes and pushed the door open. Through the gloom he saw Karim with his back facing him. Dead is dead, face-to-face or not, raising the handgun he pulled the trigger twice. The first bullet entered Karim's neck; the second shattered the back of his skull; blood and bone showered the wall and ceiling. Karim fell spilling a vase of white flowers. Gillet ducked behind the gold brocade sofa. Jawad stared down at Karim's lifeless body, a smile of triumph stretching his face.

"One down and one to go."

Jawad turned to leave as Gillet peered from behind the sofa. Their eyes locked, Jawad's triumphant smile melted into bewilderment. He stood like an admonished child who didn't understand the basic rules of behaviour. His hand jerked up and squeezed the triggeras he made his way from the house. The bullet zinged past Gillet's head. Out on the driveway Gillet's he heard Gillet's breathing growing louder. Street lights loomed out of the darkness, leaving him exposed. In blind panic he fired off two wild shots. One pinged off the tarmac. The other ricocheted from the wall, throwing out a shower of stinging brick splinters into Gillet's face. He slowed, groaning at the pain, and rubbed his eyes.

"Wherever you go, Rupert, I promise I will find you, and I will kill you," he roared at the figure disappearing into the night.

Jawad didn't stop running until he reached his parked car at the end of the road. Cursing, he fumbled for his car keys. One after another house lights illuminated the cul-de-sac, and he felt like a naked whore in the Vatican. Ramming the key into the ignition, he pulled away, his only thoughts to be gone from Gillet's retribution.

Slamming hard on the accelerator, he drove with no thought to his destination.

Gillet pressed his hands to his face to stop the bleeding. When the bleeding persisted, he ran the cold water tap and rinsed his face before clearing the splinters from his face and eyes. Satisfied he could see well enough to drive, he checked the address Karim had written on the slip of paper and left. When he reached the car, he checked the boot and gazed at the sawn-off shotgun next to the short hooked bladed knife designed for ripping open throats or tearing out the nerves at the base of the neck. Then swallowed the obligatory handful of painkillers, aware his pain would subside for only a short period. Tugging the slip of paper from his pocket he checked the address grateful for Karim's foresight to include the postcode. Entering the relevant information into the satnav, he swung the car round and began the journey through the back roads to Waterbeach on the outskirts of Cambridge.

*

Omar's mood had receded slightly since Shafiq's refusal to do as he was bid, and he sat with arms folded listening to Jawad's rambling monologue of the night's events. The boy, he would deal with later; his punishment would be harsh, he would flog the skin from his back until the insolent young bastard learned his place. The thought raised his dampened spirits. By the large panoramic window overlooking the estate, he stared out into the dull light thrown by the security lights and listened to Jawad catalogue the death of Karim. He shrugged; the world was well rid of Karim.

Jawad had served his purposes well in the past, but was in grave danger of becoming a liability. His only contribution to worldwide Islamic domination had been to throw in with a few insurgents holed up in the mountains separating Pakistan from Afghanistan and making spasmodic forays to avenge his brother's death. Time marched on and the day was close when Islam would prune out the deadwood, leaving the strong to flourish in the great *jihad*. He looked at Jawad. In his eyes he was childlike, fickle and flamboyant in the manner in which he tried to make people dislike him as if it gave him power. He himself commanded tens of thousands of underlings, and possessed access to unlimited millions of American dollars. He had little time for the trivialities that Jawad heaped upon him.

"You have allowed yourself to become involved in an unnecessary personal vendetta with this man you call Gillet. Do not bother me with minor problems, deal with it in the same manner you dealt with the fool Karim, discreetly," he said, continuing to stare out into the darkness through the open drapes.

"And the boy, Shafiq?"

"Ask the other brats, they will know where he is hiding. I had intended to deal with him myself, but I am summoned by Allah for a higher calling. Find the boy and get him out of my sight; you know what to do with him."

When Jawad closed the door behind him; he was glad to be rid of him along with the boy, who had left him unrelieved. A village clock struck eleven o'clock in the evening and he felt weary.

Today had not been a good day. A number of North African consulates had co-operated willingly with his plans, others not so reticent, a few difficult. Yet, he allowed the semblance of a smile to cross his face. The ranks of the Muslim Brotherhood in Egypt were swelling. Soon, the time would come to strike at Egypt, and then Libya in much the same manner as Tunisia, followed by Syria. Then, in accordance with his instructions, the whole of Africa would fall under the cloak of Islam. Later, the banners of Islam would flutter across the Mediterranean Sea and into Europe, followed by world domination.

At twenty-five minutes to midnight, Gillet ducked his head and watched a car pull away from the mansion. Headlights blazing, it slowed and stopped outside the security office. The jet-black African guard dressed in shirtsleeves raised the barrier, nodded and returned to the girlie book tucked inside the open drawer. A half-smoked cigarette dangled from his lips. Following the road further down for less than quarter of a mile, the wall turned at right angles into open countryside. A wooden five-bar gate was the only access to the field running adjacent to the wall. Opening the gate, Gillet drove along a mud track until he reached a clearing consisting of sawn-off tree trunks. Through the swaying elms less than a hundred metres away, the stately house lay bathed in brilliance from strategically placed searchlights. He sucked in his cheeks. He'd have to wait until the lights were extinguished or dimmed before he made his move. Painkillers made him drowsy and, settling back in the seat, he closed his eyes.

She came too soon, as if summoned, the woman holding the baby in one hand and a grenade in the other. But this time it was different. This time his finger froze on the trigger as he gazed into the baby's eyes. They stared back, blood-red, evil and malevolent. His limbs locked and refused to move. The baby growled like a dog, its mouth gaping open, revealing long curved fangs. Without warning it leapt from its mother's arms and sank the fangs into his face. Biting and slashing at his features, he heard the crunch of his bones breaking as the sweet taste of blood poured into his mouth and began choking him. He wanted to cry out, but he had difficulty breathing as the baby ripped and clawed away his flesh. Instead, he reached out and tried to tear the baby away from him, but still it remained, its slavering foul breath filling his nostrils.

Saturated in sweat and gasping for air, he heaved the car door open. Down on his knees he spat blood where he'd bitten through the soft flesh of his inner cheek. His chest contracted, squeezing hard against his heart, and cutting off his breath. In a moment of self-reflection he felt forced to admit he was ill. From past conversations with those who suffered from the disorder he knew his nightmares would grow worse, until the day arrived when he'd no longer be responsible for his actions. Even now the speed of his mood swings took him by surprise. The erupting temper tantrums, fits of depression he tried so hard to suppress, were more and more frequent and unrelenting. His life had become like a modern-day Robinson Crusoe; alone, shipwrecked in an obscure environment empty of people, with only himself for company. With no desire to mix with others, he had become withdrawn. Cut off from the real world, drifting, a prisoner of his own mind. The intense pounding was relentless and he clutched his head in his hands. God, would it ever stop? The the light in the sky dimmed, at last the house became cloaked in darkness. Exerting all of his willpower, he pulled himself erect and gritted his teeth, grateful for something other than his torment to apply his mind. The time had come to think, act sharp. A tiny smile touched his lips as his intensity for action heightened his senses, levering away all other feelings. The welcome haunt of the past slipped into his mind, reminding him what was to follow. With the sawn-off shotgun tucked under his arm, he made his way across the damp grass. Next to a row of disused stables inhabited by the stale smell of sweating horseflesh, he stopped to check his bearings. In complete darkness the house stood silent, overlooked by stalking beech and silver birch. Minutes later he found a sash window slightly open. Inside, he waited for his eyes to grow accustomed to the darkness. The lack of elegance, the bare walls, left him stunned. What had once been grand and swathed in decadence was now plain and clinical. Burning candle wax clogged his nostrils.

Close to the wall, he moved along a narrow corridor and into the main hall; a bare wooden staircase led to a large stone balcony. To the left were two doors. Careful not to make a sound, he twisted the handle of the nearest, waited and peered inside. The room was empty, the second room the same. Further along he slowed at a strip of light shining beneath a door. Inside the sound of conversation in a language he didn't recognise. One option would be to burst in, and take those inside by surprise and kill them where they stood. For a second he brooded and considered stealth. A grin split his lips. The game was on. As long as they died he couldn't give a shit. Joy flared within him, the heat of excitement coursed through his body. The old days had returned, days when he held sway over life and death. Deciding on the latter, turning the handle he pushed the door open. Surprise mingled with disappointment sprang onto his face. An old man with his back to him spoke down a landline telephone. Dressed in a cream *chappan* and a matching turban, he turned and dropped the phone into the cradle. Frail and thin, he was weasel-like in his movements and exuded a high-strung vigour capable of a man half his age. His face displayed no sign of fear or discomfort; if anything, a faint hint of amusement shaded his eyes.

"Ah, you must be the Mr Gillet I have heard so much about," he said in a calm voice. "I have been expecting you."

Gillet stepped into the room and back-heeled the door shut. Back against the wall, he remained close to the door, blocking any attempt to enter.

"Right first time, and you are?"

"I am known simply as Omar, a teacher of the joys of the Koran to young boys who wish to serve Allah."

"You mean you beat the shit out of them, then brainwash the poor bastards until they do everything you tell them to do. The

255

same things you bastards don't have the guts to do for yourselves," Gillet snorted.

"Your imagination serves you poorly, Mr Gillet."

"There is nothing wrong with my imagination, you sack of shit. Where is Shafiq?"

A flash of anger sparked in Omar's eyes.

"Shafiq? I understood your target is Jawad."

A faint smile creased Gillet's lips.

"His time will come when I have the boy, where are they?"

"Unfortunately, they left an hour ago."

Gillet's dislike for Omar grew, and he longed to pull out the knife and slice open his throat. His thoughts interrupted by a soft tap on the door. Tense, he pulled back both hammers on the shotgun and waited. The sound of tapping came again, this time followed by the creak of the door handle turning. Gillet held the shotgun waist height, his finger pressed on the trigger ready to fire. A small boy of no more than ten or eleven years of age stepped into the room. Dressed in a simple white cotton gown, he stared wide-eyed first at Gillet and then turned to face Omar. He looked confused. His frightened eyes drifted to the shotgun levelled at his chest and he fought against his stuttering nerves, and then urinated onto the floor.

"Please, master, it was an accident," he stammered at Omar. "Please do not beat me again."

"Quiet, you fool," Omar hissed.

Gillet's eyes fixed on the trembling boy.

"What are you doing here?" he said.

"I have been summoned by the master to join him in paradise."

Gillet frowned.

"Yeah, and how do you do that?"

"Allah permits us to perform miracles on the master; it is his will."

Gillet gazed into the boy's eyes, the innocence defiled by the creature standing behind him. His hand fumbled for the knife in his pocket.

"And how do you perform these miracles?" he growled.

"With my hands and mouth. Sometimes the master enters me and we are joined as one; it is Allah's will, a great honour indeed."

Gillet snarled and turned; his eyes, cold and bleak, stared into Omar's face.

The old man seemed to fold, his energy drained from his body, and he leaned against the table for support. His thin lips stretched back tight over his rotting teeth and he looked as if he were about to burst into tears. There could be no getting rid of it now, that sucking pain in Gillet's stomach. He wanted to beat Omar to a pulp, better still rip open his stomach and watch him die with his guts spilled out on the floor. Instead, he strode across the room, yanked open the window and hurled him kicking and screaming out into the night. The thud of the body smashing onto the paving stones below echoed. Omar's crushed head lay in a pool of blood at right angles to his body.

"What is your name?"

"I am called Ahmed," the boy stuttered, swaying with terror.

"I'm not going to hurt you, Ahmed. How many other boys live here?"

"We count up to sixty each morning at lessons. Are you going to kill me?" the boy sobbed.

"No. Do you know of a boy called Shafiq?"

"Shafiq, yes, the name is familiar. He is no longer with us. His stubbornness did not please the master and he was taken away for punishment."

"Do you know where he was taken, and was there a man called Jawad with him?"

"Yes, yes," the boy wailed. "There was a man by that name; it is he who has taken Shafiq to a place of worship close to the sea. The Imam is young and beats the boys until they repent their ways. Sometimes, if they are good he takes them to a place of great joy."

"A place of joy, what do you mean?"

"It is a place called Yarmouth, a wondrous place full of happy people and fairgrounds, with bright lights and loud music," the boy stammered. "Promise me Allah will not punish me for telling you these things?"

Gillet knelt and gripped the boy by the arms.

"It's over now. No one will harm you again; you and the rest of the boys can go home."

The tears stopped.

"Allah thanks you. Our parents were forced to hand us over to these bad men. Many boys have come from countries we have never heard of. Every night they cry for their mothers. Rather than live, some choose to die by holding their heads under water on bath nights."

Gillet gazed into the sad eyes and saw the evil that men do. Of his own nightmares, they were fragments of a troubled mind brought about of his own choosing. But these boys, alone in the stark surroundings of the once stately house, had lived through a horrible nightmare day after day without choice or opportunity to live like humans.

"Are there more grown-ups in the building?"

"Yes, on the second floor, by the toilets."

"How many?"

"Four."

"Wait here for ten minutes, then collect the boys and wait for me inside the main doors."

The four men sat eating from a bowl of dates and reading from battered copies of the Koran in the white-walled room on the second floor of the stately house. Each wore a long unkempt grey-streaked beard, making it impossible to tell their ages. Their sole aim in life to poison the minds of children. To Gillet they were sub-human filth responsible for grooming, abusing and, in most cases, raping and trafficking small boys of the Muslim faith. Kicking open the door, the force of both barrels sent the two closest hurling backwards across the room minus their heads. Taking his time to reload, he sent the two remaining miscreants into the arms of Allah, with half of their chests blown away.

Five minutes later he led sixty children between eight and fourteen years of age outside the front doors of the stately home.

"Make your way to the security gatehouse at the bottom of the drive and tell the guard to call the police. If he refuses, turn right and head for the nearest village a mile away."

"Allah blesses you," Ahmed called.

They passed by him in an orderly fashion, as if the faintest rustle of clothing might disturb the breath of evil that inhabited the building, their faces were clothed in bewilderment. The youngest, gripped the hands of those nearest, desperate to seek a form of comfort against the cruelty heaped upon them by immoral men unfit to walk the earth.

Gillet's anger rose, when the children were out of sight he re-entered the house.

In the car and, with a benign expression, he watched the orange flames lick at the stately house. He felt better than he had for a long time. He had much to celebrate; no matter how small or large, a limb from the evil of *Bacha Bazi* had been severed.

CHAPTER ELEVEN

Great Yarmouth wasn't too long a journey from the smouldering remains of the stately house in Cambridgeshire. Jawad, in no particular rush, made good time through the darkness, unaware the house was about to collapse into a pile of ashes. If he had known he wouldn't have cared too much. Omar's death would have cheered him so much so he might have taken the time to push Shafiq from the car in the middle of nowhere, and make his way back to the safety of Pakistan, and freedom from the everlasting threat of Gillet. As a nemesis, Gillet would forever be a fulminating menace to his security, there was no doubt about that. Sucking his tongue against his teeth, he glanced across at Shafiq; the flesh around his swollen eye had turned a dark shade of blue and his swollen split lip disfigured his mouth. One day, he promised himself, the day would come when he would kill Omar. Over the last few weeks he had proved that he had the nerve to kill up close, instead of employing hit-and-run tactics from a distance. He'd killed the hooked-nose man on the mountain without compunction, and Karim in cold blood from less than a couple of metres away. He had almost managed to kill Gillet. Things were looking up, and he felt an exaggerated sense of power.

"Hungry?"

Shafiq shrugged.

"Suit yourself, I'm starving," he said, pulling into the car park of a fast-food outlet.

A quick study of the neon-lit menu, Jawad ordered two quarter pounders with large fries, plus two large colas with ice. Seated by the window he looked around at the stereotyped customers synonymous with places such as this. In one corner, an overweight mother sat with her two obese daughters, dressed in oversized pink tracksuit bottoms, their T-shirts strained at the seams preventing rolls of flab making a frenzied bid for freedom. A solitary stick-thin youth with a face full of spots ready to explode sucked on the straw of a soft drink. An ample-bosomed peroxide waitress with a slim waist made her way over with the order. Her expression bland and uncompromising; nothing could be worse than Albania, who knows, this time next week I'll be an international fashion model. She flashed a practised friendly fluoride smile and displaying a hint of a black lace bra, dropped the Styrofoam containers onto the table and moved away, her walk jaunty and brimming with confidence. Shafiq pushed the plastic knife and fork aside, grabbed a handful of fries and stuffed them into his mouth. The last of the quarter pounder disappeared in seconds, then licked the fingertips of his right hand and wiped them down the front of his grey sweatshirt. The overweight mother stopped eating and stared up in disgust, her open mouth displaying the mangled remains of fries and tomato ketchup.

Jawad stared out into the street. Unsettled, he felt as if he were in a place he didn't belong. Or maybe it was the reverse and this *was* where he belonged. He'd always kept to himself, aloof and distant from those around him, his heart so ice-cold that no one could melt it. It was best that way, he told himself, safer, more secure. Attachments were a folly that brought a vulnerability which might bring him down. As a teenager he'd been reckless and stupid, doing all the things he shouldn't have done, and then revelled in the consequences like a spoilt brat in need of a firm hand. Worried for his future, his father had paid a small fortune to put him through medical college in the hope the responsibility might help to calm him. It proved to be fruitless, and after eighteen months he still didn't know the difference between a clavicle and a clarinet. To his chagrin, his father washed his hands of him and severed his allowance. Angry at being deprived of what he considered his, he 'dropped out', and wandered through life, living in squats with the homeless and unwanted. But all that changed the day he heard the news his brother had died serving in Afghanistan. The death left him in a state of severe shock, later, when he discovered the truth of how he had died, he felt bitter and angry. Since that day, his life of boredom and frustrated impotence, took on a different meaning. His anger festered until at last he found something he could centre his inner rage on – the British Army.

"Had enough to eat?"

Shafiq shrugged.

"Well, have you or haven't you, because you won't get this treatment where you are going?"

Without speaking, Shafiq raised his shoulders, then allowed them to slump.

Jawad smiled, and beckoning to the waitress ordered the same again. Captured in a bubble of amusement and with his hands locked behind his neck, he watched Shafiq devour the meal in the time it took the waitress to clear the table. When Shafiq asked for more, he glanced up in astonishment and leaned to ruffle his hair. No matter how full Shafiq's stomach, like a hungry dog he would never refuse the offer of food. He would eat until sick. Surprised by his unprovoked display of tenderness, Jawad pulled his hand away.

"Enough," he said gruffly. "It's greed you suffer from, not hunger. Time we made a move."

At the first sign of a gap, Jawad pushed down on the accelerator and pulled out into the flow of traffic, from the corner of his eye he glanced at Shafiq. On more than one occasion it had crossed his mind that since leaving Afghanistan, Shafiq had never complained of the chain of events that had led him to become homeless in a foreign country. It stood to reason that the brutal manner in which his parents and sisters died was more than enough to traumatise any boy for the rest of his life. Even at the tender age of eleven he possessed the intrinsic ability to take everything in his stride as if it were an everyday occurrence. Maybe it was his unshakeable belief in his religion that helped bind him together throughout the trials and tribulations of his boyhood. Whatever it was, he knew the boy had an inner strength worthy of even the strongest of men. His privileged childhood, a well-placed pout would suffice to obtain whatever it was he wanted. A mock cry of anguish followed by a rush for his mother's all-embracing arms excused all misdemeanours, no matter how spiteful or heinous his crime.

By degrees he pushed the emotion-invoking thoughts to the back of his mind and turned on the radio. An enthusiast rambled on about jazz in the thirties. Pushing a button, he settled back to listen to a news bulletin. At first he paid small interest, and then reeled with shock at the precise clipped voice of the newsreader. A stately house in Cambridgeshire, thought to be used as an early learning centre for young Muslims, had been burned to the ground. Dozens of young male Muslim children had been found wandering the countryside lost and unattended. A security guard operating the main entrance had been arrested and taken to London for questioning. Further investigations revealed the stately house had been used as a centre where young Muslim boys between eight and fourteen years of age learned to dance prior to use as sexual gratification for wealthy Muslims residing throughout the UK. Police were searching mosques in all parts of the country for further proof of the re-emergence of an ancient Muslim tradition known as *Bacha Bazi*. It is thought the head of the centre, Omar-al-Haddad, a suspected Al Qaeda terrorist, died jumping from a top-storey window while attempting to escape the flames. Investigations are ongoing.

Dark images flashed though Jawad's mind. Who else but Gillet possessed the capability to cause an amount of chaos in a short space of time? Unsure what to do next, he pulled into a lay-by and, resting his forehead on the steering wheel, contemplated his future.

He tried to clear his mind. But everything had become too far-fetched, too mental, and before he knew what he was saying, the words came out of his mouth like bullets from a gun.

"I've had enough of all this shit; let's get out of here."

Shafiq gripped the small of bottle of dust from the Shamali Plains and unscrewed the cap; holding it to his nose, he inhaled.

"Take me home, to Afghanistan, where I can pay my respects to my dead parents and sisters," he whispered.

Jawad's face creased into a bemused frown and he stared at Shafiq.

"What are you doing?"

"I am remembering my homeland, a place where I can live among my own people in peace with Allah."

Jawad wished his own life might be that simple. Somewhere in the future the time would come when he would need to piece together a meaning to his own life, find a direction. At that moment, if anyone had asked him what good had come from his past he would struggle for a an answer. One thing was for sure, he couldn't spend the rest of his life killing British soldiers, he had sworn to Allah that the death of Thorne would bring an end to all of that. Always remember the past is a lesson for the future, his father told him again and again while remonstrating over his wasted life. But he had paid no attention. Now it was too late, he felt trapped in a sweeping tide of guilt. He had become less than nothing, a procurer of small defenceless boys to be sacrificed for the immoral and heinous deprivations of those unworthy to kneel before Allah. But what of Allah? What had he done to punish the evil doers? Where was he to right the wrongs? The realisation that he was as guilty as those he condemned plunged into his soul. His union with Islam he had once believed intractable was splintering at the seams like an overripe fruit.

Shafiq gazed at him with pleading eyes, silence squeezed the air. All Jawad could feel was despair merged with despondency.

"Allah, why do you always desert me in my hour of need?" he murmured aloud.

"You blaspheme, for this he will not protect you from the wrath of Mister Sergeant," Shafiq cried, sitting upright.

Jerked from his thoughts, Jawad forced amusement into his eyes, but the old images flooded back, in a fit of false bravado rolled his eyes in mock fear.

"You speak like a fool, little one. I'm not afraid of Gillet."

He knew his words were meaningless and without weight, and under a dark threatening sky they entered the coastal resort town of Great Yarmouth. An elderly man walking a small black and white dog gave then directions for Kitchener Road. It was the time of night when everyone was in their homes, and it took him longer than expected to find a place to park. Gripping Shafiq firmly by the arm, they made their way to the mosque, fidgeting from one foot to the other he rapped on the rear door. Turning locks accompanied by the rasp of bolts withdrawing grated through the night air. Consistent with his ilk, bareheaded he wore Islamic dress. An unkempt grey-tinged beard covered his face. Suspicious eyes glinted above a hooked nose.

"It is late. Wait here and I will inform the Imam," he said, shuffling away, his sandals squeaking on the tiled floor.

"Then hurry, I don't have all night," Jawad snapped.

Once rid of Shafiq, his business with the Imam was complete, and placing his hands on the boy's shoulders he pushed him into the narrow passageway.

"This is as far as I go. Do as they say, and maybe you will be okay. Good luck," he mumbled as he turned to leave.

Shafiq's hand reached out and clutched at his fingers, refusing to let go. Jawad pulled away. In desperation Shafiq squeezed tighter, then lost his balance and cannoned face first into the wall. His body shook; brimming tears ran down his cheeks and spilled onto the floor. His upturned face like a lost puppy, soulful, full of hopelessness, streamers of snot worked around his mouth, mingling with spittle, his grip refused to yield.

"Take me home, please?" Shafiq said between gushing sobs. "I do not wish to stay with these people that do bad things against the will of Allah."

Jawad closed his eyes, his mind tangled in the thick reeds separating sanity from madness.

"The Imam will see you now."

"Take the boy; I have no further need of him, he is a burden."

The man's distorted nose twitched and he sneezed; then grabbed Shafiq's arm. Shafiq cringed, shrinking back tight against the wall he yelped like an animal caught in a trap. Jawad blocked the sound from his ears, determined not to look back. By the time he reached the car, guilt dripped from his conscience like melting snow and he wondered if he would ever again distinguish right from wrong. He sat staring through the windscreen, aware that his experiences in life were the stuff of shame and the burden of unwanted secrets.

Shafiq concentrated his gaze on his feet. Afraid to look the Imam in the face, his eyes sank back deep into his skull. Chilled numbness spread into his chest, smothering his heart, and raising his hands to protect himself he waited for the stinging blow to his head. A sudden jab of pain seared into his ankles as his feet were swept from beneath him. Screams of pain gushed from his mouth and he collapsed; again and again the Imam's foot smashed into his head and chest. Outside, Jawad, unable to block the pitiful sounds from his ears, slammed the car into gear and drove away. Stopping once for petrol, he headed for his home town.

In Luton, he walked the familiar streets where he had been raised as a child until dawn peeped over the horizon. Night turned to day, and for one suspended moment he felt lost in a frenzy of unanswerable questions. In a public house on the corner of a road he didn't recognise, he sipped a still orange and tinkered with a plate of tuna sandwiches. The first mouthful stuck in his throat, pushing the sandwiches to one side, he stood and left. Everything had changed. The codes of practice that he once adhered to, even his iron belief in his way of life that had served so well in the past, seemed distant and isolated. He wondered how these things could happen, without warning, as if it had never mattered. Seated on a bench in Dunstable Road overlooking a park he watched a group of children playing football using two coats as a goal. A West Indian towered above the others, using his weight to keep hold of the ball until the others converged on him he fell laughing and shrieking.

A chill wind caused him to hunched his head between his shoulders. Deep down he knew he could never stop Gillet. Whatever he was wasn't enough. He needed to become someone who could rip off his clothes and become someone else, someone like Superman; strong, intrepid and invincible, anyone but himself. Aware that the defining moment in his life would soon arrive, his mind hovered. To make matters worse, it wasn't just Gillet he thought of; everything inside of him seemed to deteriorate. The very foundations of his belief, the words of the prophet Mohammed, all fell apart, crumbling and disintegrating with every moment of passing time. That part of his soul he once put to one side to harbour his beliefs and creed lay empty and void.

*

It mattered little how hard Shafiq tried to halt the trembling in his body, he failed and struggled for survival. At last he succumbed to the merciful luxury of sleep. Darkness held him in its grip when he woke and blinked in the cramped windowless room. He prayed for strength to survive the coming ordeal, and then stood, trying to ease the pain in his back from the severe kicking. All feeling in his feet and his fingers were absent. Fear tightened his skin and he felt as if he had no influence over his body. Fretful for his existence, he wanted to call for someone, anyone, to free him from his misery. Yet even as he tried to speak, he felt as if he were being strangled by ever-tightening hands, choking the life from his aching body. Filled with despair, he uttered a muted cry of anguish and sank down to the floor, remote from any thought of hope. The door swung open and a harsh light seared into his eyes. A hard bony hand slapped his cheek, drawing a trickle of blood. The voice of the Imam stiffened his bones and he waited, this time perhaps for death.

"Soon you will learn to obey Allah's will, you son of a low-born dog."

Beneath the merciless onslaught, he curled into a ball. Blood blocked his nose, threatening to cut off the supply of oxygen. Like an animal awaiting slaughter, he lay with simple resignation, praying for his torment to be over and death a welcome relief. A corridor in his mind swung open as the pain singing out from his flesh numbed. Anger overruled the agony of each blow. They could beat him until he gasped for his last breath, but he'd never do the things they tried to force him to do. Allah was his protector, and clutching the bottle containing the dust of his homeland, his anger erupted. His body stretched taut, and he rolled out of reach of the man beating him. Blind fury fused his muscles, and struggling to his feet he leapt at his tormentor. The Imam stumbled back. Grasping his chance for freedom, Shafiq ran towards the door at the bottom of the corridor. The door resisted his efforts and then opened, and gasping for breath he lurched out into the coolness of the early morning air. Ignoring his injuries, he made his way down a side road, and then paused. The sound of hurried footsteps tightened his chest. Metres down the street he noted the lorry parked on a bare patch of ground and, crawling underneath, pulled his body up over the rear axle. Now only Allah alone stood between him and the twisted cruelties of the Imam. It came slowly at first, the shadow, and then stretched long and dark beneath the lorry. It seemed impossible to cling to the greasy axle for another minute, and unable to summon the strength he slid down onto the road. Darkness closed over him. Allah had forsaken him for something more important. It mattered not if his eyes were open or closed, but he closed them all the same and waited. Then he knew that Allah would never desert him in his hour of need, as the footsteps grew fainter. He was free. Free in a foreign country with nowhere to go. Free as a shackled soul condemned to solitary confinement.

*

Gillet pushed the key in the lock of his front door and turned his attention to the front garden. What had once been a place of natural beauty now a stagnation of nature's prodigality. The lawn, long since past mowing, sprouted a variety of thistles and weeds almost waist high. Used confectionary wrappers, empty plastic coke bottles along with a generous helping of 21st-century litter stood on the spot once cared for by Amy. All around the stifling summer eased its stranglehold, and with the heat inside the house unbearable, he swung open the windows. The usual routine followed – coffee with one sugar and easy on the powdered milk. Settled on a tall stiff-backed kitchen chair, his mind drifted to his son, to the look of disappointment when he'd dropped him off at his parents'. It was the first time he'd ever seen Luke lose his temper.

"Why can't we stay together for at least a couple of days before you leave?" he snapped at his father.

Luke's grandfather, taken aback by the outburst, sprung to his grandson's defence.

"I don't know what the devil's going on, but it's about bloody time you started acting like a proper father. What the bloody hell was all this nonsense about sending for him while you were in Afghanistan?" he raged. "Bloody daft, never heard the likes. He's not a soldier you know; he's a twelve-year-old lad for God's sake. About time you forgot the army and grew up, start bringing him up, or me and your mother will."

Gillet didn't know how to respond to his parents' display of anger. So he did what he thought best and walked out of the house without uttering a word. His father stood opening and closing his fists, then gestured to Luke with his head.

"Go to your room, there's a good lad, I need to talk to your gran."

Sitting down, he rested his elbows on the table and peered into the empty teapot.

"I'll make a fresh brew," she said.

"No, sit down for a minute, there's a few things you ought to know."

"Don't fret, dear, you know what Tom's like."

"It's not that daft bugger I want to talk about, it's young Luke."

Mrs Gillet clasped her hands to her apron and studied her husband's face.

"Do you know where I caught him yesterday?" he began. "In the cemetery, that's where."

"Whatever was he doing there?"

"Doing? I'll tell you what he was doing; he was standing at attention in front of a grave, that's what he was doing. Holding a small Union flag and wearing one of his father's old paratrooper berets on his head. When I asked him what was going on, he said he was practising for the day his father died; didn't want to cry during the funeral he said, wanted his father to feel proud of him."

His wife brushed imaginary crumbs from her pinafore.

"That's not all. The surname on the gravestone was Thomas. Seventeen people of the same name buried there, Christian and surnames both mind you, counted them himself he said. Well I thought, that's funny, seeing how he can't count to save his life. I don't believe you, I said, you count from the top of cemetery and I'll count from the bottom and we'll meet in the middle. Eight I counted; when I asked him how many he had counted, he said nine, nine plus my eight makes seventeen, he said, quick as a flash."

Mrs Gillet shifted in her chair, trying to clear that part of her mind she needed. The speed of her husband's declaration had left her stunned.

"What shall we do?"

"I'll have a word with Dr Frobisher after surgery tomorrow night, see what he has to say on the matter. Pretty obvious that young Luke's feigning his disability, looking for attention he is. There ain't much wrong with him that a settled life wouldn't cure," her husband said. "If you ask me, it's all the carryings-on with his mother and father responsible for all of this. Poor little bugger don't know whether he's coming or going. Once they got married they should bloody stay married; treat marriage like a bloody pawn shop they do these days, chopping and bloody changing whenever it suits them. But that's not all."

"What do you mean, that's not all?"

"Well, I weren't going to tell this, but I suppose I'd better. Day before yesterday I caught him upstairs in Amy and Tom's room wearing make - up Amy must have left behind. Plastered all over his it was, told him to get it of before I gave him slap round his ear."

"What did he do?"

"Do, he ran in the bathroom laughing, and started singing in a voice I've never heard the likes of."

*

Gillet didn't bother to turn on the lights, instead he sat in the darkened room with his head cradled in his hands, and wishing things might be different. Something at the back of his mind was nagging him, warning him to ease up, take things easy. But in his confusion there was one constant emotion present, his rooted devotion to find Shafiq. It wasn't just a mere pathetic dream born out of boredom, it was real and drove him on when he should have turned and walked away. Undressed, he climbed into bed.

The following morning he felt drained and turned on the shower, then changed his mind and sloshed his face under the cold water tap. A wondrous place called Yarmouth where everybody is happy and music fills the air the boy had said. It didn't take rocket science to figure out the place of worship was a mosque. Better if it was beneath the sea rather than by it, he thought with vicious satisfaction. Unable to suppress his frustrations, he squeezed his eyes tight shut until they hurt, trying to ease out his tiredness. But there was no ridding himself of it, no God-given release. The tenuous thread of willpower that had kept him going threatened to snap and send him spinning into oblivion. It began with his hands, first the tremble, then the light piercing his sight and turning everything different shades of dancing red. The shiver clattered his bones. Fumbling his way to the landing and gripping the banister for support, he descended the stairs. Now buried in the timeless realms of incapability, on his hands and knees he crawled to the corner unit in the lounge and pulled out a bottle of brandy. After a brief struggle the cap came loose in his hand, and raising the neck to his lips he drank until he could no longer hold his breath. Waiting for his lungs to fill with oxygen, he raised the bottle again, feeling the neck crash against his front teeth. With no thought other than the pain in his head, he guzzled down the contents until his stomach rejected the fiery liquid and sent it hurtling up through his mouth. His eyes danced with mischief and he blinked at his drink-stained trousers. Light-headed and struggling to his feet he collapsed onto the sofa. Tension melted away to nothing. His eyelids fluttered and his breathing became regular. For the first time in months he slept through to early evening. When he woke, he went upstairs, ripped off his stained clothing, climbed into his bed and slept until morning.

*

For the rest of that morning, until sunrise, Shafiq slept on the beach behind a wooden hut surrounded by folded deckchairs. At dawn, a man dressed in tight blue denims and leather jacket stopped, stared, and hurled a mouthful of obscenities at him before unlocking the wooden hut. Shafiq, reluctant for any form of confrontation, moved and hunkered further down the beach. Gradually, morning pushed further into day, a hot sun with a cooling sea breeze wafting over the golden sands. With his back to the sea wall he sat whispering a silent prayer and gazed out over the sea. No money or food and nowhere to go he had but one choice, return to the mosque and accept the violence along with the degradation from the Imam. Fear brought tears to his eyes. Distracted at the angry sound of a woman's voice, with boyish curiosity he watched a plump woman cursing three sad-eyed donkeys further along the beach. From a large hessian sack she pulled a tangled mess of bright-red harnesses and struggled to slip them one at a time over the uncooperative animals' heads. Finally, she managed to saddle the animals and stood with her feet apart, panting for her efforts. A surge of holidaymakers headed for the nearest stretch of beach determined to make the most of the hot sun. The sight of the donkeys aroused the children and parents formed an orderly queue. The plump woman hoisted a ginger-haired child onto the back of the smallest animal. No more than four years of age, the boy sat stiff as a poker and afraid to move. No matter how hard the woman tugged the halter, the donkey dug its feet into the sand, straightened its front legs and refused to move. Disgruntled, the boy let out a loud wail and turned to face his parents with tears streaming down his face. Shafiq smiled. he had learned from his father the idiosyncrasies of a donkey's obstinate nature towards the needs of the human race.

Walking over, he fondled the donkey's ears.

"Hut-hut-hut," he said, pulling the halter from the woman's hands.

The donkey trotted to the marker and back. The boy's tears dried and Shafiq handed the halter to the plump woman and turned away.

"Hold on, lad, my assistant's not turned up," she said. "Twenty quid if you stay till five o'clock."

Shafiq shrugged, confused.

"Alright, you awkward little sod," she puffed. "Twenty quid and a fish and chip supper, final offer."

"You wish me to help with donkeys, I help," Shafiq said.

For the remainder of the day, under the plump woman's beaming smile, he led the donkeys two at a time up and down the beach, grinning at her futile attempts to imitate his command. Later in the afternoon, a bell tolled the hour and small boats strained on their moorings against the incoming tide.

"Right, lad, that's it for the day, let's eat. By the way, what's your name?"

"I am called Shafiq."

"Well, chaffinch, I don't know about you," she said, "but I could eat a horse."

"Horse, you eat horse? I have never eaten horse."

"The world's full of bloody comedians," she sighed, shaking her head. "My name's Bellarose, you can call me Bella."

Bella watched him press handfuls of chips into his mouth with his right hand, his left hand out of sight resting on his thigh. Finished, he ran his finger around the plate hopeful of missed morsels. She possessed a warm expression along with a healthy glow to her skin; though her hair was lank and mousy and lacking any form of style, it portrayed a woman at ease with herself. In her mid-thirties, months ago her husband left her for a scrawny woman with a flat chest, who wore too much make-up and ran an amusement arcade on the seafront. She never missed him because he was dirty and never washed, and breathed a sigh of relief when he packed a holdall with his few belongings. When he started to apologise for his weakness she trembled at the thought he might change his mind and stay. Her home was a smallholding on the outskirts of Yarmouth, where she housed five more donkeys, each with varying degrees of health. Considered unsuitable for use on the beach, she cared for them the best she could, ignoring the fact their upkeep drained most of the profits made from the three fit and able enough to work.

"Where do you live, chaffinch?" she asked.

He shrugged, smiling sheepishly. She waited for his answer. When he didn't respond, her gaze hardened.

"You must live somewhere. Where did you sleep last night?"

"On the sand."

Opening her mouth to speak, she changed her mind. Over the years she'd seen her fair share of runaways and strays. From various parts of the country they came, each trying their best to eke out an existence during the summer season. Most returned home of their own accord before the summer season started. The rest, under-age runaways, rounded up by the police or welfare services were returned protesting to their parents. The next year she'd see the same faces again.

"You can stay at my place for the night," she said. "Help me bed those damn donkeys down for the night, seeing as how you seem to have a way with the stubborn sods."

That evening she stood with arms folded beneath her ample breasts and watched as he coaxed the donkeys from the horsebox and into the large corrugated barn. The words he used she didn't understand or even try to remember for another day. Motionless, they waited one at a time as he washed the sand from their hooves to prevent sores and chafing, all the time talking and encouraging them to do his bidding. Of the remaining five he told her one was too old for work and the other four plain lazy. She bent double, choking with laughter when he remonstrated in a loud voice and wagged his finger in a comical manner at the lazy animals, until one raised its head and rent the air with a sequence of hee-haws loud enough to be heard for miles Balling his fist, he punched the donkey in the jaw, leapt on its back and bounced up and down until it shuffled into a trot with the other four following close behind. Next day, seven donkeys, fed, watered and saddled, waited ready for work.

CHAPTER TWELVE

Gillet suffered from a hang-over the next morning. Bleary-eyed, he studied the lampshade suspended from the ceiling – pink with white tassels. Pink was Amy's favourite colour. *No comfort there*, he thought, pushing her from his mind. No matter which way he looked at it he knew the cause of his discomfort was drink. But as the saying goes, every cloud has a silver lining, he'd found a method of escaping from his moods of depression. With a stomach like a bucket of shit in a cement mixer, he slurped hot coffee and waited for the miracle of sobriety. When it didn't he felt ashamed. Blinking, he leaned back and he sucked in a great breath through his nose, hesitated, and exhaled through his mouth. He was ill, troubled, unwell, or whatever they called it – Post Traumatic Stress Disorder. He'd seen it in soldiers serving at the front a hundred times. Those who swore blind they were fine, just a little tired, they said, with staring eyes. His eyes gleamed, and he raked his fingers through his hair and smiled a wry smile; now he was a doctor, offering a self-diagnosis. To place himself in a better frame of mind he left the house, made his way along the beach road and sat facing the sea. His thoughts centred on Shafiq. Jawad was a sly bastard and maybe, just maybe, he wouldn't head for Yarmouth. He'd hole up somewhere else, somewhere familiar. He toyed with an idea, punched in the numbers and rested the phone against his face.

"Pinkie, you old bastard, what are you up to?"

"Tommo, as if you didn't already know." The reply came in a low voice.

"Yeah, I heard a few rumours. Reckon I'll pop over for a couple of days, chew over old times," Gillet said, attempting to sound casual. "Give me your address and I'll see you later this evening."

*

Pinkie lived in Luton, and it was the first time that Gillet had ever visited his home. Parked on the gravel drive he looked up at the large Georgian-fronted house and gave a low whistle. Six bedrooms, a double garage and manicured gardens, no way did it look the kind of place a hairy-arsed Para could afford. The large oak door opened and he glanced at Pinkie framed in the doorway. He looked much the same as the last time he'd seen him, apart from the fact he moved differently than before; not jerky, but with slow stork-like paces.

"Good to see you. How's it going, mate?"

Pinkie's eyes flitted over every aspect of his friend's face as if struggling to form recognition.

"Fucking hell, you look ready for the knacker's yard. I suppose you know all about me and my fracas with the army?" he said, raising a defensive wall.

"Some. How the fuck did you get away with the drug rap?"

"I told them I couldn't remember anything due to stress. Drink?"

"Beer. And they believed it?"

"Come on, mate, you know the score, regimental honour and all that shit. By the time I'd spilled the beans about what really went on they couldn't throw me out quick enough."

"What about the stress bit?"

"Yeah, well that's something else," Pinkie said in a quiet voice. "I didn't know I was suffering from it until the doctors told me; it creeps up on you. Been on medication ever since."

Gillet took a pull from the can and looked around at the room. Pinkie had always been the clever type, smart, always in the know, with sharp opinions on the way the world should be run. If he had a fault it was his downright untidiness, he was the kind of man who could enter a throne room and turn it into a rubbish tip by just standing there. Yet the house was neat and tidy. No old newspapers, magazines or dirty plates strewn around like you might expect from a man that lived alone. Pinkie watched Gillet's eyes rake the room. He wasn't here on a social visit that was for sure. Gillet didn't do social, and sooner or later the stunted conversation would come to an abrupt end and his former comrade-in-arms would post what it was he wanted. Gillet took a couple of shambling steps and joined him by the window, his hands forced deep into his trouser pockets.

"This PTSD, or whatever they call it, what's it like?"

Pinkie's anticipation rose; now they were closing in on the trurth.

"I attend counselling twice a week; apart from that I take anti-depressants and try to forget about the past. You ought to try it sometime."

"Why would I want to do that?"

"Stop kidding yourself, Tommo. You displayed all the symptoms the minute you walked through the door; the way you move, your eye movements, your aggressiveness. Take my advice and get help, before it's too late."

Gillet stared. He knew he needed help, and so did Pinkie. A burgeoning sense of optimism prompted his response.

"I can't, not yet," he said gruffly. "I've got things to do."

"Bullshit! *Won't*, you mean. For God's sake, don't tell me you are still wasting your time chasing after that kid? Let it go, he doesn't give a shit for you."

Gillet stood as if imprisoned in a room without windows or doors. His world once so coherent had disappeared into the farthest confines of his memory. He slumped into a chair, diminished, afraid to face his friend, afraid that he was able to see all the things he refused to admit to himself. Pinkie had seen it all before and wasn't going to waste his time offering Gillet comprehensible advice he was certain he'd ignore. Careful of his own fragile condition, he avoided looking at Gillet. Over the years, he and Gillet had formed a steady friendship in spite the opposition of character. It seemed like fragments of another era.

"Okay, let's just say I did treatment, where can I buy these anti-depressants?" Gillet grunted.

Pinkie smiled, and shaking his head from side to side rummaged in a drawer inches from where he sat, and pulled out three small white boxes.

"These are only available on prescription. Take them, I don't need them anymore. But I'll tell you something for nothing, Tommo, when you called this morning I didn't want to see you, because I knew with you around I might suffer a relapse. But it's worked in reverse; seeing the fucking state you are in has made me feel stronger."

"Cheers, mate, glad to be of help," Gillet half sneered.

"Don't be stupid. The doctors told me to try and recall my nightmares during the day, then change them around to the way I would like them to be; that way they cease to be nightmares and become dreams," Pinkie said in a soft voice. "I don't see three kids by the roadside with their throats slit any more, thank God, I see them waiting for more sweets when we return from patrol. I see three Taliban bastards in a ditch with their throats slit, and that makes me as happy as a fucking pig in a sty full of truffles. It might sound silly, but it works."

"Yeah, I'll give it a try. So what do you do with yourself these days?"

"What I've been doing for the past few years, pushing drugs. Where the fuck do you think all of this came from?" he said, gesturing with his arms.

Gillet greeted the remark with measured calmness. There had been times in the past when he'd considered Pinkie an enigma, unsure which way he'd turn at a moment's notice. He shook his head from side to side before answering.

"You always were a slow learner, Pinkie, that's what held you back in the army."

"Fuck the army, they didn't give a fuck for me, nor I them. Where's the moral justification in sending soldiers to die if the poor bastards don't have a clue what they are trying to achieve? My time in the Paras was a front. Eh, who'd suspect a soldier serving in Afghanistan would be running a drug ring?" Pinkie chuckled. "I've got police forces from five counties on my books, plus magistrates and councillors. The pious dickheads that beat their gums about the evil of drugs have kids on my books. Haloes are ten a penny these days, Tommo, but honesty and integrity; you couldn't buy that with all the oil in Saudi Arabia."

"Yeah, well, you are not in the army anymore."

"Makes no difference, mate, I was planning to buy my release anyway. I have six carriers bringing heroin in from Afghanistan, including an officer in a Guards' regiment and a medical officer. And I'm making inroads to supply North London. Few months from now I'll be living a millionaire's life in Portugal, and you can stick this piddling little knackered country up your arse. Blair and Brown didn't have a fucking clue, and Cameron doesn't know which way his arse hangs. That's what fucked this country, third-rate wankers fit for fuck-all who consider themselves politicians."

"Leave it out for fuck sake, what are you going to do in Portugal, sit round a pool drinking cold beer for the rest of your life?" Gillet smirked. "You won't last five minutes."

"We'll see. Now the niceties are over, perhaps you can tell me why you are here."

Seldom did Pinkie out-argue Gillet. But he did that day, and he decided it best not to press the subject; nothing was normal anymore and the past never went away, it just waited, patient, like a relentless ticking clock.

"I need your help to find someone, someone who might be here, in Luton."

"Sure, got a name?"

"His name is Rupert Singh, calls himself Jawad. Mixed race, English mother, Indian father; he's involved in the *Bacha Bazi* set-up. Slave-trafficking children from Afghanistan for under-age sex in the UK. He was raised in Luton, and I have a hunch he is here hiding with Shafiq."

Pinkie listened to Gillet's account of the last few months without interruption. He didn't feel open to any sentimentality concerning Shafiq or his predicament, but because of their past military association he would help Gillet. Now that he was on the road to a full recovery the quicker he was out of his hair the better. He didn't tell Gillet the tablets he had given him might take anything from two to four weeks to kick in, even then there was no guarantee the response would be beneficial. The psychological aspect might help, like a doctor giving an elderly lady a bottle of multicoloured sweets and telling her all her pains will disappear after two days.

"Kitchen's through there." He nodded. "Make the coffee while I make a few calls. If this guy uses the mosques, it should be easy enough to track him down."

*

Jawad walked across the shopping precinct towards the town centre. The sound of early morning traffic and pavements crowded with people rushing to places of employment did little to disturb his thoughts. His eyes lacked sparkle. Behind him, Luton's central mosque loomed up into the stark vaporous sky, its cold uninspiring shape besieged by teeming early morning worshippers. That which he had thought long dead and buried rose to haunt him and he quickened his pace, as if he might leave it behind. In his subconscious he racked his memory for the ten *Thou shalt not*'s of God's commandments; he managed six, the others refused to come to mind. The once formidable front door of his mind had slammed shut, blocking out all past thoughts of Allah, Mohammed the Prophet and all that concerned Islam. He had tested his resolve by entering the mosque in Bury Park, and the moment he heard the call to prayer he felt like a stranger in a land where he didn't belong, and turned and left. Now his mind teemed with memories of gentler boyhood days in the huge St Mary's Church in the town centre. The time spent with his mother, late brother, and sister, Jazzy, who had married a Dutchman called Adrian and lived and worked in the diamond houses of Amsterdam. Every Sunday they sang to tunes like 'Onward Christian Soldiers', and many other inspiring renditions. Later, during the journey home, they had stopped at the beef-burger bar.

On the spur of the moment he took a taxi to the west side of Luton, as if lured back to a place where he might cleanse his soul and make his wrongs right. Hands pushed deep into his pockets, he stood and stared up at the large detached house where his parents had raised him. It hadn't changed, apart from the different curtains installed by the new owners. It was still the same Victorian house where his father had berated him for being a bad son to his mother and a disappointment to his family. Solid and formidable, the house was built like a fortress ready to repel unwanted invaders. Forgotten memories returned with crystal clarity, and he picked out the good bits of his childhood, discarding the rest into the waste bin of oblivion. In the beginning he thought perhaps it was too late to change. But he knew it was never too late to start a new life, free of violence in the name of a religion that had diminished in his mind. The world of Islam as he knew it had turned sour with its unseen consequences; its constant violence disgusted him and he felt confused over which was wrong and which was right. At the end of the street, he turned for one more look as if he would never again set eyes on the font of his upbringing. Time stood still, yet time, still or otherwise, was the greatest of healers. He didn't feel remote or perturbed at his sudden unforeseen loss of faith; if anything, he felt somehow relieved. He'd made up his mind; he would return to India and make his peace with those whom he loved the most, and in return loved him.

*

Shafiq slept with an uncluttered mind. At seven o'clock the following morning, he searched for his clothes he'd left scattered on the bedroom floor. They lay laundered and folded on the table by the window. Fearful of disturbing the fresh crispness of his trousers and softness of the sweatshirt he dressed, and in spite of the early hour made his way to the barn housing the donkeys.

"Cast your eyes upon this, my four-legged friends," he said, waving the bottle hanging from his neck in front of their melancholic eyes. "Before you is the soil from the land of my forefathers, and who knows, perhaps even yours. Someday I shall return and again breathe the cool fresh air from the mountains, away from the smell of fumes and big cities."

The old donkey unfit for work raised his head to let out a breathless rasp.

"Ah, so you mock my words. We shall see."

Bella leaned against the open door to the barn, coffee in hand she watched him groom the donkeys. She failed to understand the donkeys' ready response to his commands, as if already an invisible bond had grown between them.

"You love animals, I can see that," she said as he slapped the last donkey across the rump and sent it trotting to rejoin the others in the outside pasture.

"Are they not God's creatures the same as us? Do they not carry the burdens of men for little reward and without complaint?" he said in a serious voice. "For this alone they should be held in high regard and treasured."

Bella fidgeted with the empty cup, and without a word walked away. Her face flamed with embarrassment at what she took to be a sharp rebuke for the manner in which she eked out a meagre living. Five minutes later, her guilt turned to astonishment as she sat at the kitchen table, watching him devour his third bowl of porridge. A wry smile crossed her lips.

"Cheeky little sod," she muttered to herself, and left the table to answer a knock on the door.

The small man standing in the doorway dressed in a well-cut black suit with a matching skullcap on his head smiled. In spite of this, the intensity in his eyes never wavered and she felt the stirring of trouble.

"Can I help you?" she said.

"Good morning, madam, I believe you have a young runaway by the name of Shafiq staying with you?"

"Do you?"

"Yes, I do. I am his uncle and I wish to return him to his parents. You know what young boys are like," he said, attempting flippancy.

"Chaffinch," she called, blocking the doorway with her plump frame.

Shafiq appeared. His eyes widened and he staggered back at the sight of Imam. His foot became entangled in the thick hessian doormat and he fell to the floor.

"Please, Miss Bella, do not let him take me. This is the man who beats me and forces me to do bad things against the will of Allah," he cried, covering his face with his hands.

"Come, Shafiq, enough of this nonsense," the man said, reaching out. "Your parents worry over you."

"Please, you must believe me, he lies. My parents are dead, killed by the Taliban. This is my home now."

She pulled the boy to his feet and turned to the Imam.

"Get off my property."

"Please, I beg you do not be so foolish. If I must I will put this matter in the hands of the police."

"Alright, you've said your piece, now sod off."

His smile hardened.

"I warn you, madam, you are making a great deal of unnecessary trouble for yourself," he said, walking away.

Shafiq sat with his elbows rested on the kitchen table, his chin cradled in his palms, and in his own time he told Bella the whole sad story. Almost unable to understand his incredible tale, she gave up and stared into his face. He raised his head and returned her stare with pleading eyes, and with a runny nose he slid his hand across the tabletop and grasped her fingers. The tremble in his shoulders extended to his hand and she tightened her grip and raised his hand to her lips. Her action caught her by surprise. What did she know of children? Years ago, to her husband's disgust, her doctor told her she was unable to give birth. Since that day she had refused to allow herself nature's call for carnal demands and a wide abyss separated her from maternal thoughts; because of this her marriage had floundered. But this day something inside her stirred, something she had never experienced before, a motherly tenderness. She moved around the table, and holding him in her arms soothed away his fears until the floodgates opened and hot salty tears streamed down her face. He squirmed and his arms slipped around her neck, afraid any moment she would push him away.

Noon that day, Shafiq watched the 4x4 pull into the yard. Three men stepped from the vehicle. Dressed in leather bomber jackets and denims, they made their way to the house and entered without knocking.

"Hello, Bellarose," John Flynn said in his thick Irish brogue. "I hear you've had a spot of bother."

"You could say that, Pa. It's good to see you've bought my two handsome brothers with you."

"Will you be wanting us to hang around for a few days, just in case this weirdo turns up with the police? If there's one thing that puts the shits up the police it's travellers, and there's plenty more where we came from. Now show me the boy."

As they sipped hot coffee, they listened as Shafiq related much the same story he'd told Bella. John Flynn pulled his fingers through his wild greying hair.

"Mother of Mary, I've never heard the likes," he said, pulling out a tin box of tobacco and rolling a thin cigarette.

"One thing's for sure," Danny, Bella's eldest brother, said, "from what the kid has told us, whoever the foreign bastard was that knocked on your door I'm certain he won't come back with the police."

"It's settled then, he'll more than likely return with a gang of his cronies and try to take the kid by force," Billy, the youngest brother, said, taking the tobacco tin from his father.

John Flynn raised an eyebrow.

"Take the boy back to the site for the time being, Danny, and tell my darling wife Jess not to let him out of her sight. You know what to bring back, and you might bring Biff."

"Okay, Pa. Come on, kid."

Shafiq didn't move and rocked back and forth, rubbing his hands up and down his thighs.

"You can stay here if it makes you feel better, chaffinch," she said in a gentle voice. "But you have to promise me you'll keep out of trouble until this mess is sorted."

*

"Best stay away from alcohol when taking the tablets," Pinkie warned Gillet.

He was wasting his breath; it was like telling a drowning man not to drink the water. Gillet pushed his drink to one side and watched Pinkie check his phone for incoming texts. Leaning across the bar, he asked the barman for a bottle of Evian and popped the pills into his mouth.

"No sign of this Jawad fella. Sure he's in Luton?"

"He's here, I can feel it in my bones."

"What are you going to do with him when you find him?"

"If he doesn't tell me where Shafiq is, maybe I'll cut his balls off and leave him to bleed to death. Come on, let's get out of here."

"Yeah, I know a couple of clubs in the town centre where the classy pussy hangs out."

"I'm not bothered with all that shit right now."

"Come on, let yourself go for once. If you can't score, you can always knock one unconscious with your gammy foot."

"You can be a right prick at times." Gillet grinned.

It was the usual for a Thursday night; quiet, everybody at home gearing up for the coming weekend. That or the benefit money had run out. Turning a corner with a patisserie on their left, they made their way down the sodium-lit street. Halfway down, Pinkie stopped, tapped on a black painted door and waited. The sound of wood sliding on wood produced a narrow strip of light.

"Yeah, who is it?" a voice said. The accent wasn't local, more northern; Manchester, or somewhere in that area.

"Pinkie."

Gillet never heard the crash of drawing bolts. His interest was in the man crossing the road carrying a plastic bag of groceries from an all-night corner shop. His muscles tensed. Laughter mingled with loud music poured out onto the street, disturbing the stillness of night. The man turned and stared, his eyes hooked into Gillet's face, and he blinked as if someone had thrown a handful of sand in his face.

"Jawad, you bastard," Gillet breathed, lunging forward.

The bag slipped from Jawad's hands, the contents spilled onto the road, his jaw sagged as if he'd seen a ghost. Revulsion surged up through Gillet's chest. He stepped forward, and broke into a hobble cursing his artificial foot for holding him back as the distance between them reduced. Jawad staggered back, sensing the fractional difference between life and death. Through the cold rays of the moon streaking down from the night sky, he saw those same unforgiving eyes intent on his death. He turned and ran, listening to the uneven sound of Gillet's pounding feet close behind. Gillet tried to reduce the distance, but hindered by his false foot, Jawad pulled easily away into the dark shadowy side streets. Heaving for his breath, Gillet abandoned the chase and limped to the corner where the main road ran past, and hailed a passing taxi. He recalled Pinkie's words and took the key concealed beneath a brick, entered the house, phoned Pinkie and waited. His head felt empty, like a balloon on a piece of string, and raising his foot onto a stool he inspected his leg. When he pressed his thumb to his ankle he winced; it hurt like hell and he cursed his inability to run Jawad down. Pinkie's advice to take matters easy for a few days had become no more than a passing fancy, and his face hardened. Turn the bad dreams around in your mind during daylight, Pinkie had said. It had a ring of sense about it. At least he was in the right place, and his nightmares might become a dream made in heaven when he had his hands around Jawad's neck. His elation was short-lived; it might take weeks, even months to rid himself of his ailment. He needed to act now, before it was too late. A key grating in the front door lock interrupted his thoughts.

Pinkie grinned, like always.

"Don't tell me, let me guess, you caught him and ripped his head off?"

"Bollocks."

"He'll run for Yarmouth now, hole up in that mosque the kids told you about."

"Yeah, that's what I thought, probably on his way there this minute; time I was gone."

"Don't be a fool; we'll leave together tomorrow after light. Try to relax."

If Gillet harboured the slightest hint of gratitude it didn't show; instead, he pondered on what to do next, but Pinkie's words made sense.

"Sounds good, I'll see you in the morning," he said.

Pinkie listened to Gillet's irregular steps thumping on the staircase. It had been a long day, and he flicked on the TV to watch the late-night news. He knew it was going to happen, under the circumstances it was inevitable, and clasping his head between his hands he felt dread grasp his insides.

"Fuck you, Tommo, you bastard," he said, feeling the old familiar wave of depression creep into his bones and suck at his mind. "Fuck you."

*

Time, and fear for his life was uppermost in Jawad's mind. His fingers had felt like sausages as he fumbled to pack his sparse belongings in readiness for the journey to Yarmouth. Gripped with a mixture of misery and fear, he thumped his fist against the steering wheel. Gillet was a persistent bastard, a manic depressive who had threatened to find his parents and flush them down the toilet, and he believed him. He discarded the word persistent, and added the word insane. Or maybe he wasn't either; perhaps he was unstable, deranged, with homicidal tendencies. Whatever it was, it didn't stop his face muscles from twitching. Tonight was a matter of needs as needs must, he would stay in the mosque for personal safety, after which he'd relinquish his Muslim faith forever. Before dawn the following morning, he'd leave for Heathrow Airport and the comparative safety of India with his parents. If Gillet attempted to make good his threats, he knew of ways and means to stop him once and for all.

CHAPTER THIRTEEN

Gillet had swallowed two of the anti-depressant pills the previous night in the hope of a decent night's sleep. Whether or not they were the reason for his peaceful slumber, he couldn't hazard a guess. Nevertheless, as Mondays went, he felt relaxed. At last day turned to night; ribbons of pink and gold stretched across the dark blue sky. The coffee tasted good and raised his spirits. At the sound of Pinkie stirring, he dropped a spoonful of the dark brown powder into a mug and added hot water; black with no sugar, he recalled, was how Pinkie liked his coffee.

Pinkie glowered over his second mug. He'd had a shit night tossing and turning, and wasn't in the mood for light conversation, especially not with the likes of Gillet. Right now he preferred the company of rabid dogs.

"We'll take my car and stop for breakfast, my treat," Gillet said, tugging on his jacket. "If you want to change your mind, that's fine by me, I understand."

"Did I say I didn't want to come? Did I?" Pinkie grunted.

"No."

"Then don't do my thinking for me, alright?"

Gillet shrugged, climbed into the car and waited. Pinkie hadn't changed. Not even Kylie Minogue in the buff could raise a smile from him at this time of the morning. At Newmarket, after chomping through a full English breakfast, he began to display signs of normality.

"We could be in deep shit if you kill Jawad," Pinkie said.

"Maybe."

"No fucking maybe about it. I don't want to be involved in a murder case, you lunatic."

*

Jawad wiped a clammy hand over his sweating brow and looked at the Imam as if he had just been poked with an electric cattle prod. He knew who he was and of his reputation as a cruel weasel of a man with a penchant for inflicting pain on small boys. Rumour had it he'd buggered a couple of nine-year-old boys to death.

"What do you mean, he's escaped?" Jawad said, his eyes widening.

"He is sheltering with a woman on the edge of the town. She is nothing, a stupid bitch operating a herd of donkeys on the beach," the Imam said, his penetrating eyes staring into Jawad's face. "Soon four men will arrive. Go with them, and don't return without the boy. How you do it is up to you, but I want the boy back here alive."

Realising that any further involvement with Shafiq would increase his odds of coming face-to-face with Gillet, uneasiness crept into his bones. The flight he'd booked from Heathrow for that morning now worth jack-shit.

"Fuck Shafiq and fuck you, you murdering bastard," he mumbled under his breath, regretting his decision to return to the mosque.

He wanted to tell the Imam he didn't like him and never had; hebhad a stench of self-delusion about him, like a small-town politician keen on forming the next government. His first thought was to distance himself from the everlasting brutality he had allowed himself to become embroiled in. But that would make his position more precarious; he daren't allow them to discover that his union with Islam had become frayed and estranged. With his knowledge of the child trafficking operation he would never be allowed to live, and he slunk away to a small anteroom, away from the main hall, and sat with his arms folded on a metal table. For all his misgivings, his world was crumbling. No longer the master of his own destiny he listened to the Imam rant about the evils of the Western world to a group of young boys with no other thoughts than to play the latest shoot-up game on PlayStation. Every other word accompanied by a series of kicks and slaps, followed by yelps of pain. The door swung open and he stared up at the four heavyset men. His nervousness turned to anger. He wanted to tell them that in future, knock on doors before entering. A huge black African with flared nostrils pressed flat against his face stared at him with eyes the size of billiard balls. The others, white, untidy and unshaven, slouched behind him; the local hard cases were out to play.

"Let's get it done, man," the black man said.

The car pulled to a stop on the mud road leading to Bella's bungalow. Jawad's nervousness reached fever pitch, and the hairs on his neck stood upright like the quills on a hedgehog's back. A flock of starlings, startled by the slamming car doors, rose as one from the thick gorse hedgerow. Their fluttering wings, like a muted drum roll, turned his legs to rubber. The image of Gillet speared into his mind and he stared at the bungalow, certain that he was inside watching his every move.

"Okay, one of you remain in the car in case we need to leave in a hurry," the black man said, jerking his head. "Jawad, you do the talking. If she refuses to hand over the boy, we'll take him by force."

Jawad, feeling as if he was having an out-of-body experience, pulled himself together, swallowed and prepared to meet his nemesis. Ignoring the broken brass door knocker, he rapped on the door and stepped back. Inside the sound of footsteps drew nearer, his heart rate increased and his Adam's apple lodged in his throat. The door swung open, revealing a woman with bulging breasts. When he opened his mouth to speak, his tongue was dry.

"I have been sent by the authorities to take the boy into care. Please, it is in your best interest to hand him over without any fuss, and we can be on our way," he said, forcing out the words in a nasal whine.

His words meant little or nothing to Bella. All her life she had been a traveller used to dealing with authority; quarrelling a part of her everyday life.

The sound of a shotgun from the direction of the car, followed by the piercing shriek of an injured man cranked up the dread surging throughout his body. When Bella slammed the door, he heaved a great sigh of relief.

"Is there something you'll be wanting?" a voice drifted from behind him.

Jawad swayed, and he prayed to both Allah and the Christian God for a painless ending. Whether through fear or cowardice he remained stationary, staring at the closed door as if it led to hell. His three accompanists turned to face John and Billy Flynn. A donkey brayed, the rasping sound softened by the distance.

"We don't want any trouble, man. Give us the boy and we'll be on our way," the African spoke first.

John Flynn chuckled. "You are already in trouble, sonny, unless you fuck off and take your black arse and your dozy morons with you," he said.

"Hey, man, you don't listen too well, we don't want any tro..." the African started.

John Flynn raised the shotgun and pulled the trigger.

"That was a warning, lads. I'll take your heads off with the second barrel, so I will." John Flynn smiled.

A stream of obscenities fell from the African's mouth. He recognised Flynn and knew of his reputation. He was a man the police avoided. For a second he imagined what it might be like to stand up to him, ignore his threats and call his bluff. Overnight he'd become a local hero able to charge twice the amount for his services. Sticky sweat formed between his shoulder blades and pins and needles ran down his arms to his fingertips. Then the cold twist of vexation when he realised he didn't possess the bottle to put his thoughts into action.

His mood dipped as the bungalow door swung open and Shafiq hurled himself at Jawad cowering on the ground.

"Pig, pig, you filthy pig. Allah will punish you and those like you that beat innocent boys and make them do bad things," he screamed, raining kicks and feeble blows at Jawad.

Jawad raised his hands to protect himself and his hand brushed Shafiq's face, sending him tumbling to the ground with blood pouring from his nose. The African lunged at Shafiq and scooped him up, with his knife point pricking into the boy's throat. John Flynn lowered the shotgun and pulled the trigger. The African's left foot disappeared in a mess of bloody flesh and he crumbled to the ground, whimpering. White-faced, the remaining two men backed away with their arms outstretched. Jawad scrambled to his feet, eager to join them.

"Stay where you are, bastard," John Flynn roared.

Jawad stopped in his tracks; fear hung on him like a wet woollen robe.

"You two, take the black man with you. If I ever see either of you again you'll end up the same," Flynn said, turning his attention to Jawad. "You, my friend, are coming with us."

Jawad felt the need to plead his case, tell anyone who would listen that he no longer recognised Islam as his divine inspiration. Convince them that the godlessness and profane practices he had witnessed, had shattered his faith in the Koran forever. And he wanted to make amends, reparation, anything that might help to clear his conscience. But his feelings became crowded with nothingness. What was done was done, the time had come to pay for his past mischief.

Altogether there were thirty caravans spread about the site. An old disused parking lot behind an empty factory awaiting redevelopment acted as their home. Scattered around the litter and mess were expensive vehicles, Mercedes cosied next to 4x4s with no visible tax discs displayed on the front windows. Dogs sniffed at Shafiq for unwanted food, growling at anyone they considered a threat. From somewhere the smell of frying sausages filled Jawad's nostrils, reminding him he hadn't eaten that day. On the perimeter, away from the site, a large bonfire made of burning tyres served as an incinerator for plastic bags of waste. Nearby, three tethered ponies shook their heads and whinnied at the thick black smoke invading their sensitive nostrils.

John Flynn stepped from the pickup, jerked his thumb and waited as Jawad clambered down from the back.

"What are we going to do with him, Pa?" Jimmy Flynn said.

"We'll keep him for a few days and wait to see what happens. In the meantime, lock him in the horsebox out of the way."

"And the kid?"

"He's free to come and go as he pleases. It's up to him whether or not he stays with Bella."

Shafiq sensed a tremor of exhilaration. It wasn't Afghanistan, but it was the nearest to home he'd seen for a long time. In place of mud dwellings, metal caravans, horses replaced donkeys, goats and dogs, the same everywhere, searched for food to satisfy an eternal hunger. A little more dust accompanied by a searing sun and he might be back in the village of his birth with his parents and sisters. Billy Flynn brushed his shoulder as he pushed Jawad towards the horsebox. Shafiq's right hand curled around the handle of the bread knife he had stolen from Bella's kitchen earlier. The bruises on his body ached. His hatred for Jawad and the Imam obliterated all forms of reality from his mind, tenderness and common decency purged from his soul. Right now, more than anything he wanted to even the score for the pain he'd endured. When a firm hand gripped his shoulder he shook it away, resisting the urge to pull the knife concealed in his waistband. He could smell it, taste it and breathe it, the sweet cut of revenge. Everything turned cold within him, his eyes flashed and he panted like a dog straining on a leash. A hand grabbed at his waistband and pulled the knife away. He stood with his feet apart, breathing heavily through his nose. He didn't want to calm down, he needed his anger to fuel his hate as pressure swelled inside his head, forcing against the walls of his skull. Bella's shadow blocked the heat of the sun. He didn't want to look into her eyes; at that moment he no longer cared what she or anyone else thought of him. She never spoke, but moved away with the knife in her hand, and the sun's rays returned to heat his face. All he had was her; there was no one else to care for and protect him. Apart from his religion and the blessing of Allah, there was nothing to stop the coldness of loneliness ripping his soul apart. She was his only friend, apart from Luke, and he was somewhere secure and safe with his father. His unrelenting weariness challenged all other feelings, his shoulders sagged and a sneer hid his face. How dare something as

307

common as tiredness rob him of the one thing he wanted more than anything else in life, the chance to see Jawad kicking and screaming as he had when he tried to avoid the Imam's stinging blows? But he wanted more; he wanted to see him mutilated, covered in blood, twitching and writhing for his last breath before he jerked and lay still.

"Chaffinch!" Bella called. "What do you want to eat?"

"Burgers and chips," he said, his sudden smile breaking his brooding thoughts. "With baked beans, please."

Reluctantly he stepped forward, and stored away his memory for another time. It would come when needed; it wasn't over, not yet. Drawing level with her she held out her hand, and without thinking reached out and slipped his small fist into her meaty grip. She smiled to let him know she was aware of his feelings and would always be there to care for him. Instead of returning the smile, he shuddered. How could she know how he felt? His eyes were lifeless, dull and as cold as a dagger's blade.

It was cold when Shafiq slipped from the caravan in the dead of night. The wind honed sharp, rolling eastward across the North Sea, taking all before it. He knew where they were, he'd seen them the moment he had entered the campsite. The two Dobermans that acted as guard dogs during the night were chained to the rusting hatchback used as a kennel against any sudden change in the weather. The clink of chain leashes dulled by darkness as he squatted and waited. They came hesitant at first, then willingly. Earlier, after Bella had cooked him burgers and chips, he'd slipped the burgers into his pocket without her knowing and fed them to the dogs. Now they trusted him, and he spoke in a soft hushed voice, pushing his face into their shoulders to muzzle his scent into their nostrils. They licked his face with wet tongues and raised their paws. Satisfied they were at ease, he slipped off the chains. They looked up into his face, their mouths open and panting, eyes expectant.

"Hut-hut," he snapped, walking away.

Briskly crossing the site and heading for the horsebox, they trotted at his side. Rather than snap a command, he raised a finger, and they sat watching as he loosened the bar holding the horsebox tailgate in place, then lowered the ramp. He did not look at Jawad struggling to his feet. Instead, he crouched and whispered to the two dogs, then pointed to the interior of the horsebox. As if they understood his words, their slavering lips quivered over razor-sharp teeth. Their heads turned to stare at Jawad pressed against the rear of the horsebox. He knelt and faced Shafiq, and when he saw the look of naked hate he knew his time had come. He was a sinner, condemned, unclean. A frown creased his brow and he looked up at the dark sky.

"Jesus, son of God," he whispered. "Forgive me my sins."

"Hut-hut," Shafiq snapped.

The dogs bounded up the wooden ramp. Razor-sharp fangs sank into Jawad's neck, tearing at the flesh, cutting off the scream. The second dog clamped its jaws into Jawad's thigh and shook its head from side to side until Jawad sank to the floor. Frenzied, the dogs tore flesh from bone until Jawad lay still, in a spreading pool of blood. Shafiq watched, part of him excited; then returned the dogs to the wreck and replaced the leashes. Satisfaction hauled across his mouth and lightened his features as he watched the dogs clean the blood from their faces and paws. Throwing caution aside, he raised the tailgate and locked it into position, and kneeling, faced towards Mecca. He thanked Allah for the strength and fortitude to punish those who had sinned against him.

*

Pinkie tapped his knee in time to the drone of the present-day music filtering from the car radio and glanced through the gloom at the mosque. He didn't know the name of the artist singing the song. It all sounded the same, mournful, depressing crap, fit for a funeral, and enough to drive the sane to suicide. Next to him, looking ready at any moment to fall into a deep sleep, Gillet sat with his mouth open.

"They must have stopped praying by now," Pinkie said, glancing at his watch.

"Yeah," Gillet grunted. "I'll go around the back and look for a way inside; you wait by the front entrance, just in case Jawad is in there and tries to make a break for it."

It was dark at the rear of the mosque, unlit, without shadows. Gillet waited for his eyes to become accustomed to the gloom before moving. Two black fire doors he discounted; they opened from the inside. A few feet either side of the doors two windows protected by metal security bars concreted into the brickwork also made entry impossible. To his right, he craned his neck and glanced up at the ten-feet-high wall separating the mosque from the building next door. It reached halfway up to the flat roof, even on his toes he would still be a couple of feet short of the roof. Pulling the box of painkillers from his pocket, he pushed three into his mouth and with a gob of saliva forced them down his throat. At first he gave scant regard for the pile of plastic milk crates stacked next to a wheelie bin, and then paused to stare up at the wall one more time. Maybe it would and maybe it wouldn't, but it was worth a try. Hooking two crates over his arm, he climbed onto the bin and made his way along the wall until level with the mosque. With one crate placed on top of the wall, he stepped up and heaved his body onto the roof. Of the three reinforced glass skylights, two glowed through the frosted glass, signalling the rooms below were lit and inhabited; the third unlit. For ten minutes he struggled to prise open the darkened skylight. A wind fresh from the sea rose and swept across his face, cool and refreshing, and he gave up his futile efforts; it was impossible to force a way in without breaking the reinforced glass. Nerves jumped beneath his skin like tiny voracious insects, their claws and teeth tearing at his flesh, eating him alive. Sweat sprung from his face, and ripping off his jacket he laid it across the window. In a fit of temper he stamped down with his foot; nothing. He stamped again, this time bringing all his weight to bear. At last the window fractured, unclasping his knife he prised away the shards of glass until he'd formed a hole large enough to wriggle through. Peering down into the darkened room, he reminded himself that caution being the mother of survival, only a fool would drop through into the darkness. It had to be ten, maybe fifteen feet down at the most, no problem for a trained paratrooper. But what would break his fall? This wasn't the time to break a leg or sprain an ankle. A five-minute search produced two scaffold poles left behind by careless sub-contractors. One pole he passed through the broken skylight and shimmied down, listening for sound.

Three metres square, the room was shelved on three sides on which stood canisters and plastic bottles smelling of cleaning chemicals, against the wall a row of mops. He eased the door open. A muffled voice, followed by the sharp sound of a slap, preceded a long drawn-out groan which echoed along the corridor. In a crouch he made his way towards the end of the corridor and peered through the round glass porthole window. Unable to believe his eyes, he stood transfixed. A boy of no more than twelve years of age, naked apart from a pair of dirty trainers, stood with his legs apart, spread - eagled over a table. Behind him, a man with a flimsy unkempt beard in the process of loosening his clothing. The boy's legs buckled and he shrieked in fright of what was about to happen next; then jerked upright sending the table skidding across the room. Isolated in sexual frenzy, the man naked from the waist down, hurled words Gillet failed to understand. With no thought than to rid the earth of the inhuman creature, he pushed open the door and charged. The man sidestepped Gillet's clumsy attempt and their eyes met. Gillet's hands clutched at fresh air, and the throbbing pain in his head disappeared. His mind shut down and his eyes flooded with shock.

"Tubeh," he roared, crashing into a row of stacked chairs.

Anger tore him from the rest of the world; nothing mattered, just revenge against the man who had somehow survived drowning in the North Sea. Hurling the chairs barring his path to one side, he made his way towards the door through which Tubeh had disappeared. Plastered in sweat, his uncontrollable rage was so strong it threatened to rob him of his sight. He pushed down on the handle; the door was locked. Whether through divine providence or demonic intervention, he stood back and then threw himself at the door. The third time, it shattered. Now the death of Tubeh was of no consequence to him, merely an obligation to rid the world of scum. Way too late to change a habit of a lifetime, he brokered death like a judge with a hangover. Metres away, the front doors of the mosque swung loose and unattended in the cold easterly breeze. An image of Pinkie conjured up in his mind and he smiled. Good old reliable Pinkie, nothing would get by him. Outside, he inhaled and spat a gob of phlegm onto the pavement.

"Save the bastard for me, Pinkie," he roared into the night.

He heard him before he saw him, staggering with his hands clasped around his neck, trying to staunch the blood flowing through his fingers.

"Sorry, Tommo, bastard took me by surprise," Pinkie whispered.

Gillet stared at the knife handle jutting from his friend's neck. The curved blade had entered clear through one side and protruded from the other. Gillet tried to think of something to say, something that might make sense, but nothing came, no words of wisdom. He felt as if he was disintegrating, made of sand, and a great wind waited to blow him away.

"The beach, he headed for the beach, don't let the bastard get away," were the last words Pinkie uttered.

Gillet turned to face the beach. All signs of humanity inside his body incomprehensible. Only Tubeh's death would satisfy his lust and feed the force of man's most powerful weapon, revenge. He walked at first, steady and disciplined, and then broke into a determined jog.

Tubeh gripped his tunic and pulled it higher to allow his thin legs more freedom. Gillet would come for him; there were no two ways about that. In retrospect it may have been wiser to remain in the mosque, barricade himself in and call the police. They would come like they always did; the fools lived in fear of riling the Muslim community. The idea drained from his mind; if the police questioned the boy, his worldwide child trafficking operation would be exposed, bringing untold damage not only to the to the Muslim community of the UK, but the rest of the world. Beneath his naked feet the cold uneven pavement jarred and cut into his flesh. Unable to keep up the pace, he stopped, bent and rested his hands on his knees, then straightened at the sound of uneven footsteps drumming on the pavement. The intermittent slap followed by a thump drew closer. Like a frightened child he whimpered, hitched his tunic higher and ran for his life. His imagination played tricks with his mind, and he imagined he could feel Gillet's hot breath on his neck. His whimper changed to a strangulated sob and his plaintive wails rent the night air, much the same as the defenceless boys he buggered night after night to satisfy his demonic sexual appetite. Those same boys he defiled, and then tossed to one side as if they were no longer human. Then, without warning the ground gave way and he paddled in mid-air like a disjointed marionette with broken strings. Screams of terror poured from his chest and excrement burst from his bowels. He fell into something soft and looked around. In blind panic he had fallen from the concrete sea wall onto the beach. Just feet away the black menacing sea lapped towards him, as if seeking to pull him down into its deep depths, and then ebbed, stroking the churning sands smooth. On all fours he scrambled up against the side of the concrete wall, and scuttling like a crab made his way towards the pier jutting out into the sea like a long dark shadowy finger. After a few minutes he stopped and raised his head. Apart from the sound of the shifting sea, silence; an air of tranquillity reignited his calm. Part of him became excited and he closed his mouth to stifle the uncontrollable giggle. He had survived, and bested Gillet. Later, when certain he was clear of danger, he would return to the mosque, pack his belongings and continue his work in Cologne, Germany. Things always have a way of working themselves out.

His giggle rose to a cackling laugh and he buried his face in his hands to muffle the sound.

Further along the sea wall he slowed and strained his ears. Unsure, he held his breath and waited. Soft footsteps moving across the sand filled him with dread and his fear returned. Sucking for air, he stared at the pair of legs barring his way. Gillet stared down, his eyes slitted, devoid of sympathy. His mouth somehow different, twisted, deformed, shaped into a sneer of malevolence that even the strongest of men might balk. Tubeh worked his mouth, unsure whether to beg for forgiveness or curse his murderer before he died. No sound came and it no longer mattered. He closed his eyes, listening to the rise and fall of the sea blocking out all sound. He was going to die and nothing anyone said could alter that. Gillet gripped him by the back of his neck and forced him face down into the soft sand. Tubeh's legs straightened and jerked as if trying to free themselves from their joints. His hands scrabbled, sending up clouds of sand as he fought for air. Gillet pushed harder, until his struggling ceased and he lay lifeless. Gillet's head slumped with his chin rested on his chest. Tears ran down his face onto his lips, leaving the saltiness on the tip of his tongue. Inwardly he battled to bring his feelings to order, but nothing happened, and in desperation he beat his face with his fists. He no longer knew who he was, but what he had become. The inner regions of his mind tumbled with incoherent thoughts and he began to drag Tubeh's body towards the sea. Heaving the body into the cold murky water he pushed it down to make sure that this time Tubeh wouldn't survive. Satisfied, he watched the body drift away and sink out of sight.

The water felt cold and he thought it might wash him of his sins, swill away the taint of an executioner. He sneered and discounted Jawad's death as a favour to all mankind. Hollow-eyed, he stared into an abyss of darkness and tried to remember the past. To put a label on the places he'd seen, things he'd done and people he'd met. Always it was the same, nothing, as if he had never existed. Ready to put everything behind him and seek a permanent peace, his powerful strokes pulled him out to sea. He swam until his feet no longer touched the seabed, then turned to face the shore. In the distance the twinkle of yellowed street lights, the occasional sweep of flashing headlights disappearing from view. The ceaseless ebb and flow of the tide sucked at his body. His memory jarred. He'd been a soldier once, and a father, but not now. How could anyone ever love him? Not Luke and not Amy. He had brought about his downfall by refusing to accept his symptoms, his nervous disorders, or more bluntly his part lunacy. But that was how he was, the great invincible Gillet, the man that could steal the world from the shoulders of Atlas and hold it aloft with one hand. Coldness probed his bones, stiffening his muscles. He wasn't mad, he told himself, he was sane; he wasn't mad, he had a son to care for, and his life wasn't his to do with as he pleased. Relinquishing the black shadows lurking in the corners of his mind, he struck out for the shore.

CHAPTER FOURTEEN

Daylight came, slowly at first. Then rapidly, in a rush to expose the world for what it was – a place of contradictions, where men pushed against the flow of the tide, to fall at the ebb. Stretching and yawning he pulled himself to his feet. The sea had retreated into the distance, leaving the sand damp and smooth with scattered pools, a haven for tiny marine creatures waiting to rejoin the ocean when the moon returned. Glancing out at the horizon, he thought of the Afghan he'd drowned the night before. He neither smiled nor sneered, but no longer cared. Throughout the night he'd sat statue-like on the sea wall, working out which part of the past few months were reality and which were delusionary. Sure, he'd suffered from the stress of fighting on the front line in Afghanistan, who didn't? All soldiers in that environment suffered, that's why they were allowed a cooling-off period in places like Cyprus before being shipped home. It would never do for the population to see the truth – husbands, fathers and sons shaking and twitching like escapees from hell. Right now he felt fine, perhaps in the future he wouldn't. So what? Who would know the difference, or even care? Deep down his attitude towards life had become dominated by frustration. Shafiq had been an excuse to vent his anger, pay the world back for taking his foot. To his way of thinking that was reality, or maybe, after all, it was delusionary.

Right now the only thing he knew for sure was that he was cold and hungry. Even the death of his friend Pinkie seemed meaningless; men die, remorse no more than a waste of energy. Anyhow, a man who had the gall to use the regiment as a means of procuring drugs for profit was unfit to live. Then he rebuked himself for his spitefulness.

The sun broke through, and on the opposite side of the road a man from a corner café wedged the door open and dragged out a sandwich board extolling the day's culinary delights. A full English breakfast including a pot of tea for £4.99, written in bold multicoloured chalks, excited his hunger pangs. Delving into his pockets, he pulled out a wad of soaking wet ten-pound notes, flung them to the ground and made his way to the corner of Northgate Street. Skulking in the shadows, he watched the paramedics lift Pinkie's dead body onto a stretcher and then load him into the back of the waiting ambulance. Shuffling his feet, he waited for the police to disappear into the mosque. Later they would check every vehicle in close proximity, slipping into his car he parked further down in a side street. Opposite the mosque, a crowd of curious onlookers watched in silence, faces void of understanding. Others drifted away in twos and threes, whispering their verdicts, their morbid curiosity satisfied.

"Hello, anything interesting happening?" Gillet said, forcing a grin at an elderly woman walking her dog.

"Found a body they have, blood everywhere. Bloody Muslims are nothing but trouble," she answered.

"Anyone else come out, kids or anything?"

"No, just a boy with a blanket wrapped around his shoulders, crying his eyes out he were."

It was a long shot, but worth the chance. By a pillar box he hung around hoping Jawad, or Shafiq might make an appearance. The crowd dispersed, and those with business to attend to melted away with a gory tale to tell the family over dinner that night. Others remained, huddled in small groups discussing the sorry state of the country before moving away, shaking their heads with mock resignation.

Morning drifted into afternoon, his lonely vigil proved fruitless. Hands in pockets, he made his way down the road leading to the seafront. Unlike the self-deception of the previous night, now the death of Pinkie hung heavy on his mind. With elbows on the metal rails, he looked out over the sparkling sea, thinking how the starkness of daylight brought a different perspective to past events, made everything clearer, more concise; like trying to read a book in the gloom, then switching on a light and seeing the words and their meaning.

*

Billy Flynn half lowered the horsebox tailgate and stopped in his tracks at the sight of the mutilated body. A pool of thick black blood stained the vehicle's wooden floor, and the ramp slipped from his grip and crashed down in a cloud of dust. Bile jumped into his throat, rushing into his gaping mouth and he almost choked.

"Mary, mother of Jesus," he rasped. "Pa, you'd better come and see this for yourself."

John Flynn glanced up from the engine of the pickup, wiped his hands on an oily rag and strode towards the horsebox. No stranger to death, his younger days spent with the Real IRA had hardened him to atrocities. But the sight of Jawad took his breath away.

"Jasus. Find a secluded spot away from here and bury the body deep, then come back here and set fire to the horsebox," he said.

The door to Bella's caravan was unlocked. In no mood for niceties, John Flynn wrenched it open.

"Where's the boy?" he snapped at her.

"He's asleep, why?"

"Wake him," he said, muttering a string of curses. "It's gone eight; this isn't a fucking holiday camp."

John Flynn sat folding and unfolding his worn cloth cap. Behind the partition he heard movement, and pulling the cap over his head he began drumming his fists on the Formica tabletop. It had to be the boy; nobody else would dare do such a thing without his prior knowledge. Shafiq emerged from his makeshift bedroom, his eyes flickering beneath John Flynn's truculent stare. No one spoke as Shafiq's tongue darted in and out of his mouth, moisturising his dry lips.

"You young idiot, do you realise you have endangered every person on this site?" John Flynn said in a low voice. "Get your things together and get out of here."

Shafiq stiffened, and felt the need to curl up into a ball and hide under the nearest rock where no one would ever find him. He wanted somewhere safe to keep the constant misery of his life at bay, somewhere he could close his eyes and never have to open them again until the release of death beckoned him to a better place. Raising his hand to his chest, he gripped the bottle containing the soil of his homeland.

"Hold on, Pa, we can't just throw him out. He can come back to my place," Bella interrupted.

"Then leave now, I've others to think of," John Flynn said, slamming the door behind him.

The remainder of the day Shafiq stayed alone, trying to figure out a way to hold his life together. Time had passed since his worldly innocence had been wrenched from his fragile mind. Rejoicing in the knowledge that Jawad was at last dead he felt glad he had died in a horrible manner. Allah would smile on him for his actions, of that he was certain. Until that day he must find the strength to confront his present ordeal, the one that left him free from all hope. When they arrived at Bella's house, he declined the offer of a bed and slept in the barn with the donkeys. Next to them he felt closer to his homeland, he told her, and she never argued.

Next morning, before the advent of the dawn chorus, he rose and groomed the donkeys. As he talked and whispered, as if they understood each word he uttered, tears ran down his cheeks. The animals twitched their ears and waited for him to finish, then trotted outside to feast on the freshly dew-soaked grass. Bella, for all her faults, wasn't the kind to set herself up as a champion for the human race; most she'd known would better serve the world by leaping off the end of the pier with a bag of bricks tied round their ankles. Meanwhile, biting her lip to dam her emotions, she watched Shafiq and sensed a great wrongdoing that should be righted. If it made him happy, he was more than welcome to stay and act as her assistant, later perhaps become a partner. She'd never met anyone who could hold a candle to the manner in which he worked the animals. The way they responded to him was almost religious. But deep down, she knew he would never stay.

Zipping her coat up to her chin, she entered the barn. He greeted her with a tiny smile, the kind that requires effort, then stepped towards her and held out his right hand. His fingers slid across her roughened palm and she fought against the rising tears bubbling up into her eyes. Without thinking, she knelt and squeezed her eyes shut.

"Tell me, chaffinch," she said softly, "would you like to go home, back to Afghanistan?"

"Oh yes, I would like that very much," he said, withdrawing his hand from her grip and sliding his arms around her neck.

"Then so you shall," she said a little shrilly. "But first we will take the donkeys to the beach one more time, and later eat a fish and chip dinner with two helpings of your favourite dessert, mushy peas."

*

The sun had burned off the fragile mist hanging over the sea like a grey blanket, and Gillet stepped into the midst of the bewildered multitude of day trippers cramming all their energy into the short stay. Whatever the consequences, whatever the weather, they would show no reticence in an admirable display of British determination to enjoy their annual pilgrimage to the coast. He shuddered. Not at the cold, but the lingering stench of fish and chips, onion rings, kebabs, hot dogs, burgers and hot frying fat. He watched those around him gorge their carelessly cooked food, then stick their fingers into their mouths to lick away the glistening film of grease. At first he hesitated, waiting for it all to flow through him, wondering what he should do next. The crowd milled and uncoiled past him like a never-ending snake. Behind a bunch of teenage girls he waited at the crowded bar of the busy pub and ordered a pint of best bitter, before retreating to a secluded space a few paces from the door. Three pints and three whiskies later, the melancholy of loneliness rose inside him, dampening his already flagging spirits. When he saw her watching him a shadow flitted over his face. She spoke to her two companions and they turned and giggled. Somewhere in her early thirties and a little drunk, she smiled a friendly smile and gave a small wave as if to say, no need to be alone. Her make-up was minimal apart from a splash of pink lipstick, the same colour Amy used to wear, sticky, the kind that had made his lips want to cling to her forever. Briefly he mourned his loss, placed the glass on the bar and left.

Thanks to the weather, most holidaymakers thronged to the beach. On the opposite side of the road he found a cast-iron bench, and sat beneath a tree and looked out over the sea like he did on the north Norfolk coast. Overcome by the power of his memory, everything became clear again, as if he were reliving it. Then in an instant everything changed and his life raced, turning in ever-decreasing circles, and although he tried to keep up, everything seemed to be sliding away. Jawad could be anywhere by now, even back in Afghanistan. As for Shafiq, he dared not hazard a guess as to his whereabouts, and struggled to produce an image of his face in his mind. Then he did something he'd never done before, he searched for a hunch, like a gambler forced to trust his instinct. Nothing came, and puffing out his cheeks, he stretched the ache from his legs, stepped onto the yielding sand and walked in a straight line towards the receding sea. When the water lapped over his ankles, he stopped and closed his eyes. It was over; whatever it was he had hoped for in the past had died before the first green shoots had time to rear their heads. Throughout the day he walked, stopping to rest and clear his mind. Luke, poor old Luke; how much as a father he owed his son would take an age to calculate. How much his son missed him whenever he was away he never bothered to consider, he had sabotaged his schoolwork by acting dumb in the hope he would return from whichever theatre of war his career thrust him into. Drained, empty and washed up like the flotsam left by the retreating tide, the simple belief that he could make everything right no longer existed.

*

Almost unable to live with his joy, Shafiq leapt from Bella's horsebox, his heart bursting with happiness. Should his smile expand any further, his face would split in two. The sweet illusion that displayed a mask of innocence had returned, raised from out of the pit of uncertainty with a fierce determination. Once more he became Shafiq, the boy who had assisted the likes of Mister Sergeant for a few scraps of food and a way of passing the time. It was a game he played, he and the other boys. Each with their adopted hero, they lied and bragged of his bravery, his limitless courage that exceeded all bounds of possibility, until they fell about laughing. They had been good times, feeding information to both the Taliban and the coalition forces at the same time. The Americans were the best payers, keen for mobile phones taken from dead Taliban after fire-fights. They used the phone numbers to trap insurgents and gain information. On the day Mister Sergeant had lost his foot; he had lied to both him and the Taliban leader that both sides had weakened forces. Then, Mister Sergeant, his main meal ticket and an easy touch, had ruined everything. Along with the other boys, his one tangible thought was survival from a war where everyone killed everyone else for reasons no one understood. In the meantime, without conscience, he filled his pockets by playing one side against the other until the Taliban discovered his scam and murdered his family in reprisal. The British killed the Taliban, the Taliban killed the British, and the Americans killed anything that moved; so what? Amidst this kaleidoscope of catastrophes, the people of Afghanistan looked the other way and made money by any method available to them. Compensation for property damaged either by war or by intent paid well. Above all else it was his country and he loved it, and no one had the right to take it from him. He could have escaped the clutches of Mirza Khan anytime he chose to, but decided to stay for as long as it suited him. It was the fool Mister Sergeant that had ruined the opportunity for him to steal from the Khan and make good money on the side. It was Mister Sergeant who had brought him to this country where he had been beaten and abused. But even for him revenge is sweet, and he had left Mister Sergeant a legacy he would never forget until the day he died, his day would soon when he would regret his return to Afghanistan. Back in his homeland, when he was old enough he would enrol in the ranks of the Taliban and join the *jihad*.

Bella watched him scurry across the sand, ready to lay out the markers each donkey would travel to before returning to the start. She smiled a sad smile. If she was honest, all of her wanted him to stay. In the short time she had known him he might have grown into the son she could never have. One time she had remonstrated with herself for allowing him the opportunity to return to his homeland. But sometimes, children are best left innocent and unspoiled, and she had been taken by his innocence combined with a determination that would one day carry him through life. She drew on the strength in the knowledge that she was doing the right thing.

*

Wrapped up in his world of raging confusion, Gillet contemplated going back to the north Norfolk coast and home. It was finished. Seconds later, he searched his mind for a reason not to do so and instead strolled along the seafront, content in his mind he'd done all he could for Shafiq. But on the surface he knew he hadn't, and his suppressed violence turned against him. The words, starting over afresh is easy, jumped into his mind; whoever said that was either a liar, or delusional. As he passed the ostentatious shops displaying tack and cheap souvenirs, along with decaying facades hidden by gaudy illuminated signboards, he forced himself to walk slowly. Why wouldn't it go away to leave him in peace, this unreal world? His sight fogged; his limbs felt light and detached from the rest of his body. He searched for a place to hide from the puzzled stares of those passing. A woman gripping a stick of candyfloss held out her free hand to prevent him from falling to his knees; he snarled and pushed her aside. Unable to control his momentum, he staggered from side to side down the concrete ramp leading to the beach and slumped in the shade thrown by a horsebox. Grateful for the coolness, he sat staring straight ahead as the apathy of indifference darted in and out of his stomach. Fear and self-hatred welled inside him. She came from behind the horsebox, the heavily built woman with mousy hair and smelling of horseshit, her pointed nose portraying an air of haughtiness.

"Oi, get out of here, you drunken sod," she snapped. "I'll be unloading a string of donkeys in a minute and I don't want you lurching around frightening them half to death. Go on, clear off, you drunken sod."

"Fuck off, you fat bitch," he sneered, looking up at her.

"Chaffinch, get a move on," she called.

On the other side of the horsebox, Shafiq dropped the tailgate and shooed the donkeys out onto the soft sand. The crash of the tailgate hurtled into Gillet's skull, his sight faded and he held out his hand as if seeking assistance.

She looked down at him, her lips curled into a sneer. He stared back and imagined the words she wanted to hurl at him: disgusting, a disgrace to humanity and any other profanities she could lay her tongue to. Struggling to his feet, he staggered up the concrete ramp. Overhead, the shrieking call of seabirds magnified, hammering all cohesive thoughts from his mind as he lurched further along the beach. Something he had never experienced before tapped a well, a feeling of self-pity, of uselessness, lowliness. With his back pressed against the sea wall, he gazed out over the hazy sea. Why wouldn't it go away, the everlasting sense of guilt riddled with confusion? Racking his brain he tried to remember what he was doing in a place where people dressed in shorts with sunglasses balancing on pink noses. There was nothing left; he had passed the point of no return. Without inhibition or conscience, he struggled to his feet, his car, he remembered his car. The pain in his head increased beyond human endurance. By the time he reached his car greyness had turned to darkness, and wrenching the car door open he sat with his chin resting on his chest. It was there, where he had left it, taped inside the glove compartment. It was the one thing of which he was certain. Fumbling to pull it free of the adhesive tape, he pushed the safety catch to off, pulled back the hammer and pushed the barrel into his mouth.

"Whoa there, Gillet, you crazy son of a bitch, we have some goddam unfinished business to attend to."

Gillet felt the gun pulled from his hand; the voice sounded familiar, recent.

"Jesus, I always knew you needed treatment."

Gillet raised his head and stared at Riley, the CNN news hound. Behind him, looking concerned, was Uma, the woman that had helped him in Kabul.

He tried to make sense of it all, to put it together by fractions, make the picture real, complete.

"What do you want? Go away and leave me alone," he mumbled through closed lips.

"Remember Fisher? Damn fool got himself killed by an IED, so the agency sent me over here for a break. And this lady has a conference in London the day after tomorrow, so we travelled over together, got talking, and your name came up. The moment we landed, the newspapers were full of a guy named Pink, ex-soldier found stabbed outside a mosque in Yarmouth. Goddam it, Gillet, I just knew you had to be involved, and we got here as soon as possible. Spotted you stumbling off the beach, but weren't sure whether or not to approach you the state you were in. Looks like I was just in time."

Gillet turned at the scent. Female; it wasn't rosewater, but familiar.

Uma smiled down at him. There was something vulnerable about him, like a little boy struggling to leave the deep end. She had noted it in Kabul. During the time they had spent together she had felt afraid to communicate with him, afraid her feelings might get the better of her.

"Hey, how about we get you home," she said in a soft voice, "and back to your son? Guess he'll be pleased to see you."

Luke? He wanted to answer, but couldn't think of anything to say, and even if he could, his mouth refused to work. Instead, he nodded and smiled a crooked smile.

"Not so fast Gillet. You goddam bastard, I want my goddam story," Riley growled.

*

No one spoke during the journey. When they reached Gillet's house he stumbled from the rear of the car and headedg for the kitchen. Uma told him to sit and made coffee. Riley disappeared looking for the toilet. It was minutes later when Riley returned with a sheepish look on his face.

"I think you had better come and see this for yourself, Gillet."

Gillet looked up and followed Riley through the utility room and into the garage, then stopped with a stunned look masking his face.

"*Salaam Alaikum,* my father, you are in time to see me dance."

Gillet stared at the painted fingernails and toenails, the make-up smothering Luke's face. His eyes shaded with thick mascara and the red gash of lipstick. Stripped to his pants he held a tambourine, bells on his wrists and ankles tinkled. On the floor a prayer mat faced the east. An image of Shafiq appeared crystal clear in his mind, and he sank to the cold concrete floor unable to control his trembling limbs.

THE END

Printed in Great Britain
by Amazon.co.uk, Ltd.,
Marston Gate.